AWARD-WINNING AUTHOR
MARCIA ARMANDI

ALIVE

SHADOWS OF A
FORGOTTEN PAST

PART TWO

ALIVE

SHADOWS OF A FORGOTTEN PAST

MARCIA ARMANDI

CITY OWL
PRESS

ALIVE
Shadows of a Forgotten Past, Part Two
By Marcia Armandi

CITY OWL PRESS
www.cityowlpress.com

Cover Design by MiblArt. All stock photos licensed appropriately.

Edited by Lisa Green.

For information on subsidiary rights, please contact the publisher at info@cityowlpress.com.

Print Edition ISBN: 978-1-64898-517-1

Digital Edition ISBN: 978-1-64898-516-4

Printed in the United States of America

To my mother, Marina, who taught me that love is worth fighting for.

CHAPTER 1
~ SHADOWS OF THE PAST ~

THE NEW FOREST, HAMPSHIRE, ENGLAND, 1939

Amid the complexities of life, one truth I knew without a doubt: the beginning is the end, the end is the beginning. Even when the tombs at the Breamore cemetery told a different story, one story—my own— attested to my conviction.

Florence Contini Sterling—
Forever My Lady
1894–1917

Standing before my grave, I wondered if anyone could ever understand how dreamlike this moment was. Twenty-two years ago, I had been laid to rest here. This burial ground witnessed Alexander Sterling's grief. It also provided a mysterious ray of hope when it later proved to no longer hold my remains. The empty tomb revealed an unfathomable truth: I had been released from the bonds of death.

Soon after I awakened to my past identity, Alex married me once more. With little notice from the world, Father Thompson performed the ceremony at the monastery in Geneva, New York. Reading from an ancient manuscript, the priest taught, "The souls connected with perpetual love have no cessation. They live on forever." If only he'd known how profound that statement was, his world would have turned topsy-turvy.

The setting sun deepened the twilight, and shadows spread across the graveyard. My gaze drifted to the headstone beside mine.

Sterlings' beloved baby boy,
sleep in peace under the nurturing
love of your dear mother.

My baby didn't have a name.

The knowledge of my past life was a blessing, yet it could not reconcile my grief for the departed nor ease my longing for what might have been. True, after my brother Lucca's visit, I found comfort in knowing that the spirits of the dead indeed dwelled in another realm and that, someday, I would join them. Still, the ache of their absence lingered.

Then, in contrast to the memory of my loved ones, thoughts of Deborah White, the cold-blooded murderess who remained at large, set my nerves on edge. She had stolen my son at birth, robbing me of the opportunity to behold his face. Her obsession with Alex, her resolution to end my life, and her callous indifference to my baby's fate haunted me. Had my baby died of natural causes, or had Mrs. White taken his life to sever the ties between Alex and me? That she was an iniquitous woman was beyond question, but would she go that far?

I didn't know what transpired after she took the baby. On more than one occasion, I had almost mustered enough courage to ask Alex, but the fear of reopening old wounds stayed my tongue. After all, there was no reason to wander back through years that were gone or chase something not meant to be. Still, the memory of my son's birth refused to fade, and I yearned to learn more about his death.

"I'm sorry, miss. I don't mean to intrude," a raspy voice broke the stillness.

Startled, I spun to face the cemetery keeper. Pale, dressed in black, and jingling a ring of keys on his belt, he looked as though he'd risen from one of the tombs he tended.

"The cemetery is now closed," he said. "I should've locked the gate twenty minutes ago." As if to underscore his words, the last rays of the sun slipped below the horizon, draping the graveyard in shadows. The closure of another day obscured the names, lives, and memories of those who lay asleep here.

"Do forgive me, Mr. . . .?"

"Morris, miss. Morris is the name."

"I apologize. I'm afraid I lost track of time."

"Indeed, you've been here for an awful long while." He gestured to a copse of trees beyond the Elmores' Victorian mausoleum. "See, I've been watching you from over there."

"You have?" I felt uneasy.

"Goodness, yes," he replied with a crooked smile. "I thought you were a haunt at first."

I supposed he could have. The nudge to come here had been so compelling, I hadn't bothered to change into riding clothes. My white dress, in the diffused light, likely made for a peculiar sight. And apparently, I wasn't the first ghostly figure Mr. Morris had seen on these grounds.

"You aren't from these parts, are you?" He gave me a measured look. "At least your accent is not."

"I'm from America."

"Hmm, a recent arrival, then?" he said with a hint of skepticism.

"That's right." A recent arrival to my previous life, I thought wryly. Had Mr. Morris known the Contini family? I didn't remember him from the past. "Have you worked in the cemetery long?"

"Since I was a young lad. I know these grounds and everyone who lives here like the palm of my hand."

Lives here. Interesting choice of words. To settle my curiosity and deflect suspicion, I turned toward my grave and asked, "Did you know her?"

"Florence Contini?"

"Yes."

"Saw her once or twice from a distance. Very refined lady, she was." He fidgeted with his keys. The sound drifted across the tombs as if summoning their inhabitants to rise. "Are you related?"

"Me?" I smiled nervously. "Well . . . no, not really."

"Hmm." His gaze bored into mine. "I'd have sworn you were family."

His words held truth, mine deceit—but then again, what choice did I have? I couldn't very well tell him I *was* the deceased.

"The way you looked at her and her child's grave, you know," he continued. "This place is acquainted with sorrow. I recognize it whenever I see it."

"Ohh." Relieved he wasn't referring to a physical resemblance, I offered a half-truth. "You see, I married Alexander Sterling—her husband and the baby's father."

"Ahh." He nodded slowly, as though my presence finally made sense. "It was but yesterday I heard talk of the general's return to the forest. So, it's true, after all these years. Who would have thought he would ever marry again?"

"Why do you say that? He is young. Besides, it's never too late, is it?"

"Oh no, don't misunderstand me. It's just that their story is so tragic. For years, he came to see her rain or shine. He spent hours kneeling beside her, sometimes weeping, sometimes staring into space. It was heartrending to behold."

If I weren't his late wife, I might have worried that Alex would never love me as much as he had loved her. As it was, I marveled at the wonder of my current existence, of being with him again. My heart had belonged to him ever since I first saw him in the fields of Forti Radici. Despite my childish antics, insecurities, and grief, he stood by me with undying affection.

"He moved to America after he retired," Mr. Morris concluded, breaking my reverie. "Of course, you knew that already."

"That's where we met."

"He visited not too long ago, though." Mr. Morris rubbed his chin thoughtfully. "Even now, I'm not sure what took place that day."

"What day? What took place?"

"It was early morning . . . winter it was. The ground was frozen." He motioned to my headstone, shifting uneasily on his feet. "Scotland Yard ordered me and another chap to dig up her coffin."

"You don't say!" I feigned astonishment but remembered Alex's sudden trip to the New Forest while I worked at Oak's Place.

"Nasty business, I thought."

Had he seen the empty coffin? "I'm sorry you had to see that," I said, hoping for a little more information.

"No, miss. We didn't see anything. Me and the other chap were dismissed after we unearthed the box. Scotland Yard, the local police, and the general himself were the only ones who saw inside. I don't know what they were looking for. Some presumed it might have been valuables buried with her," he said with a shrug.

"Do you believe that?"

"Not for a moment. He loved his wife too much to disturb her rest for something so trivial. And besides, the man does well enough regarding money."

I clasped the bracelet around my wrist, the only thing that had been buried with me. Even that, they hadn't found in my coffin.

"I must say," Mr. Morris continued, "Scotland Yard's secrecy flustered me. They came here in their well-pressed overcoats and polished badges, yet didn't have the decency to explain why on earth we were digging up corpses. 'It was a family matter,' they said, and left it at that. In other words, they hushed it up." He looked at me intently, as though he expected the general's new wife to elaborate.

As the last hints of day dissolved into night, I seized the opportunity to end the discussion. "I'm sorry to have kept you this long, Mr. Morris. It was nice chatting with you."

"I'll walk you to the entrance, or exit, same difference. It can get spooky after nightfall." Before I could object, he added, "I need to lock the gate anyway. Not that anyone with half a brain would wander in at night, but protocol is protocol."

We started on the pebble path. In addition to the click-clack of our shoes and the clink of his keys, the evening was filled with unspoken things—about the graveyard, about me, and about my family.

When the iron gate materialized ahead, I lengthened my steps.

"Thank you. My horse is just by the trees."

"Your horse?" His gaze flicked over my attire. "You didn't drive here?"

"I prefer to ride."

"A woman shouldn't be riding alone through the woods at this hour."

"I'll be all right." I stepped through the gate into the glow of a nearby lamppost.

"I'll say!" His eyes widened as if struck by a revelation. "Most extraordinary."

"What is?"

"You, miss. I could be mistaken, but your resemblance to the general's late wife is . . . most remarkable."

I pursed my lips. He remembered after all.

"Quite remarkable," he reiterated.

"Good night, Mr. Morris." With a polite smile, I hurried to Betsy, who munched on the foliage as if she had just arrived.

"Wait, miss, you haven't told me your name," he called from behind the iron bars, turning a large key in the lock. "How rude of me not to ask."

"Florence, Mr. Morris. Florence Sterling."

Shock rippled across his face.

Though I had tried to keep things quiet, the gossip was sure to spread like wildfire. Not only did I resemble Alex's first wife, but I also shared her name. No doubt people would pity me, convinced he'd married me because I reminded him of the love of his life. If only they knew. But how could anyone ever believe such an extraordinary truth?

CHAPTER 2
~ FORTI RADICI ~

Forti Radici beckoned as Betsy broke through the tree line. The silver moonlight bathed its sprawling roof and stone façade, softening the edges of the night. I was home.

Once more, I felt like I'd never left the New Forest, like my existence in New York had been a dream from which I'd woken to find myself back in 1917. It would have been easy to believe if not for the tragic losses of my father, General Marcus Contini; our dear housekeeper, Mrs. Allerton; and Mr. Leroy, our tenderhearted gardener.

My heart ached for them.

I could picture Father in the courtyard, discussing the latest news in the car industry with Mr. Lewis, our chauffeur. The image faded, replaced by Mrs. Allerton and Mr. Leroy quarreling about the garden's design—her white hair neatly pinned into a bun, her spectacles catching the sunlight. And the short, French fellow, adjusting his cap in exasperation. Their arguments, though fiery, were born from love and mutual respect—a bond that carried them even into their final moments as German soldiers pursued them.

The poignant memory brought the brutality of the Great War into focus. With it came Alex's reflections on Europe's current instability. *"There is a terrible evil growing in Germany—one so immense I'm afraid it will find a way to creep past its borders and threaten us all. The contempt for human life is germinating into madness. And madness never ends well,"* he had said. I hoped we wouldn't come to regret our decision to return home.

Betsy's hoofbeats echoed through the final stretch toward the house.

"We are almost there," I encouraged, sensing she'd had her fill of exercise for the day. "Almost there."

At the stable, I dismounted and caught sight of Zaira and Clarence Bolton, who cared for the horses. They conversed near the hay bales at the far end. Clarence, about Zaira's age, had fine, dark features, bright eyes, and an undeniable bond with the animals he cared for.

When Zaira and Oliver's relationship didn't work out, she moved back to Europe—for which I was grateful. Zaira, though unaware of my past life, proved a trustworthy friend and a comforting connection between past and present. She understood the harshness of being uprooted from one's homeland and replanted elsewhere. While I called both countries home, England had moved on without me, and Zaira had bridged the gap, helping me navigate the nuances of modern English society.

Guiding Betsy inside, I got a better look at the couple. They seemed at ease with one another, especially Clarence. Though, no doubt, I suspected Zaira's red curls and spirited personality posed a fair challenge to his confidence.

"I've got her, Mrs. Sterling." Clarence met me halfway down the aisle and took Betsy's reins.

"Thank you. She did well today—she's earned a double treat."

"Yes, ma'am." A smile crossed his face as he patted Betsy's neck. "Hear that, girl? Let's find some apples. But don't tell the others. I've already settled them for the night, and they'll be mighty jealous of your late snack."

As I watched Clarence lead Betsy away, the tranquil bond between man and animal unfolded before me—a scene that clashed with a haunting memory. I could still see Mrs. White slipping the snake into Sunny's stall, still hear Sunny's thrashing and panicked neighs. I could almost feel the pounding of her hooves on my back. I flinched; those moments had wounded Alex and me, leaving scars that time could never fully heal.

"Where were you? I'd started to worry you were lost." Zaira's voice pulled me back to the present.

"You shouldn't have. I . . ." I caught myself in time, concealing my acquaintance with the region.

"You were, weren't you?" she assumed.

"Something of the sort."

"You must be careful. This is not Geneva, you know. The forest is beautiful but desolate. If you get in trouble, no one will come to your rescue. At least, no one with decent intentions. Good, law-abiding citizens don't roam the woods after dusk." She frowned in clear disapproval of my foolishness.

"You are right. Thank you." I embraced her briefly. "Is Alex home?"

"Yes, he arrived not long ago. I dare say he was surprised, maybe even disappointed, that you weren't home. If I were you, I'd hurry inside before he comes looking for you."

I understood her meaning. Since our move back, Alex worried about me more than was necessary. "You are right again."

"Do you need anything from me?"

"No, thank you."

"Well, if you change your mind, Martha will be more than happy to help. The poor girl is terribly bored in the evenings," Zaira said. Martha, an attractive middle-aged woman with a cascade of black hair and alert eyes, helped around the house with an array of tasks. Having come from the bustling city of Salisbury, she found the slow pace of the countryside challenging—there was never enough to keep her entertained.

Betsy nickered softly, and I nodded toward the cubicle. "Clarence might appreciate some help with her though."

A soft pink spread across Zaira's cheeks.

"He's quite a catch," I added.

"You can say that again," she replied, the pink deepening to scarlet.

I gripped the door handle and smiled. Unlike my awakening, when my spirit had passed right through the wood, I was now here in the flesh. Turning the knob, I stepped into the entry hall. The marble floors, towering walls, and hand-painted ceiling never failed to amaze me. But my attention was drawn to the man leaning against the banister, dressed in dark trousers and a white button-down, his sleeves rolled up.

Alex's blue eyes took on the shine I had come to love, and for a second or two, I stood rooted to the spot, marveling at the miracle of being with him again. Since our wedding, his health had steadily improved. He had even resumed his morning runs through the forest.

"Good evening, Miss Contini." He smiled that mesmerizing smile that had broken countless hearts over the years.

"Are you holding the post in place?" I asked playfully.

"No. As always, I'm waiting for you. I'm beginning to think you like it that way."

"Good things come to those who wait, Mr. Sterling." I removed my gloves and set them on the credenza.

"Such as?"

"Such as this." I weaved my fingers through his hair, pulled him close, and kissed him soundly.

"Where have you been?"

"I went for a ride."

"At this hour?" His tone was curious but edged with suspicion.

Did he suspect where I'd been? Since arriving in the New Forest, I found myself drawn to our son's grave. When Alex voiced concern over how much time I spent there, I began to keep the outings secret. As much as I hated lying to him, I saw no reason to trouble him with my unresolved emotions—not yet.

"It was a pleasant ride," I said casually. "I'm afraid I didn't realize how late it was." Then, to divert the conversation, I added, "On the other hand, you are home sooner than I expected."

"I took the express. Disappointed?"

"No . . . maybe . . . well, it depends."

"Depends on what?"

"On how well you behave this evening."

His eyes lit with amusement. "I assure you, Miss Contini, my behavior will erase the word *disappointment* from your vocabulary."

"We shall see," I taunted.

Alex cupped my face in his hands and leaned in, his lips brushing mine. As the kiss deepened, I knew I'd lost the battle. But, the sound of footsteps forced us apart, the spell broken as Mrs. Haywood joined us.

From Alex, I had learned that Mrs. White, an acquaintance of Peter and Agnes Haywood, had hired them to manage Forti Radici when he moved to America. That connection alone was enough to temper my sentiments toward the Haywoods. However, there was nothing in their conduct to justify my reservations.

Agnes, a plump woman with white-blonde hair, radiated kindness in her smile. Her husband, Peter, reserved and observant, had red hair streaked with gray and a dedication evident in his long hours of hard work.

"Good evening, General. Mrs. Sterling," Mrs. Haywood greeted cordially. Her gaze traveled between Alex and me before settling on him. "Would you like a late supper?"

"It's up to the lady of the house," Alex said.

"Surely Mrs. Sterling would enjoy some roast beef and Yorkshire pudding. If I may say so myself, it turned out wonderfully." She gave me a quick, assessing glance, her unsaid verdict: I was too thin and could benefit from her cooking.

"Sounds like we must, Mrs. Haywood. We'll come to the kitchen as soon as we wash up," I said.

"Nonsense! I've already set the table in the dining room." Before I could protest, the housekeeper had bustled eagerly down the corridor.

Alex and I settled at the end of the grand table. I ran my hand over its polished wood, worn with scratches and burnished spots. Unlike the old days, when laughter and chatter filled the room and Mrs. Allerton arranged place cards for guests, the dining room now felt too quiet and elaborate for just the two of us.

"Mrs. Haywood wasn't exaggerating about the food. It's very good," Alex commented, digging into the pudding.

"It is, but not as good as Zaira's," I said quietly.

"Even so, I'm sure Zaira is enjoying the break from the kitchen."

"Of that, I have no doubt." I thought of her friendship with Clarence and the hours they spent together. Contrary to her time at Oak's Place—where Mrs. White's strict schedules strained her relationship with Oliver—Zaira now had the freedom to meet Clarence whenever she pleased.

Alex took another bite of the meat. "Mm, delicious."

"You haven't told me why you went to London."

"You'll know in the morning."

"In the morning?" I repeated, the wait sounding like years to me. "Don't be a bore—tell me."

"You are a curious creature," he teased.

"That's why you shouldn't make me wait."

"Oh, but I will."

Knowing his stubbornness, there was no point in pressing further. With a sigh of defeat, I dropped the subject. Tomorrow would come soon enough. Alex shot me a sideways glance, his lips curling—he knew he'd won—and helped himself to another serving of Yorkshire pudding.

We savored the meal in comfortable silence, never needing meaningless words to fill the void. However, as time passed, I noticed a shift in Alex's demeanor. His cheerful air gave way to quiet tension, his thoughts seemingly lost in a labyrinth of worry. I knew that look.

"What's troubling you?" I placed my hand over his, an assurance that I was here for him. When his eyes met mine, I saw apprehension there. Never a good sign. "Whatever it is, I'd rather know."

"I didn't want to ruin our evening by telling you." He pushed his plate aside. "But sooner or later, I have to. Being forewarned is being forearmed."

"What is it?"

"A telegram from Scotland Yard arrived. They spotted Deborah White on the outskirts of London."

"Mrs. White . . ." saying her name aloud summoned a flood of dark memories. "She's back in England, then."

"They believe she has been for quite some time."

"And Mr. Vines?"

"Nothing about him. They might not even be together anymore."

"I doubt that. If he didn't leave her after the atrocities she committed, he never will. He is obsessively attached to her. It's a sickness."

"Even murder." Alex groaned, rising abruptly.

Murder—her husband's, mine, nearly Alex's, and maybe even my son's. I joined him by the window and followed his gaze into the obscurity beyond. I could almost see Mrs. White there, hidden in the tangled undergrowth, her cunning eyes trained on the house, watching, waiting. She had walked the road of treachery superbly, and at its end, she had brought death. I shivered. "Let's hope they catch her soon and lock her away for the rest of her miserable days."

"Let's hope they find her before I do. When I think of all those years she lived under my roof, posing as a friend while she was the root of our family's suffering . . ." Alex pressed his fist against the windowpane, his voice low with restrained fury.

"I understand your feelings—you know I do—but we are together now. That's what matters most, and we must protect it." I forced myself to stay grounded, though heaven only knew the battle raging within me. The nuns at Higher Grounds warned me that unchecked anger could evolve into revenge-fueled hate. And hatred was a corrosive force that consumed reason and compassion. "Now, don't misunderstand me," I went on. "Mrs. White absolutely deserves to be punished—she does. But we must let the authorities handle it. She is the one who belongs in prison, not us."

"You are right. To level yourself with a snake, you'd have to crawl on the ground. That we'll never do." His features softened, and his fists unclenched, though I feared the storm within him still brewed.

I opened my eyes to find Alex already awake, his gaze loving as he watched me.

"Good morning." He brushed a few strands of hair from my face. "Today, we forget about the world. It's just you and me."

"And what will we be doing?"

"We are going to Keyhaven," he announced.

"Are you serious?" In my first life, I had spent some of my happiest days in the fishing hamlet near Hurst Castle, the artillery fortress from which Alex had sailed to deliver Father's classified information to France. "Is that why you went to London?"

"Yes, to get something for you." He left the bed and disappeared into the powder room. A moment later, he returned with a round box. "Open it."

"Alex, it's beautiful!" I rotated the burgundy, wide-brimmed hat in my hands, admiring its embroidery. "Thank you."

"I'm glad you like it." He grinned. "You'll need it at the beach. When I was planning the trip, I realized you didn't have one."

"In New York, hats aren't as prevalent." With a flourish, I placed the hat atop my head.

"I also brought you a catalog. It's in my office." He hustled to change out of his pajamas. "Makes it easier to order more if you'd like."

"Thank you! I can't wait to show it to Zaira. She's infatuated with hats." I pulled the brim lower over my eyes. "It'll be perfect for shielding the sun at the beach—and excellent for avoiding unwelcome scrutiny."

"Oh, am I unwelcome now?" he joked, lifting the brim just enough to meet my gaze.

"Believe me, you are the always-wanted man."

"If I didn't have another surprise for you, I'd continue this discussion," he said with a wink.

"Another surprise?"

"That's right. I'll wait for you downstairs." He rushed from the room.

I pulled on a pair of black slacks and an indigo blouse. Pleased with my choice, I sat before the mirror, my heart racing with anticipation. I drew the brush through my hair, each stroke reminding me of Mrs. Allerton. I could almost see her standing behind me, speaking of "the art of making oneself presentable," as she called it, often followed by a lecture on how I might improve at it.

With a longing sigh, I left the bedroom, making a mental note to write to Granny. Throughout my two lives, I had been blessed to be surrounded by stalwart women—not just Granny and Mrs. Allerton but Zaira, Sister Callahan, and Margaret Sterling.

Unbidden, a recollection of Mrs. White surfaced. She'd played a significant role in my life as well, and still did, though her influence stood in contrast to that of the others. A realization struck me: Women held endless power to shape lives, for good or ill. Their challenge lay in loving and being at peace with themselves. Then, they could extend those gifts to their fellow beings—a tall order at times.

As I rounded the corner, Zaira nearly collided with me, her steps hurried as she surfaced from the staircase.

"Good morning!" she exclaimed.

"Good morning. What's the rush?"

"Mr. Sterling is impatiently waiting for you out front." She smirked.

"Out front?"

"Yes, out front. I'll pick a few things for you to pack."

"Oh, so you know."

"Yes, yes. Go now." She tucked her hair behind her ears and strode away with purpose.

I descended the steps, crossed the foyer, and stepped out into the morning sun. There, gleaming in the courtyard, sat a red-and-black convertible, its polished curves dazzling in the light. Beside it, Alex and a middle-aged gentleman were deep in animated conversation. Their fascination with the vehicle in full flare. I stood, letting the moment linger until their discussion naturally waned. At last, Alex turned to me.

"What do you think?" He motioned to the car like a child showing off a new toy.

"It's magnificent." My father's 1910 Rolls-Royce Silver Ghost had been impressive, but nothing like this.

"Florence, I'd like you to meet Albert Brown. He'll be looking after the Lagonda and attempting to resurrect our old cars."

"It's a pleasure, Mrs. Sterling." The man doffed his gray beret, revealing a well-kept black mane. I noticed a slight accent—French, perhaps?

"How do you do, Mr. Brown?"

"I'm well, thank you. Thrilled to work at Forti Radici."

"Lagonda?" I asked Alex.

"It's the name of the car. Lagonda V12 Rapide."

"I see."

"It can reach up to one hundred miles per hour," Mr. Brown chimed in. He reminded me of Mr. Lewis, our former chauffeur, and his intimate attachment to the Silver Ghost. What was it with men and these machines? I doubted I would ever understand.

"One hundred and five, to be exact," Alex clarified. "Mr. Brown will have it ready for our trip."

"I'll get to it straightaway." Mr. Brown hopped into the Lagonda and turned the key. "Ahh, hear that? Like the roar of a thousand lions!" With that, he drove off around the side of the house.

"I hope the chap doesn't run away with it," Alex joked.

Trying to sort out what just unfolded, I peppered him with questions. "I didn't know you were getting a car—a sports one at that. Did it cost a fortune?" We had discussed purchasing a vehicle, but I'd imagined something practical that could accommodate a family with children, not a sleek two-seater. "Where did Mr. Brown come from?"

"Which question would you like me to answer first?" Alex teased. "There are quite a few."

I opened my mouth to add another, but he silenced me with a kiss. If he hoped to charm his way out of this one, he was mistaken. "Your choice," I said. "Just answer them."

"It's not like I'm a spendthrift. The cars we have are old and haven't been driven in a long time. I figured we could use a new one and didn't think you'd object if I went ahead and got it. I'll admit it did cost a fortune—but that's a conversation for another time." He cleared his throat, clearly choking on the memory of the price tag.

Though I valued frugality, I chose not to dampen his elation. After all, my disappointment lay less in the cost and more in the car's size. But I reasoned that we could trade it in when the time came. "And Mr. Brown?"

"I wasn't looking for a driver. It kind of happened. He's a recent arrival from Belgium and needed work. Besides, he comes highly recommended by an acquaintance. Satisfied?"

Not French like my dear groundskeeper, Mr. Leroy, had been. "For now." I produced a gracious smile.

"I can't wait to take it out on the road." Alex grasped my hand. "Let's go pack."

The Lagonda's engine rumbled down the winding forest roads, so different from the day we escaped the German attack on the manor. Back then, we were hunted souls overshadowed by grief and fear. Today, those shadows were far behind us. In their place, we reveled in each other's company, carefree and content.

"Your arm is going to fall off if you don't let it rest," Alex called over the roar of the engine.

"Better than losing my hat," I shot back, irritated by the wind tearing at me. I was no fan of driving with an open roof.

He reached over, plucked the hat from my head, and set it on my lap. "There. Now, rest your arm, and I'll watch your hair wrestle with the wind."

Gusts of air rushed through the cabin, sending my tresses into a wild flurry. Alex chuckled. I swatted his arm, unable to suppress a grin. We were like children on an adventure, eager to bend the rules, anxious to discover and please each other.

Alex continued to test the car on sharp curves, braking suddenly at unexpected signs of wildlife. Shouting and laughing, we whiled away the minutes until the air began to change. It grew damp and heavy, infused with the salt of the sea—like the sudatoriums I had read about in history books.

I closed my eyes, reminiscing: Alex's family cottage, the steady drone of insects as we fell asleep each night, sunny afternoons at the sea, his love, his passion. It all came back with searing intensity. I glanced at him —his fine features, muscular frame, and indomitable spirit—an irresistible combination. I felt just as crazy about the man as I did over twenty years ago.

"Where are we staying?" I asked, assuming the dilapidated cottage had been torn down long ago.

The corners of his mouth curled up. "Care to guess?"

"Really? The cottage?"

"That's right."

"You can't be serious." I pictured the sagging roof, layers of dust, and cobwebs in every corner.

"Don't act so excited," he teased, veering off the road onto a narrow path. "It's just beyond those trees." A few yards later, he made a final turn and parked. "This is as far as we can go."

Nature had aged as well, reproducing and expanding in every direction. The sequoias' branches interlaced in verdant splendor, shading the undergrowth. We stepped out of the Lagonda, and I spotted a roofline peeking through the foliage.

"Come on, let's go." Alex led the way through the brush, his stride confident.

Not far ahead, the cottage emerged before us. Its brown wooden walls and grayish roof looked fresh and alive, blending seamlessly with the landscape. Stones now skirted the perimeter, and a porch sheltered it from the elements.

"It can't be the same place . . ."

"But it is," Alex said. "I've maintained it over the years, and before I moved to America, I had it fully restored. I knew that someday I would return looking for you, for memories, for something to hold on to. Now I have something even better—you." He kissed my forehead. "I didn't think I'd get this sentimental."

"Nothing wrong with that." I understood. My own emotions simmered just beneath the surface.

He bounded across the porch and opened the front door, signaling for me to follow. Inside, he went to the window and drew the shutters. Daylight streamed in, vanquishing the darkness.

"Wow!" I turned in a slow circle, taking in the transformed interior. "This is beautiful." The polished floorboards, stone fireplace, and built-in cupboards were a marvel. A rustic table and chairs, along with colorful rugs completed the ensemble.

"I'm glad you like it, but don't get too attached to modern conveniences—there's still no electricity."

"The window helps—it's bigger than the old one."

"I replaced the one upstairs too. No more worrying about critters." Alex grinned. "Well, at least not as much."

My gaze shifted to the ladder that led to the attic. It was now a solid, built-in piece. "Ah, that was long overdue. I held my breath every time you climbed it."

"Are you implying I was too heavy, or that the ladder was too weak?" He raised an eyebrow, his tone playful.

"The latter, Mr. Sterling, the latter."

"Right, then. Shall we test this one?" He started up the steps, pausing briefly. "Listen—no creaks at all"

I climbed after him, the solid footing reassuring beneath my steps. Daylight streamed through the open shutters, highlighting the metal bed and large chest filled with bedding, just as I remembered them. "You kept them."

"I couldn't let them go."

I came to the window. The woods stared back at me. They brought memories of the days I had stood here, gazing beyond the trees to the sea, waiting for Alex to return from France. A wave of nostalgia washed over me. "All of this feels like a dream—one from which I hope to never wake . . ."

"Let's not, then." Alex's voice was warm, steady. "Right now, out here, we are free from every care. And now that I think about it, this is our second honeymoon. Ironic as it sounds, I wouldn't want it any other way."

"Our hiding place. Our haven."

"*You* are my haven." Alex leaned in, and as his lips connected with mine, the world fell into perfect harmony, a moment of perfect belonging.

CHAPTER 3
~ KEYHAVEN ~

A beautiful boy with dark hair and a mesmerizing smile dashes through the grass, untouched by the world's worries. My heart burns with love.

Wolves howl from the trees, catching his attention. He rushes toward the sound. Dread swallows my contentment. I race after him.

I push my legs harder. It's no use—I can't catch up. He disappears into the brush. Then—he reappears, taller, older. Time is stealing him from me.

The trees close in, their branches intertwining, locking him away. Loneliness crashes over me. "No! No! I have to find my son!"

A voice broke through the fog of despair, accompanied by gentle shaking. "Florence, wake up. Wake up! It's just a dream."

Drops of cold sweat slid down my neck. I opened my eyes to a pre-dawn stillness.

"Are you all right?" Alex spoke again, his voice edged with concern.

"I think so . . . it was a vivid, painful dream."

"It's over now." He pulled me into his embrace.

"I saw him." My voice trembled with longing.

"Who?"

"Our son. He was running in the fields, playing, laughing, alive. He was alive." The dream had felt so real, the connection so intense, that waking seemed like losing him all over again.

"I know it's hard," Alex whispered. "I, too, wish he were with us."

"Why won't these dreams leave me alone?" The pain drove me to pursue the long-overdue conversation. "When he was born, Mrs. White carried him from the room, leaving me with the aching desire to be with him, to hold him, even when physically I couldn't. It left a hole in my heart that never healed," I said. "Later, the sadness in your eyes told me he was gone. There were many unanswered questions—I wondered who cared for him, how long he lived, and where his remains were. Please, Alex, tell me about it."

A brief silence ensued—the same silence that on previous occasions ended the discussion before it even started.

"Alex, please."

He drew a long breath, his arms tightening around me as though to anchor himself. "When I arrived at the manor, the baby had already been rushed to the dispensary. The attending nurse was trained to care for him."

"Who took him there?"

"Deborah White."

"But she was there when I . . . left you."

"Vines drove her. I'm not sure how long they were gone. You were unconscious for quite some time. Florence, it was the best thing to do. The best chance our son had to survive. You couldn't . . ."

"I know. I know."

"I learned of his passing soon after I returned to you."

My heart ached at the indescribable loss. Had he lived, he would have been a source of peace and love for Alex.

"All of it was a terrible blow," Alex continued. "Nothing could have prepared me for that day. In a matter of hours, my world collapsed, and I was set adrift. Things happened too fast. At the mercy of circumstance, I had no time to think, to react." Alex, trained to be stoic in the face of the harshest trials, had nearly been broken by our son's death and mine. Though the miracle of my reappearance brought healing, scars clearly remained. "I should've returned to you earlier. If I had, the accident could have been avoided."

"Don't," I said. "Mrs. White has a murderer's heart. If not then, she would've found another time, another way." Though true, my words offered little comfort.

"That wretched woman," he spat. "Someday she'll regret all she's done."

"Tell me, when did you see our son?"

"When we brought your body to the church, his remains were already there," Alex replied. "Now, try to rest. We have a long day ahead."

The topic was bitter for us both. I snuggled deeper against his chest. Replaying his account, I couldn't shake the feeling that something either fit too well or didn't fit at all.

"Come on, Florence! We are almost there," Alex shouted, yards ahead.

I left the moss-carpeted forest and stepped onto the golden sand, the fresh scent of seawater filling my nostrils. Black-headed gulls soared against the azure sky, dipping close to the waves. And not far in the distance, Hurst Castle rose from the narrow spit of land stretching into the sea as massive as I recalled. I dropped my bag next to Alex's. He was already engaged in setting up camp for the afternoon.

"We are far better prepared than last time," I said, observing Alex spread the flannel cloth Zaira had packed for us over the sand.

"You can say that again. At least this time, I don't have to beg the fortress for food." Alex chuckled.

"I almost forgot about that."

"I didn't. Just like I haven't forgotten that you refused to join me in the water then—but that's going to change today."

I laughed. The idea hadn't even crossed my mind. The sea might look inviting, but I dreaded its chill. "You couldn't be more wrong."

"You *will* swim with me, lady, I assure you." He gave me a roguish smile.

"Even if I entertained the idea, I couldn't. I'm not wearing a bathing suit."

"Why not?" His gaze darted to me. "I asked Zaira to pack one. Did she forget?"

"She didn't."

"I see. You were defiant."

"You can call it that—or clever enough to avoid freezing to death."

Alex began unlacing his shoes.

I unpacked our meal. "Would you like a cucumber sandwich or a Cornish pasty?"

"Are you trying to starve me?"

"We also have apples." I smiled, holding one up.

"Look at the size of this. It wouldn't feed an ant." He took a sandwich and polished it off in two bites while his attention settled on the fortress. "I'll say, that's interesting . . . interesting indeed . . ."

"What is?"

"The movement at Hurst Castle. Those vessels on the far side, the vehicles in front—it's unusual." He rubbed his chin thoughtfully.

"Why?"

"Since the Great War, it's been a low-key location," he replied, grabbing another sandwich. "Even more so in recent years. Hardly any ships come through here anymore."

"It might be a naval exercise or gathering of some sort." I swallowed the last piece of my apple.

"That's what I'm worried about."

"It's probably nothing." I leaned back on my elbows, soaking in the sun.

"I could wander over and find out what's blowing in the wind."

"And why would you do that?"

"Pure curiosity."

"Since you're no longer in active service, I think we should leave it alone. The military doesn't take kindly to civilians snooping around."

"You are right." With a sigh, he lay back and closed his eyes. Before long, the heat prompted him to peel off his top layers. "I'm ready to tackle the *freezing* water."

"Have fun."

"Take courage," he pleaded. "Come with me."

I shook my head decisively.

"You are acting like a fraidy cat," he taunted.

"And I'll gladly remain one, thank you."

Chuckling, he headed to the ocean and dove in with ease, each stroke carrying him farther out into the shimmering waves.

I placed my hat over my face and must have fallen asleep because I startled awake when Alex dropped beside me. Voices drifted through the trees, and I looked over my shoulder. A group of youngsters—three girls in colorful dresses and three boys in dark, weathered overalls—emerged onto the beach. Laughing and shouting, they darted across the sand, the girls' dresses swirling as they ran, and the boys chasing one another with sticks in hand.

"We have company," Alex remarked.

The group smiled and waved as they passed us.

"They are so full of life and joy," I remarked.

"I hope they find some good ones," Alex muttered.

"Good ones?"

"They are looking for shells. The tall boy is carrying a collector's pouch."

"I missed that." I watched as they wandered farther, occasionally stooping to examine their finds. "Where do they come from?"

"Probably from one of the fishing hamlets along the shore."

A breeze carried their laughter to us, stirring an ache in my heart. Maybe it was the longing for my son, but I felt prompted to broach a sensitive subject—one we had discussed before with little success. "You know," I began tentatively, "having children would add so much to our lives."

As if prodded with a spear, Alex sat upright, his body rigid.

When he didn't respond, I pressed on. "Wouldn't you agree?"

"Florence, you know how I feel." He stood abruptly, dressed, and offered me his hand. "Let's walk."

We strolled along the water's edge.

"You haven't answered me," I said.

"You know I love you more than I can ever understand. Sometimes I look at you and wonder if you are truly here or if I've lost my mind entirely. I'm still adjusting to the miracle of having you back. I'm not ready to have children. I'm not ready for things to change again." Why did I feel he left something unsaid?

"Sometimes I also feel that our reality is too amazing to grasp. But like you said last night, we have been blessed beyond reason. Shouldn't we embrace it without fear? Shouldn't we make the most of being together? What could be better than knowing a part of us will live on after we are gone?"

"I'll be gone sooner than you. Don't forget, I'm older than you," he said with an edge. "Maybe a bit too old to have children."

"Don't be absurd. People nowadays have children much later in life. We'd be fine. Now, be honest. Why are you apprehensive?"

"Do you know how many?" He gazed at the sky, where a few stars began to flicker.

"How many what? Stars?"

"No, nights."

"Nights?"

"Yes. Do you know how many nights after losing you, I returned to Forti Radici, yearning to find you there? I lost track. Even surrounded by people, I was empty, numb. I'd leave the house in agony, always headed to the same place—the cemetery. There was a deceptive peace there. In the end, there was no escape, I had to return to my dark world." Tears pooled in his eyes.

Mr. Morris's description of Alex's visits wasn't an exaggeration. "*For years on end, he came to see her come rain or shine. He spent hours kneeling beside her, sometimes weeping, sometimes staring into space. It was heartrending to behold.*"

"Then I escaped to the war. There were endless nights when I sat with my men, watching these very stars, wondering where you were and why you had to leave me. Wondering how much longer it would be until I finally joined you."

My heart pounded against my ribs with anticipation as he opened the door he'd kept shut for so long.

He went on, "I didn't have to be in the trenches. I could have stayed hidden from the front lines. I chose to be there. Do you remember what you made me promise right here, at this beach, so long ago?"

I could never have forgotten. "You promised you would hold on to hope no matter what."

"That promise kept me grounded, kept me from doing something foolish. It would have been easy to run into a minefield or the line of fire. So easy." Alex heaved a weary breath. "Besides, it was my responsibility to help my men survive. To do that, I had to stay alive. I saved some lives, lost others, but I did my best. And through it all, I was somehow strengthened beyond my own ability, staying on the battlefield until the very end. Later, I realized that helping them softened my grief."

"And then?"

"Then I joined the effort to build and expand our military intelligence. By the time I retired, we had developed several prototypes for weapons of mass destruction. I could have stayed on that path, but during a visit to the manor, I took a walk in the forest and ended up by the stream—"

"Where I took a dunking, thanks to you?" I smiled, lightening the mood.

"The very one. As I watched the water flow, my heart burned with an overwhelming urge to retire, to return to the New Forest for good. So I did. Soon after, White convinced me to move to America. And, well, you know the rest."

I halted, my gaze holding his. A halo of light surrounded him as the now-red globe behind him slipped below the horizon.

"How amazing is that?" I said with awe. "Think about it. In her attempt to erase your memories of me, she brought you to New York, where we would find each other. Just like I was promised when I died, our paths would cross again in life."

"Florence, I can't bear to lose you again."

The unspoken confession pierced my soul—he connected the idea of having children with losing me. "Alex, I'm here to stay. We'll grow old together this time. And when it's our turn to move on from this world, I promise I'll let you go first." Peace settled over me. I hoped he felt it too. I didn't know if my feelings were a reassurance to my words, after all, there were few things we could control in life, but I would hold on to them.

"We should head back. It's growing late," he said, ending the speculation.

We retraced our steps to our picnic spot.

"Look!" I pointed to the lighthouse. "The light is on now."

"It's permanent and always reliable, like my love for you, my lady. Don't forget that." He swept me off my feet and ran into the sea.

"Alex, no!" I shrieked. "Don't you dare!"

"Don't fuss." He laughed. "Since you are always admonishing me to conquer my fears, it's time you conquer yours."

"No, no, no!"

He dropped me into the water. I gasped at the chill swallowing me whole, my arms flailing, my legs kicking to stabilize. My feet found solid footing, and I drew a steady breath. To my dismay, Alex was already wading back to shore, his grin infuriating.

"You are a brute of a man!" I feigned anger as I stumbled out of the water.

"There, there, easy now." In between fits of laughter, he retreated as fast as I advanced on him. "See, the sea is nothing to be afraid of."

"I have no problem with the sea other than how cold it is! And who is the fraidy cat now? Stop running!" I gathered the hem of my dress and pulled it up to my thighs to chase after him.

"Are you going to hurt me?"

"Why don't you come over here and find out?"

"Only if you promise to be civil."

"Civil?" I shot back, breathless. "You don't even know what that means, *Lieutenant*. Let me show you."

"Lieutenant?" He laughed. "You must be truly flustered." He retrieved the cloth from the sand. "Here, take this. You'll feel better."

My pride made me hesitate, but the cold won out. I let him wrap the cover around my shoulders. But then, I balled my fists and pounded his chest. "You'll pay dearly for this."

"Oh? What do you have in mind?"

With a wicked grin, I stomped on his foot.

"Ouch!" he yelped.

I dropped the cloth and bolted. He caught me, pulling me down onto the sand, where we rolled together. He kissed me. I hit him. We laughed. He kissed me again. I kissed him back.

Morning found me where I had fallen asleep—in Alex's arms on the shag rug before the embers of the fireplace. The scent of wool mingled with the aroma of charred wood, welcoming the new day.

"Florence." His voice pierced the stillness like an unwelcome alarm. "Do you hear that?"

"No."

"Listen . . ."

I strained my ears. Silence.

"There it is again." Alex sat up. "Do you hear it now?"

"I think so." A growing rumbling in the distance. "What is it?"

"Planes!" Alex sprang to his feet and dashed outside.

I scrambled after him. We halted beneath a patch of blue sky. Within seconds, two aircraft flew overhead, the roar drowning the rustling leaves and birdsong.

"Warplanes." Dread curled my stomach.

Three more streaked above us, their metallic forms glinting in the sunlight.

"Not just warplanes—Spitfires," Alex said. "Our newer short-range bombers. They are extremely fast, and powerful enough to rain hell from heaven."

"What are they doing here?"

"There is only one reason why they would be mobilized." His eyes locked onto mine with a truth I didn't want to face. "We are at war."

CHAPTER 4
~ THE UNCERTAINTY OF WAR ~

Alex's premonition loomed before us. *"There is a terrible evil growing in Germany—one so immense, I'm afraid it will find a way to creep past its borders and threaten us all."*

We were at war, and Germany wasted no time proving its intent. A German submarine torpedoed the *Athenia*, a British passenger liner. The Nazi war machine then set its sights on the battleship HMS *Royal Oak*, anchored at Scapa Flow in the Orkneys to aid the Home Fleet. Another German submarine evaded the defenses and fired three torpedoes—each finding its mark.

Of the 165 sailors under the age of eighteen, 125 perished. England mourned those precious souls, but never more than their mothers. I became convinced that when Shakespeare wrote, *"Hell is empty, and all the devils are here,"* he had foreseen our time.

England, determined to protect its youngsters, initiated the evacuation program, relocating them to safer areas. London especially saw a great number of its children removed. The city bore the brunt of the air raids, each more brutal than the last, designed to crush the spirit of resilience in our people.

At the manor, we prepared for the repercussions of war. Our plan was methodical: acquire extra tools, clothing, weapons, and seeds to expand the produce garden. Despite many helping hands, the task was overwhelming.

Adding to the strain, the incessant ringing of the telephone sent my nerves soaring. The army wanted Alex's expertise. I understood that helping was honorable, but fear crept into my chest. Would they take him away?

Mrs. Haywood surfaced on the threshold. I may as well have been a chair in the library for the attention she paid me, her feather duster flurrying over the double doors. Muttering something under her breath, she gave the panels one final sweep before rushing in to address the furniture.

Upon seeing me, she shrieked. "Goodness gracious, Mrs. Sterling! I had no idea you were here."

"All morning, in this very chair."

"Oh, is that so?" A faint blush colored her cheeks.

"I just finished this book." I signaled to *The Count of Monte Cristo* on the sofa. "And started this one." I held up the volume for her to see.

"*Clever Agriculture.*" She read the title.

"I'm afraid the more I learn about sowing and harvesting, the more I realize how little I know. I had a garden in New York, but nothing compared to what we hope to achieve here."

"Take heart, Mrs. Sterling. There is always something to be learned." Her eyes descended on *The Count of Monte Cristo.* "Was this your first time reading it?"

"No."

"A favorite, then?"

"I wouldn't say favorite. There's just something compelling about the story that draws me back."

"I can't imagine what," she replied with a shudder. "In my opinion, it's too tragic. Too much anger and revenge."

"Realistic, no?"

"Perhaps, but I think I'd prefer it if the story focused more on

Edmond's growth and the rewards he gained from his ordeal, like finding the treasure and meeting Haydée—rather than dwelling on vengeance."

"True, but it doesn't justify the injustices he suffered, does it?" I found myself defending the plot, though I wasn't sure why.

"I think circumstances must be considered, and they are all so different," she offered.

"While there is truth in that," I countered, "I don't believe circumstances give us license to harm others for personal gain. Do you?"

"Oh no," she said with a nervous laugh. "Don't read too much into what I said. It's only a novel."

"Indeed." I smiled but sensed that something beyond the story troubled her. "Mrs. Haywood, is something wrong?"

"Oh, dear. Oh, dear." She dropped her arms in resignation, shoulders slumped. "Is it that obvious?"

"Please, have a seat." I coaxed her to an armchair and returned to my own.

"War, Mrs. Sterling. War is so deplorable, especially when it touches our loved ones."

"Is it someone close to you?"

"The light of my life." Silent tears slipped down her cheeks. "My son left on a high-risk mission early this week. I may never see him again. See, he is in the Royal Air Force."

Her son? The Haywoods never mentioned children. "I . . . I'm sorry." The nation remained transfixed by reports of the week's strategic aerial campaign against Germany, aware of our numerical disadvantage. Having shared Alex, Lucca, and my father with the military, I understood too well the grief and anxiety that came with such sacrifices. "Would you like to tell me about him?"

"Yes, yes. That's precisely what I need." The housekeeper pulled a handkerchief from her pocket and dabbed at her eyes. "He's an extraordinary lad."

"What's his name?"

"William. We call him Will—our little Will."

"Do you have other children?"

"No. I was unable to conceive for the longest time. I had accepted my misfortune when, late in life, my gift from heaven arrived. I became pregnant with Will." Her composure cracked, and she sobbed as though her son were already dead.

"I've heard many stories from my husband about war and the miracles he's witnessed," I said gently. "You mustn't lose hope. You are your son's greatest support."

"I keep telling myself that, but my emotions betray me now and then." She sniffled and wiped her nose, composing herself somewhat. "Will is an excellent pilot, you know. He was selected to fly one of those high-performance planes—Spitfire, I believe they are called. He's been infatuated with airplanes since childhood. I couldn't keep him indoors. From sunrise to sunset, he would dash through the fields with his arms outstretched, pretending to be a plane. Time went by too fast.

"When Will came of age, Haywood and I used our life savings to send him to Cranwell for a proper education. But, of course, that meant we couldn't retire. That's why, at our age, we jumped at the opportunity to work here." The creases at the corners of her eyes deepened, her thoughts seeming to drift from the room. "Oh, Mrs. Sterling, you must believe me—we did all we could for him."

Her words held an undercurrent of—guilt? Maybe it was the timing. Having a son in the RAF would have been her greatest pride if not for the bloody war. The danger he now faced might have eclipsed the joy she once felt in supporting his ambitions.

"I have no doubt you've done your best, and likely much more," I reassured. "Now, you must be strong for Will. As far as we know, he is alive and doing well. Hold on to that hope."

"Yes, yes, he is alive. He'll stay alive." She stood at once. "You must forgive me. I shouldn't have dragged you into my personal affairs."

"The suffering and sacrifice of a mother are never in vain. They are accounted for in the heavens above, and whatever happens, all will be well." My words surprised me more than they did her—I sounded just like Granny.

"Thank you, Mrs. Sterling. I must get on with my chores." She turned to leave, her voice trailing behind her like a prayer. "He'll come back to me...heavens above..."

The wind howled, and rain battered the house through the night. Restless, I left the bed and peered out the window. Darkness yielded to the first hints of dawn. And fog's tendrils wove through the trees, smothering everything in their path—much like our menace, Adolf Hitler. The thought turned my mind to Mrs. Haywood's son.

"What is it, Florence?" Alex mumbled from the bed.

"I'm sorry. Did I wake you?" I slipped back under the covers.

"I don't think so." He yawned and stretched, his arms reaching over his head. "The rain stopped."

"At last. But it's another gray day."

"That's all we've been getting lately."

"Not ideal for our pilots."

"The poor fellows," Alex groaned. "The battle in the sky is a ghastly affair."

A sudden idea struck me. Could Mrs. Haywood have been hinting for me to intervene on her son's behalf? "Hypothetically speaking," I said, "how difficult would it be to ground a pilot?"

"What do you mean?"

"Could a pilot be assigned to a safer post?"

"Who are you thinking about?"

"The Haywoods' son. He is a Royal Air Force pilot."

"I'll say, I did not know they had a son," Alex exclaimed.

"They do. And as you can imagine, they are distraught over safety."

"As are countless other parents."

I heard the implication: the Haywoods weren't alone in their fears, and recalling one pilot wouldn't solve the greater crisis. While I understood the fallacy of my pursuit, if my son had lived, he might be a soldier now, and I would try to keep him from harm. "He's their only child, Alex. Could you look him up? Pull some strings? I mean, there must be other places he could serve."

A heavy silence ensued.

"I'm not active in the army," Alex said at last. "I don't carry the influence I once did in higher circles."

"And that's why the army won't stop calling you day or night, isn't it?" I said with sarcasm.

"That's different."

"No, it isn't," I insisted. "You have connections. A few calls, reminders of old favors might make a difference."

"Florence, be serious," he said, exasperated. "It's not as simple as you think. It's unprofessional. And it's inappropriate."

"Mrs. Haywood. She's gotten into me. She is terrified of losing her son. Do you remember the men you helped in the trenches? The stories you shared about their longing to return home, to see their mothers? I assure you—the longing of their mothers is far, far worse."

Alex sighed, rubbing his temples. "Do you know where he is stationed?"

"All I know is that he flies a Spitfire."

"Hmm. He must be very skilled. Did he fly this week?"

"I believe so."

"I heard only fifty percent of the pilots made it back."

"For Mrs. Haywood's sake, I hope he was among them. Please, Alex, look him up."

"All right, but I can't promise anything."

I headed to the kitchen, a storm of worries accompanying me. Alex had locked himself in his office. Again. The calls and telegrams from London refused to abate. The signs were impossible to ignore. The military crept back into our lives, and I couldn't understand why they so desperately sought Alex's advice. Surely, they had no shortage of clever strategists at their bidding. All I knew was the persistent premonition of separation—a loss taking root before it began.

I found the Haywoods and Zaira gathered around the radio atop the counter. The apparatus was our lifeline for news, though it mostly delivered updates that only added to our already flagging spirits. Even so, we remained tethered to it, needing to stay informed. A burst of static interrupted the communication, prompting Mr. Haywood to mutter a string of colorful words.

"Good afternoon," I greeted.

Startled, Zaira and Mrs. Haywood whirled around with muffled gasps, while Mr. Haywood's gaze snapped to me. They had been so engrossed in the broadcast that my arrival had gone unnoticed.

"Mrs. Sterling, forgive me—the signal is impossible today." Mr. Haywood fidgeted with the dial.

"No need to apologize." I pulled a chair and sat at the table. "I'm just as eager to hear the latest news."

"Would you like some tea?" Mrs. Haywood offered.

"No, thank you."

"Wretched war." Zaira settled in the seat beside me. "The BBC is insistent that the German offensive is victorious everywhere. And they've confirmed that France has surrendered."

"Heaven have mercy on us!" Mrs. Haywood threw her arms in the air, punctuating her words.

"France needs it more than us," Mr. Haywood croaked.

"I'm not so sure about that," Zaira refuted. "We are next in the Nazi's list—and after our defiance, they won't show us any mercy."

"I'm afraid you are right." I agreed. If France—better equipped to fight them than we were—had fallen, what chance did England have? With France occupied and only the English Channel between us, a swift and brutal invasion seemed inevitable. If that happened, nothing would stop the Nazis from dominating all of Europe.

"It was also announced that the conscription of men will continue full steam ahead," Zaira said with sadness.

"Oh, my dear friend. I'm so sorry." I held her hand. "You are thinking of Clarence."

"He is almost thirty-nine, and in excellent health. Two more years would have spared him."

"Maybe, but I'm afraid the government will raise the age limit if this conflict doesn't come under control soon." My stomach churned; Alex might not be spared either.

Mr. Haywood uttered a triumphant exclamation as the radio waves came clearly once more. An urgent voice announced: *"Britain continues to plead with the United States to join our efforts for liberty."*

The voice faded, again overtaken by a series of sharp pops and crackling. With a growl, Mr. Haywood toyed with the dial until the signal returned.

"Years of Nazi indoctrination continue to bear fruit against minority groups, particularly the Jewish community. Reports of their businesses being shut down, their work licenses revoked, their homes and valuables confiscated, and their families torn apart multiply daily. So too does the number of missing or deceased. This, ladies and gentlemen, is a blunt campaign to obliterate life and its attendant rights."

The announcement ended, replaced by soft music—a balm to encourage listeners to carry on. There was no other option.

"I ought to get back to work." Mr. Haywood gathered his gloves from the counter, looking haggard by the news.

"I'll join you in a little while," I told him. "I'd like your opinion on the seeds stored in the west cellar. I'm thinking of expanding the garden. If we are to survive this war, and help others do the same, we'll need every inch of it."

The fire in the hearth died sometime during the night. Even under the bedding, the chill seeped into my bones. I scrambled to Alex's side, wrapped my arm around his chest, and flung my leg over his, absorbing his warmth.

"You are trembling," he whispered, his voice thick with sleep.

"It's freezing."

"It reminds me of the night of the storm at Oak's Place—one of the best nights of my life."

"Mine too." The rain had lashed the streets of Geneva, turning them into rivers. I'd stayed overnight at the mansion, ending up in Alex's arms. It was the beginning of our relationship in New York, our second connection in life. "You know, it's not fair that you are so comfortable wearing less clothing than me."

"If you keep holding me like this, that might change," he said playfully. "Then, I can warm you up properly."

"How about another option?"

Alex laughed and rolled off the bed. Seizing the fire poker, he stirred the ashes in the hearth, then added a few pieces of newspaper. Once the kindling burned, he tossed in a couple of logs. Soon, the bedroom filled with a lively glow, and heat wrapped around us.

"There." He slid back in bed. "I think you'll survive now."

"I suppose I've no right to complain. Our soldiers would gladly trade my problems for theirs." The thought made me recoil. I couldn't imagine the horrors they endured.

"That's true," Alex agreed. "Training and determination help, but war, especially the battlefield is ugly."

"Speaking of soldiers, did you find out anything about Will?"

"Only what you already know. He is a Spitfire pilot with an exceptional record. Unfortunately, his prowess makes him invaluable to the RAF. That complicates your request."

I mulled over his words, searching for a loophole. Finding none, I said in frustration, "Honestly, how much of a difference can one man make in such a large conflict?"

"A significant one. A skilled pilot can save countless lives."

"And break his parents' hearts along the way. The Haywoods have only him—"

"Florence, you have taken this to heart."

"I can't stop thinking about the Haywoods," I admitted. "And how cruel it would be for them to lose him."

"Don't fuss—I pushed some buttons."

"Seriously?"

"Yes."

"Thank you."

"Don't thank me yet. I have no idea what might come from it, if anything. And even if he's reassigned, he'll still face danger."

"Hopefully, less danger."

A rumble, like the rolling motion of an earthquake, rattled the house.

"What in the world?" Alex flung the covers to the side and dashed to the window. "I can't see anything."

"Thunder? Again?"

"No, it's not that." He pulled on his trousers and hustled from the room.

I thrust my arms through the sleeves of my bathrobe and followed him downstairs, stepping into the icy dawn.

"Bloody hell!" Alex exclaimed.

To the east, the sky was lit with bursts of light, plumes of smoke rising ominously.

"Southampton," I stammered, horror dawning. "The Luftwaffe found the port."

"They are bombing the docks, the ammunition depots, and, most likely, the Spitfire Supermarine factory," Alex growled, having foreseen this very moment. "It will leave us at an even greater disadvantage—one we might not recover from."

"Good heavens—so much destruction." I imagined the bombs shaking the city's foundations, the scorching fires, the screams of the injured—a scene from hell that would repeat itself, I feared, countless times before the war's end.

"I can't stay on the sidelines any longer," he stated resolutely. "It's time to get involved."

"What else can we do?" I thought of the area's service projects and our Victory Garden, as we had named it. The produce would help families in need, and the surplus could be traded for essentials. Yet, in the face of so much devastation, our efforts felt woefully insufficient.

"The military is about to undertake a high-profile mission." Alex took my hands into his. "They've requested my help. I might not make much of a difference, but at least I can try."

"A mission?" I repeated, stunned.

"Yes."

"What kind of mission?"

"One that will take me out of the country. That's all I can tell you for now."

The premonition I had dreaded came to pass. I felt as if I were sinking into quicksand, the world shifting beneath me. Alex would leave me again.

"You are shivering. Come on, let's go inside before you get sick." He maneuvered me into the house. His worried eyes looked down at me as his hands braced my shoulders. "Florence, I wasn't going to tell you this. It's not public information, but you should know. It'll help you understand my decision."

I stared at him, reminding myself to breathe.

"The Nazis have launched an operation called 'mercy killing.' It's a euphemism for euthanizing anyone, young, old, even newborns who don't fit their standard of perfection. On top of that, the reports of labor camps in Nazi territories are mounting. Of course, *labor* is a generous term, given the inhumane activities we fear might be taking place. And the terror they inflict on the nations they invade, it's beyond comprehension. We must do all we can to stop this."

Shame washed over me for how little I understood the state of the war. The world groaned under Adolf Hitler's madness, and the call to rise and defend human life had been sounded. Alex would answer it, and so would I—his departure a refiner's fire as I wavered between hope and surrendering to the void his absence would leave.

"Florence . . ." Alex searched my eyes for approval.

I nodded, pressing my lips together to hold back a sob.

Another war. Another mission, history repeating itself.

CHAPTER 5
~ FATE ~

Alex had gone to London again.

The sun grew hot, and my knees ached from the unforgiving ground where I planted seeds. I removed my gardening gloves, wiping a damp hand across my sleeve. I needed a break. I started toward the house, the newspaper headlines swirling in my head.

Nazis Raid London and 13 Towns

After relentless waves of German raiders failed to break through the RAF's defenses on South-East England, Nazi bombers renewed their raids across the country. London continues to endure endless nights in alarm.

I recalled the story of one of our bomber pilots next. He had come dangerously close to a German target before searchlights spotted his plane, turning it into the focus of the enemy's fury. Undeterred, the pilot dived eight hundred feet through a barrage of hellish fire and ordered the bombs released. "*I thought we couldn't go back having gone so far, so we carried on,*" he had said, his courage remarkable.

The pilot survived that day—a rare outcome. The loss of life and innocence on all sides of the conflict was incomprehensible. War was not confined to distant battlefields; it seeped into homes and hearts, leaving scars that would endure for generations. Yet, we had to *carry on*.

Predictably, I found the Haywoods and Zaira huddled around the radio. This time, the calm, instructive voices came from the experts at Kew Royal Botanical Gardens. They spoke of shortages of pharmaceutical plants, once supplied by Germany.

One of these essential plants was *digitalis purpurea*, commonly known as wild foxglove. As I listened, I pictured the dappled glades of the New Forest, where it thrived. Beautiful but dangerous, foxglove was notoriously toxic. It required careful drying to preserve its medicinal properties, a lesson Mr. Leroy had taught me years ago—the knowledge still lingered, sharp as ever.

Our nation now called upon its citizens to grow and, where possible, forage these plants. Zaira and I exchanged a glance, excitement flickering between us.

"We'll need baskets, clippers, and thick garden gloves," I said, mentally compiling a list of essentials.

"And maps." Zaira unfurled one across the table, tracing her finger over the wooded areas nearby. "We can plan a proper foraging expedition."

Mrs. Haywood, ever practical, spoke up. "I'll mention it at the Women's Institute meeting this week. I'm sure others would be keen to volunteer."

"The plants will need to be dried quickly upon harvesting. I'll build a drying shed," Mr. Haywood said promptly. "We'll need a few fellows from the village to help."

"Then we have a plan." I smiled, our newfound purpose lightening my previous gloom. "Let's go scouting for glades this afternoon."

"It's a bit premature for that," Zaira said, though the spark in her eyes revealed her eagerness.

"Perhaps, but it won't hurt to look." I was anxious to distract myself with something tangible—something I could control.

"All right. We'll call it Operation Foxglove," Zaira decided.

The Lagonda returned from London, its tires kicking up dust in the late afternoon light. Alex sat behind the wheel, with Mr. Brown in the passenger seat. The chauffeur took care of parking in busy streets while Alex hurried to his meetings. And often these days, they stayed overnight at Alex's flat.

I propped the rake against the evergreens, eyeing the scattered leaves with disapproval before stepping into the courtyard. Alex hopped out of the car, and Mr. Brown slid into the driver's seat to take the Lagonda around the house.

"I'm so glad you are home." I pressed my cheek against his chest, reveling in his embrace.

"I see you missed me as much as I missed you." He lowered his lips to mine, and for a moment, our troubles disappeared.

"You were gone longer this time."

"I'm sorry." He grabbed my hand, and we strode to the bench in the rhododendron garden. The plants sprawled unrestrained, the clusters of pink and violet flowers creating a soothing atmosphere. "Anything new at home?"

"The Haywoods, Zaira, and I have decided to join the effort to gather medicinal plants."

"Of course, you have." He smiled, but uneasiness clouded his eyes.

"How was your visit to London?"

"Fine."

I knew then that something weighed on his mind. "What's the matter?"

"I'm about to learn the final details for my mission."

Final details meant imminent departure. "I didn't expect it to be this soon."

"General Thomas Frankfort will be here in a few days to finalize the plans."

"Thomas?" I gazed at Alex in disbelief. Thomas was a survivor from the past, well acquainted with me.

"The very same."

"You can't be serious. He can't see me!" I shook my head. "We can't explain my resemblance to the Florence he once knew. He won't understand."

"We can't, and we won't. Thomas knows I've remarried and that you are American. You'll have to be careful, that's all."

"Careful? I'm identical to my previous self. He'll faint when he sees me!"

"He'll be fine. Besides, what option do we have?"

"I could hide."

"No. He'll be your main contact while I am gone. You know you can trust him to tell you the truth. Listen," Alex cupped my chin with his hand, "things are as they are. We won't run from reality. It's been nearly a quarter of a century for him. We'll have to chalk this up to coincidence. After all, isn't there a saying that everyone has a double?"

He was right. If I hoped to live a normal life, even as a living specter of the past, I couldn't live in the shadows. Still, facing Thomas was daunting. "I'll do my best. I hope it's enough."

"It will be. We don't have time to worry about Frankfort. Once he arrives, the mission will roll fast. I'll be gone soon after."

"I wish there were another way for you to help, one that didn't involve leaving England."

"Believe me, I have wrestled with this day and night. I have thought of every excuse to minimize my involvement. But this is what I've been called to do, and I must see it through. We must continue to fight. If we don't help those who need us, there won't be anyone to help us when they come for us."

"You sound like my father. He fulfilled his duty at the cost of his life," I said, instantly regretting it. My personal loss loomed like a monster, clouding my vision. "I'm sorry."

"It's all right. I take that as high praise." He stretched his arm across my shoulders, pulling me close. "You mustn't fret. Things are better planned and carried out nowadays."

That, I didn't believe, but there was no point in arguing. Desperate to hold on to him, even a piece of him, I turned to the desire that ignited my soul whenever I let it breathe. "Now that our lives are changing . . ."

"Tell me."

"I'd like us to reconsider having children."

"I don't want to have this discussion right now," he snapped.

"This may be the only time we have left," I shot back. "Like I told you at the beach, I'd love to have a part of us, of you, live on, especially now that you are leaving."

"I can't leave you with more than one uncertainty." I saw the agony in his eyes but also the resolve. "I can't risk coming back to learn that something went wrong. You say I'm risking my life with this mission. I say I'd be risking yours by leaving you with child."

I got to my feet, fists clenched at my sides. I wanted to cry at his stubbornness but refused to give in to self-pity. "I disagree. In this instance, Mr. Sterling, you are *wrong*." Disappointed and hurt, I strode away. He didn't follow.

The air held a menacing, dormant energy. It was one of those days when the sun refused to show its face, hiding behind a blanket of clouds. I heaved a long sigh and turned at the sound of the shop's doorbell, its chime reverberating through the morning. Zaira burst onto the pavement, clutching a box of chamomile tea.

"Wonderful. You found some," I stated the obvious.

"You have no idea the stress I went through to get it," she said. "Did you see the woman who came in after me? The one in the red fedora?"

"I did. What about her?"

"She was after the chamomile too. Luckily, I knew where it was and dashed for it. I felt a pinch of guilt, but not enough to let her have it."

"They might have some in the store at the edge of town."

"I doubt it." Zaira shook her head. "The shelves are growing emptier by the day, and there's no restocking in sight. The owner said shipments are compromised. Many never even reach the shore."

"This darn conflict will get worse before it gets better."

"Just in case, I'm going to enjoy this thoroughly." She waved the box triumphantly. "Clarence likes it, too."

"Is that what you two were drinking the other night?" On one of my walks, I'd spotted them chatting in the stable, steaming mugs in hand. Their bond had grown noticeably stronger since Clarence received the call to join the army.

"Ah, you don't miss a thing, do you?" Zaira smiled. "Yes, it was tea. Clarence loves hot drinks, and so do I, as you know."

"Sounds like you two have a lot in common." I was overjoyed that my dear friend might have finally found her soulmate.

"I would like to think so." Her voice grew softer, thoughtful. "You know, I'm starting to truly enjoy country life, and so is Clarence. In fact, he dreams of starting a horse-breeding business. Maybe even raising some of the finest horses in England." Zaira rambled on about his plans, wisely omitting the uncertainty of his upcoming leave.

While I nodded along, I prayed they would be spared the ravages of war. They deserved the chance to build a life together, for, clearly, they were in love.

We reached the main square and hurried down the cobblestone path just as thunder rolled through the sky. The clouds brimmed with fury, ready to unleash their storm.

"Goodness gracious—that's loud!" Zaira cried.

I looked up as another thunderclap exploded, reverberating in my chest. My gaze dropped to the block ahead, where a couple moved away from us. I glanced at the display windows across the road, then back at them. The woman sported a brown dress that accentuated her curves, and a flowery scarf draped over her hair. Her companion was tall and broad-shouldered, with dark hair. At first glance, they appeared ordinary folk, but something about them tugged at my instincts, a peculiarity that demanded closer inspection.

I hastened to shorten the distance, my curiosity growing.

"You don't want to get rained on, do you?" Zaira teased, as she scrambled to keep up.

I didn't respond. My focus locked onto the woman's hurried steps— the way her hips swung just so.

"Florence, what's gotten into you? Slow down!"

"Is that who I think it is?" I asked more to myself than her.

"Who?" Zaira croaked.

"White. Is that her up ahead?" My thoughts raced over the evil the woman had wrought in both my lives. Though I had no proof of my murder—unless, of course, Mr. Vines turned on her—there was a warrant for her arrest for fraud and for poisoning Alex. All that remained was to find her.

"Hmm . . ." Zaira squinted at the pair, her brow furrowed. "I'll say, it looks a great deal like her, but it's hard to tell without seeing her hair. One thing is certain, though, that's not Mr. Vines. That chap is much younger and, needless to say, far better built."

The woman glanced over her shoulder, and I could have sworn she jolted at the sight of us. Was she simply startled to see anyone, or was it us she hadn't expected? She said something to her companion, and their pace quickened.

"Come on." I almost broke into a trot. "Let's find out."

"Wait, Florence! What will we do if it is her? She's dangerous."

"I haven't thought that far." Cause a commotion to delay her until the police arrived? Give her the blows I owed her from Oak's Place? Of course, her companion might complicate matters. Who was he?

Like a vanishing act, the couple disappeared between a row of houses. I hurried to the spot, only to find a deserted alley, shrouded in shadows and silence. Tall brick walls loomed on either side.

"Florence, wait for me!" Zaira called in a wheezy voice as I darted through the passage.

Emerging at the other end, I was met with an unexpected scene: an elderly woman sweeping the sidewalk with a broom, while a blue car sped away in the distance. My gaze jumped to the windows overlooking the road, to the shuttered shops nearby—all unnervingly still, as if frozen in time. My anticipation was dampened. The pair must have gotten into that car.

"Where did they go?" Zaira panted, clutching her chest as though to steady her heart. "Oh, goodness! I'm so out of shape."

"I'm afraid they drove off, but let's make sure." I approached the woman, who grumbled something about "horrid cobwebs" as she attacked a windowpane with her broom. "Ma'am, did you see the couple who just passed by?"

She stopped mid-sweep, peering at me under thick brows. "Good morning, miss," she said, summoning a strained politeness.

"Good morning." I forced a smile despite my impatience. "Please, did you see where they went?"

"Well, yes." She pointed at the car shrinking into the horizon. "They left in their car."

In *their* car. "Do you know them?"

"And you don't?" She was clever, there was a pressing reason behind my interest. Otherwise, why ask? A knowing look flashed across her face. "I don't believe I have seen you around here before. Have I?"

Observant.

"We just moved into Forti Radici," I answered. "We are related to Alexander Sterling."

"Oh, yes. I heard he'd returned from America."

I steered the conversation back to the pair, for it was apparent she knew them. I'd repeat the repentance prayer ten times later if necessary, but a small lie might earn me valuable information. "I thought they might be the Parkers—old acquaintances of mine. I haven't seen them in ages and hoped to say hello."

"The Parkers? Oh no. You've got the wrong folk."

So, did I get the right one? Could Mrs. White truly be within reach?

"If not the Parkers, then who?" Zaira interjected with a bright smile.

"The Burrells. I understand she is a widow who's taken up lodging in the cottage at the Ackers' farm."

"Oh." The disappointment was sharp, my vision of Mrs. White behind bars evaporating.

"And the man with her?" Zaira continued the interrogation.

"I heard it's her nephew." She looked sideways, and, with a swing of the broom, obliterated the spiderwebs on the window seal. "But I must say, I highly doubt it."

"Why is that?" I asked.

"Well, you see, I've encountered them at the market on a few occasions. He's always too close to her—I mean physically, as if ready to take a bullet for her. The poor thing seems perpetually on edge, jumping at every little thing. I have nephews, miss, and believe me, they don't behave like that."

"Hmm, that's interesting indeed," Zaira murmured.

"It is, but you know," the woman said, "they might be folks relocating from the city. They are a peculiar bunch—quite traumatized by the bombings." She had a point. It might be as simple as that.

"Adele, what's taking you so long?" a man called from inside the house, the door barely cracking open.

Adele's lips tightened, her knuckles whitening around the broom. I had the distinct impression she'd like to swat him with it. "I'd better go see what he wants. He always needs something. Good day to you."

"Wait—what color is Mrs. Burrell's hair?" I had to ask.

"Umm . . ." She thought for a moment. "White. Yes, yes, white." With that, Adele disappeared inside.

I tuned to Zaira expectantly. "What do you think?"

"If it was Mrs. White, why would she risk being so close? Someone could recognize her. I mean, she may be off her rocker, but I doubt she is eager for prison."

"True. Unless her rage toward Alex and me outweighs her fear," I countered. "If she intends to cause harm, she'll want to stay close to Forti Radici to know what's happening."

"Then why trade Vines for a younger fellow? She never mentioned nephews—or any relatives for that matter. Besides, Vines and she are bound by their past, and let's not forget he is also on the run, so why separate? I can't see that happening."

She was right. Vines would follow Mrs. White anywhere. Yet, I couldn't shake the feeling that Mrs. Burrell was none other than Mrs. White.

For hours, I wrestled with the idea that Mrs. White might be closer than imagined, ready to execute one of her wicked plans. When I finally banished the worry, my desire for a family and Alex's opposition came into focus. Ultimately, my love for him and the monumental task ahead of him persuaded me to stand down—for the time being. All I could now do was pray for his safe return and spare him unnecessary concerns. Hence, I neglected to mention my suspicions about the couple in town.

I reached for him, finding his spot on the bed empty. I rolled to my other side and inhaled sharply. Thomas. After all this time, he would see me again, just as he must remember me. For my part, I considered him a loyal friend, one who hadn't wavered in rescuing us from the ruthless German leader, Krause. The memory was swift.

We had been captured and disarmed. Alex suffered a brutal beating. Then Krause aimed his rifle at him. The anguish I saw in Alex at the failure to save us and the mission remained just as painful as the day it happened. My heart stopped as I'd awaited the shot, but when it came, thank heaven Krause, not Alex, lay dead. Thomas and his men saved our lives.

In the labyrinths of my mind, I traveled forward to the days in Keyhaven, to when Thomas taught me to fire a rifle, and we read books on the beach. I was eager to see him again and apprehensive all the same. How would he react? How would I respond? Could I carry on as if I'd never known him? I would soon learn the answers. He should be arriving at any moment, if he hadn't already.

I descended the staircase and saw Alex in the shadows of the foyer, staring out the window. "Is he here? I can't tell you how many times I awoke last night, worrying about this."

He stepped into the light, and I paused, taking in the young, handsome face.

"Good morning," the soldier said.

"Good morning," I responded at once, feeling foolish for my blunder. "Do forgive me. I was looking for Mr. Sterling."

"A pleasure to meet you. Miss . . .?" He extended his hand, looking smart in his brown military uniform,

"Florence Sterling. Mr. Sterling's wife."

For a fleeting moment, disbelief flashed in his brown eyes—perhaps because I was younger than he expected. "Wing Commander William Haywood."

At the sound of his name, the awkwardness vanished. Having championed his return, I felt as if I already knew him. "Oh, Mrs. Haywood's son!" I was overjoyed for her. Though motherhood had never fully been realized for me, it felt as innate as a fledgling's growing wings. "Welcome to Forti Radici, Commander Haywood."

"Thank you. Please call me Will."

"Have you seen your mother yet?"

"Yes. I just left her and my father in the kitchen. I'm waiting for General Sterling. He is speaking to General Frankfort in his office."

Just then, Zaira appeared around the corner. "Oh, good, good. You are already up," she addressed me. "Mr. Sterling would like you and Commander Haywood to join him in his office." Her eyes surveyed the young soldier, no doubt for the umpteenth time today.

"Thank you, Zaira." To Will, I said, "This way, please."

I guided him through the corridors, my chest tight with the anticipation of seeing Thomas. My footsteps must have matched the rapid beating of my heart because before I knew it, we stood before the door. With a warning tap, I let us into the office.

Alex and Thomas rose from their seats on either side of the desk. My gaze found Thomas's as his found me. He looked as if he had seen a ghost—his mouth agape, his face drained of color. In a brown military uniform, he still cut a striking figure. His eyes, though lined with age, remained alert as they had been twenty years ago. His red hair, now threaded with silver, framed a face with a bushy mustache—one that reminded me of my father's.

I neared them, uncertain of what to say. To have known him so well, yet now pretending I didn't know him at all, was more destabilizing than I had anticipated.

"General Frankfort, this is my wife, Mrs. Sterling," Alex said, and I wondered if he had purposedly omitted my first name.

"General Frankfort, I'm pleased to meet you." I extended my hand, reeling in my emotions.

"The pleasure is all mine." His voice was unsteady, his eyes wide and unblinking.

"I've heard much about you." I smiled reassuringly, fearing he might faint. "Are you here to take my husband away?"

"I wouldn't put it that way." Maintaining eye contact, he dropped into the armchair. "But there is some truth in that."

Will sat in the chair beside Thomas. I stayed on my feet, unsure of my purpose here beyond meeting my old friend.

"Shall we proceed with the matter at hand?" Alex proposed.

"Carry on." Thomas tugged at the end of his mustache. Again, I could see my father in him.

"Should I leave?" I asked before they could suggest it.

"No, please stay," Alex responded. "I have permission for you to learn about this."

I nodded, grateful not to be left in the dark, and took the chair next to Will.

"Commander Haywood," Alex started, "as you know, your record is flawless. Your flying skills, coupled with your knowledge of aerodynamics, make you a prime candidate for this assignment. We appreciate the Royal Air Force loaning you to us and your willingness to take on this mission, especially when so little has been disclosed to you."

Alex had warned me that Will's abilities would make it difficult to bring him home. This mission was the loophole that made it possible. And what could be better for the young pilot than to be under Alex's watch?

"My pleasure, sir." Will straightened with pride.

"As you are aware, this is a high-profile mission," Thomas emphasized, glancing at me again. "Its success or failure could very well dictate the future of our country."

I thought back to the night of my first wedding to Alex. The blissful day had ended with the announcement of a mission much like this one. The cost of success had been my father's blood and that of many others. Whose blood would it cost this time?

"Let's go over it briefly, just the main points," Alex said gravely. "Britain has developed several technical prototypes for weapons of mass destruction. In scientific endeavors, we are a step ahead of other nations. As things stand, however, we are at risk of invasion, and we cannot advance or produce these inventions in great volume. The United States, on the other hand, has the capability to do so. We are going to share the information with them."

I had imagined a myriad of possibilities, from sending more spies into Germany, to a plot to capture Hitler, to secretly seizing the French fleet to keep it from Nazi hands, but not this. My thoughts spilled out before I could stop them. "Are you saying that we are to hand over our secret advancements to another country?"

"Mrs. Sterling, out of everyone here, I would've never thought you to be the one to object." Thomas's eyebrows furrowed as he turned slightly toward me.

"And why is that, Thom—General Frankfort?"

"Because you are the only American in this room."

His declaration grounded me like a wounded bird. "Forgive me. This awful war is truly upsetting." I despised being the ghost of my former self.

"Well, we don't have much choice. We need the United States to do what we cannot. It's either this or slavery to the Nazis," Alex clarified. "We are sacrificing something important for something more valuable—our liberty."

"Is that our mission, then?" Will surmised. "To bring the intelligence to the States?"

"Yes and no. Ours is a backup task for the group delivering the physical documents. In addition to copies, we'll store as much data to memory as possible," Alex replied. "I've memorized some of the most critical designs and formulas, but it's a vast project."

"That's impressive, sir," Will noted.

"Not really. I was familiar with them already."

It suddenly dawned on me. At the beach, Alex said that after the Great War, he took part in developing weapons of mass destruction. This knowledge made him a target, and uniquely qualified for this undertaking.

Alex continued, "Commander Haywood, you understand the vulnerability of our planes and defense systems. Once you've seen the new designs, you'll assist us in identifying which advancements we should prioritize."

"To make sure I understand, are we speaking about the possibility of building better planes than the Spitfire?" Will's face lit with excitement.

"Much better," Thomas assured.

"Remarkable," Will muttered.

"You can say that again," Thomas agreed with a wry smile. "We have developments that, trust me, you can hardly imagine. Now, as you can appreciate, this is a delicate matter. If harm comes to the first group, it will fall to you to complete the mission—and time is of the essence."

"Commander Haywood, you'll remain in Forti Radici until we depart," Alex informed.

"When would that be, sir?"

"As soon as we get clearance," Alex answered.

"Your mother will be ecstatic to have you a while longer," I said to Will.

"Of that, I have no doubt," he responded warmly.

Thomas reached for the teapot and refilled his cup.

"Where should we have Commander Haywood set up?" Alex asked me. "The staff quarters are not an option. Too many distractions. We can't risk the commander losing focus right now."

Will averted his gaze to the floor, as if silently agreeing with Alex's assessment.

"Please feel free to pick any rooms upstairs," I invited.

"Including Lucca's?" Alex raised an eyebrow.

"Any room." After my encounter with my brother during my journey back in time, I was at peace with his memory.

Thomas choked on his drink, his eyes widening as he clutched his throat. Whether it was the liquid going down the wrong pipe or my audacity in offering the late Mrs. Sterling's brother's room, I couldn't be sure. In Keyhaven all those years ago, I'd told him about my disagreement with my father when he allowed Alex to occupy it.

"Are you all right?" I handed him a serviette.

"Fine—fine." He wheezed, a cough bursting from his chest.

"Right, then. I'll ask Martha to give Will a tour." Alex rose. "I'll be right back."

Alex and Will withdrew.

Thomas composed himself.

I readjusted on the chair, smoothing my skirt with uncertain hands. Now that he and I were alone, I wasn't sure what to say, especially when he regarded me for an uncomfortable moment, as if waiting for a confession.

"Would you like some more tea?" I offered.

"No, thank you. Choking once was enough."

"I'm sorry, it must have gone cold."

"Just a little."

"I'll take care of it." I reached for the pot.

"It's all right. I'm done."

"Are you sure?"

"Yes."

I beheld his eyes and felt the urgency to learn more about him. Was he married? He wore a wedding ring. Did he have children? I opened my mouth to ask but quickly shut it again.

Thankfully, he spoke first. "Is this your first time in England?"

"It is." At least, it was in my current life.

"And do you like it, Mrs. Sterling?"

"I sure do." I then said something that sooner or later he would discover. "Please call me Florence."

"I'm sorry?" His eyes protruded to an unnatural size, and for a second, I feared he might choke again. "What did you say?"

"Call me Florence. It's my given name."

"Alexander's deceased wife's name was Florence," he sputtered. "You're aware of that, yes?"

"A great coincidence, isn't it?" My responses were doomed to be truths cloaked in layers of lies.

"Quite so, but not as great as your resemblance to her. You must forgive me, but have you seen a portrait of the late Mrs. Sterling?" He scanned the room, searching for one in vain.

"I'm afraid they were stored away before I arrived."

"If I didn't know better, I'd say you were her twin, cousin, or otherwise related." His voice sharpened, as if I were an enemy under interrogation. "Are you aware of that too?"

"Somewhat, yes." Disappointed by my lies, I rambled on, digging deeper into the mire. "I suppose we can't discard the possibility of a family connection. Like many Americans, I have British roots. Perhaps my likeness to his late wife is the reason Alex married me—wouldn't you agree?"

"I'm sorry. I didn't mean to suggest—"

"It's all right. We are happy together." I pressed on before he could respond. "What about you? Are you married?"

"Yes." His gaze fell to his ring. "I have five children—three boys and two girls."

"Any in the army?"

"Thank heavens, no. They are not old enough for that. My wife couldn't bear it, nor could I."

"I have no children, but after seeing Mrs. Haywood's distress over Will, I can imagine." Had he married Catherine, the Countess of Brockenhurst's daughter, my old friend and confidant from the past? I should have asked Alex.

"Oh yes. The mere thought of our boys being conscripted gives Mary a steady flow of nightmares."

Mary, not Catherine.

A shadow drew our gazes to the windowpane. Clarence moved across the grounds, a horse in tow.

"Do you enjoy horseback riding?" Thomas inquired.

"Very much." I strode to the window, memories from my previous life surfacing. I despised this silence between us, all that had gone unspoken for so long.

Alex walked in then. "Frankfort, we have much to discuss."

"I'll leave you to it." I headed to the door.

"Mrs. Sterling," Thomas called.

"Yes."

"With the war and the risk of an invasion, I strongly suggest you learn how to use a rifle—unless, of course, you already know how." The edge in his voice made it clear he was fishing for answers.

"Thank you. I shall remember that," I responded evasively. He had endured enough shock for one day.

CHAPTER 6
~ NEARNESS ~

At dawn, Alex drove Clarence to London to join the army. Zaira wore a mask of calm for his sake, but the moment he left, she broke into uncontrollable sobbing. I understood her anguish—it felt as though a piece of her soul had been torn away, knowing that she might never reclaim it. Words felt hollow, incapable of offering solace, so I simply held her, letting her cry until the tears ceased. I then gave her a sleeping draught and watched her until she drifted into rest.

It wouldn't be long now, before I, like Zaira, walked the road of hope and prayer, wishing for our loved one's safe return. Love—a dreadfully wonderful thing.

I wandered outside, idly tracing the grounds until I reached what had once been Mrs. Allerton's garden. She had cultivated the rarest flowers in the area, favoring rhododendrons and azaleas. Now, unfamiliar plants took their place. This was also the spot where Margaret Sterling once dreamed of Alex and me having a baby. *Poor Margaret—she died without a grandchild, thanks to Mrs. White.*

I sank onto a bench and tilted my head upward, enjoying the soothing sunlight.

"It's a pleasant day, isn't it?"

"Commander Haywood, hello." I squinted, refocusing. "How are you today?"

"Better than the girl with the hazel eyes—Zaira, right?"

"Yes. She's dispirited, I'm afraid, but she'll pull through."

"Will she?"

"She's one of the toughest women I know. Besides, I trust that time will ease her pain until Clarence comes home."

Will pointed to the bench. "May I?"

"Please do."

He sat down, his long legs stretched out before him. "If you ask me, time can be a loyal friend or a fierce enemy. It's treacherous. One cannot count on it."

I found his remark intriguing. "Care to explain?"

"Ah, it's a sad story—not sure you need more of that today."

"Trust me. I can handle it."

"If you insist." His gaze lifted to the sky and lingered there as he spoke. "When I was studying in Cranwell, I met the perfect girl."

I should have guessed. Only a matter of love could bring a man to question time as he did.

"Adeline was a secretary in the Air Force office."

Was?

"Truly the most beautiful woman I have ever seen, with long, pale-blonde hair and crystal-blue eyes. No matter where she was, believe me, she lit up the place with her smile. Obviously, I fell madly in love, so I proposed. She accepted. Then, life happened. It separated us. We planned to marry as soon as I graduated, but out of the blue, Adeline developed a temperature off the charts and became incoherent. All that could be done was done, but it wasn't enough. I lost her to influenza." He paused, his voice heavy with unspoken grief. "She took half my heart with her. The truth is that I don't think I'll ever be whole again."

"I'm so sorry, Commander." I felt his pain as if it were my own. "So sorry."

"Just Will, please."

"Will."

"Well, there you have it." He exhaled softly. "I'm not fond of time because it hasn't helped me much. I'll always miss not being whole."

"Perhaps not enough time has passed?" I offered, though I knew from Alex's and my own grief that some wounds never fully healed.

"Perhaps," he said, unconvinced. "I do keep busy with hard work, though—always moving, always engaged. It distracts the mind from overthinking."

"You are wise for your age."

"You speak as if I were much younger than you . . . I'm not sure that's the case." He chuckled. "I'd bet ten pounds you are younger than I am."

"I'm afraid to disappoint you, but I don't gamble," I replied with a smile. Discussing my age was out of the question. Besides, I would lose the bet. "Anyhow, judging by your experiences, I think you and Zaira could be good friends. She's missing half her heart as well."

"For her sake, let's hope the chap makes it through the war alive."

"I can't imagine him not coming home. I keep reminding myself that Zaira is strong, but I would hate to see her face such a loss."

"And you, Mrs. Sterling? Are you a strong woman?"

His question took me aback, though I suspected he might have Alex's impending departure in mind—something I did not wish to dwell on. "I like to think that I am."

"Do you like being here in England?"

"More than I can ever tell you."

"I like your American accent. It's not as thick as other foreigners'."

"Thank you." *It may have something to do with me not being a foreigner.* Thinking of my history reminded me of the Haywoods' connection to Mrs. White. According to Alex, the Haywoods and Mrs. White had been mere acquaintances when she hired them, but I couldn't help wondering if there was more to the story. "May I ask you something?"

"Anything." His brown eyes held a golden glow, familiar yet unplaceable. Where had I seen them before?

"What is the relationship between your parents and Deborah White?"

"Deborah White?"

"She was Alex's housekeeper for the longest time. She moved to New York with him. I met her there."

"Oh, right." Awareness dawned on him. "The evil housekeeper, you mean?"

"You've definitely heard about her."

"Just that she tried to poison the general and steal his fortune. Is it true?"

Gossip, it seemed, spread faster than radio waves. "Unfortunately, it is."

"Well, let me think . . ." He stroked his chin thoughtfully. "As far as I know, there is no special connection between them, apart from Mrs. White living in our vicinity for a time. I had forgotten about her until her name appeared on Scotland Yard's wanted list. They are looking for her and some fellow. I don't recall his name."

"Vines. Mr. Vines."

"Ah, that's the one."

"I'm sorry," I said, fishing for more. "Since your mother recommended Mrs. White for the post, I assumed she knew her well."

"I don't think she did. In fact, if it weren't for the general, I doubt they would have been hired."

"Alex? What do you mean?"

"If I recall correctly, Mrs. White turned my parents down, claiming they were too old for the job, even though she knew from the village they were well-qualified. They tried to convince her otherwise, but she wouldn't budge. I suppose she didn't want to worry about this place all the way from America."

"I don't think she ever did. She had bigger problems to worry about over there." I beamed at my private joke. The unbelievable coincidence of her victim reappearing in her life had been enough to disturb her mind and challenge her conscience.

"Well, as it happened, the general came upon my parents just as Mrs. White was about to dismiss them, and he hired them on the spot. I suppose he either liked them or pitied them." Will shrugged.

"He most likely saw a powerful couple," I offered, even when something about the story didn't sit well. Something that, for now, remained elusive. "And to Mrs. White's discredit, your parents have done wonders with the place. You should be proud."

"I am. I want them to retire and, at last, enjoy our farm. The land is finally free of debt. All that's left is to build up our savings. After the war, I hope to do just that, once I secure a permanent post."

"You'll leave the service, then?"

"When the time is right, yes. Who knows? I might even meet someone who also has half a heart needing to be complete. Together, we can make a whole. Start a family. The farm could use a few children." He smiled.

"You'll do great, I have no doubt." My gaze shifted toward the lowering sun. "Oh my, I've lost track of time. I should check on Zaira."

"I'll walk you back to the house." Will leaped to his feet and offered his arm. I laced mine through it. "Do you like airplanes, Mrs. Sterling?"

"Planes?"

"Yes, planes."

"I've never given them much thought. Why?"

"Because I love them. Allow me to tell you about them?"

"Go on."

He launched an extensive explanation. Mrs. Haywood's words about his infatuation with aircraft hadn't been an understatement.

It would be a long walk.

Alex and the staff were abed, the house resting in peaceful slumber. Try as I might to be brave, the moment of his departure ate at me. I couldn't stop obsessing over his safety. However, if Mrs. White was nearby, my troubles at home might only worsen.

The woman in town—it seemed preposterous now to speculate she could have been Mrs. White. And yet, the image of the pair on the pavement refused to leave me. If it was her, who was the young man? According to Adele, he seemed obsessively protective of her. Why? What bond could forge such an intense closeness? I wished I'd gotten a better look at him, but he had been too far away. The description in my head—strong, tall, dark-haired—was too vague to be of use, matching countless men.

Mrs. White was unpredictable, her cunning impossible to anticipate. The thought strengthened my resolve to protect those I loved. I mentally replayed my conversation with Will, searching for something I might have missed.

She had been acquainted with the Haywoods yet hadn't favored them for the job. Could their age have been the reason? A nagging feeling told me there was more to it, despite Will saying otherwise. Could the Haywoods be connected to Mrs. White? Distant cousins, perhaps? Could they still be in contact with her? It was possible, though unlikely. Still, if they *were* connected, they would make an ideal channel for Mrs. White to monitor our lives.

If I couldn't uncover Mrs. White's whereabouts yet, I could at least deepen my understanding of the Haywoods. If there was a connection, I needed to know. And there was no better place to start than with Will. Alex was bound to have information about him. Before I could talk myself out of it, I left the library. What exactly I expected to find, I didn't know, but determination propelled me forward.

I stepped into Alex's office, my heartbeat thumping in my ears—a warning that what I was about to do, if not criminal, was certainly dishonest. A betrayal of Alex's trust. Notwithstanding, I couldn't ask him outright. Not if I wanted to hide my suspicions and spare him needless worry.

Daring not to flip on the main light, I opted for the lamp. Its soft gleam spilled over the desk and illuminated the immediate area. I glanced back at the open door, vacillating. I pictured Alex walking in and reading the guilt on my face. I reconsidered my plan. No use. The spirit of disobedience that had seized me at Oak's Place took hold once more.

I opened the top drawer of the desk. Nothing but a pile of military documents—useless to me. I pulled open the second and sifted through the layers of personal folders, their private nature intensifying my guilt. *Darwin—no. Peterson—no. Beckwith—oh, heavens—no. Wing Commander William Haywood—finally.*

I placed the folder on the desk and turned to the first page. It detailed a short but prolific career as a pilot—his missions flown, his abilities, descriptions of aircraft and machinery. Nothing personal. I let out a sigh.

With more patience this time, I circled back to the beginning. It wasn't long before I noticed a page inconsistent with the rest—a transcript.

"William Haywood, son of Agnes and Peter Haywood, born on the outskirts of Landford in the New Forest."

My eyes traced the numbers on the paper, pausing on his birth date. It confirmed he would have won his bet—he was older than I was. Older than my son would have been, had he survived.

My son. I could easily picture him through this stranger. Will had been born in the New Forest, grew up among our people, and now served his country with the same zeal I saw in Alex. All this I already knew, making my search fruitless. Was I letting my emotions cloud my judgment? Was I obsessed with discovering something that might not exist? Struggling with the quandary, I returned the file to its place.

A sound like leaves stirred by a breeze, drew my gaze beyond the office door. It came again. I squinted, peering into the gloom. I made out a human form. How long had they been there? Had they seen what I had done? One thing was certain: it wasn't Alex. He would have come in.

I turned off the lamp, shadows rushing back to claim the corners. I rounded the desk and hurried out of the office—the spot where the watcher had been now an unsettling void. Had I imagined it? No. Someone had been there. Would they tell Alex about my betrayal? The thought twisted in my gut, cold and sharp.

Silently chastising myself for such foolish behavior, I crept to the staircase. My hand found the railing as I looked away from the dark hallway. One, two steps, and that familiar sensation—the one I'd felt in New York before my awakening—washed over me again: the haunting feeling of being a player in a story without knowing my role.

———

Martha intercepted me in the foyer. "Mrs. Sterling, this arrived by the morning post." She handed me a telegram. "I thought you might like to see it right away."

Telegrams meant urgent business. Yes, I wanted to see it. "Thank you, Martha."

"Not at all. Oh, and I almost forgot—Mr. Sterling would like to see you in his office." She retraced her steps around the stairwell, her black hair bouncing with each hurried stride.

The words *Mr. Sterling* and *office* together roiled my stomach. Someday I'd confess my mischievous actions of the night before, but not today. I unfolded the telegram and read:

We are investigating a possible sighting of Deborah White in Salisbury. Take extra precautions. Chief Inspector Overton, Scotland Yard.

A cascade of emotions—anger, frustration, and inevitably, fear—overwhelmed me. Salisbury was less than ten miles away. Martha, in fact, originated from there and often traveled to the city on her days off. The proximity made it all too possible that the woman I'd seen—Mrs. Burrell—was Deborah White.

Should I notify Scotland Yard? Without proof, I risked a false alarm—and if that happened, they might dismiss me when it truly mattered. It was a long drive from London, and the last thing I wanted was to send them on a wild-goose chase. I had to be sure. I'd pay a visit to Mrs. Burrell.

Adding it to my future confessions, I slipped the telegram into my pocket. Alex had been agitated enough about Mrs. White potentially being in London. The idea that she might be even closer would rattle him to the core.

I walked to Alex's office with unhurried steps, hoping he wouldn't see right through me.

He was seated at the desk, staring at the papers before him. I moved closer and froze, the guilt pressing heavier on me. He was holding Will's military file—the one I had read.

"Hmm . . . odd . . . quite odd . . ." he muttered, his brow furrowed.

"What is?" I dared to ask.

"Some of these pages are in the wrong order."

Alex was meticulous, especially with paperwork, and his observation made me shrink. I had returned the folder too hastily. Biting my bottom lip, I remained silent, lest I say something that gave me away.

"No matter. My mistake." He smiled, but the disquiet in his eyes betrayed him.

An uncomfortable pause ensued as he restored the pages to their proper order, closed the folder with a snap, and dropped it back into the drawer.

"You wanted to see me?" I asked, relieved the papers were out of sight.

"I wondered if you'd like to go horseback riding." Alex rose.

"I thought you were too busy."

"I'm never too busy for you, my lady." He cupped my chin in his hand, and his lips claimed mine with a gentleness that left me wanting more. "Let's ride down to the stream. What do you say?"

"I'm afraid I may need a bit more convincing."

"I was hoping you'd say that." The light of passion flared in his eyes, and he backed me against the bookshelves. His body pressed against mine, and with it, his desire. His kisses came desperate and fervent, each stroke of his lips intensified by the love we felt for one another.

"I'm sorry to interrupt," Will's voice sounded from the threshold, forcing us apart. "I was told you were looking for me."

"Will. Come in." Alex cleared his throat, smoothing his shirt back into place.

My gaze dropped to the floor, my cheeks burning. The display of affection wasn't meant for others' eyes.

Will walked in, hands in his pockets, nonchalantly.

Alex extracted a key from his desk, crossed to the Napoleon side cabinet, and unlocked it. He retrieved a stack of papers and handed them to Will. "Please, take a look at these and let me know what you make of them. The sooner, the better."

"My pleasure, sir." With a nod, Will withdrew.

"The sooner, the better?" I echoed once he was gone.

"We don't have much time. Besides, a little reading will do him good. Keep him out of trouble."

"*Little* reading!" I scoffed. "That pile will take him days to get through."

"Hopefully, he is a fast reader." Alex smirked. "About our horseback ride—will you come quietly now?"

"Yes, I'll come quietly." I frowned playfully.

The scent of pine and rain lingered in the forest. Betsy's hoofbeats against the underbrush, the birdsong, and the hum of insects wove into a soothing melody. I leaned against Alex's collarbone, watching the patches of sky that peeked through breaks in the towering canopy. So much had changed with time, yet so much—the sky, the cycle of nature, my love for Alex—remained unchanged.

"After all these years, I finally got you to ride on the same horse with me," Alex remarked, bringing me out of my head. "You have no idea how stunned I was when you refused my offer after Sunny ran away."

"I wanted to make sure you understood I wasn't an easy catch." I smiled at the memory—the blast shook the clearing, sending birds flurrying from the treetops. Sunny bolted, and I tumbled into the stream. Lieutenant Sterling, guilty as charged, had appeared to offer me a ride back. I'd refused unless I could ride his horse while he walked. He'd left me there in the woods to find my way back to the manor alone.

"For the record, I understood it so well that it hurt." He brushed my hair away and pressed a kiss to my cheek.

Betsy's ears perked at the murmur of flowing water, and she pushed through the brush line into the clearing. The rain had swelled the stream, causing it to overflow. We dismounted, and Betsy went straight for the water, plunging her muzzle in and snorting playfully.

Alex dropped onto a patch of wild grass, stretching out comfortably. The sunlight caught in his eyes, their intensity as arresting as ever. Everything about him—his bold spirit, his passion—made him irreplaceable. I watched him in quiet awe, grateful for our relationship.

Its only flaw was its vulnerability to mortality. It had separated us before, and I dreaded that it could do so again.

"What's on your mind?" he asked.

"You." I sat beside him.

"Oh, I like that." He gave me a crooked smile.

"I'm dreading the moment of your departure."

My words erased his smile. "As am I, Florence."

Betsy nudged my legs with her head. "Sorry, girl, I didn't bring any apples."

Alex reached for the reins and guided her toward the patch of heath bedstraw behind us. Betsy took the hint. While most horses contented themselves with wild grass, given the choice, she favored flowering plants. He scooted closer to me. "I'll be back before you know it."

"You don't know that," I said grimly.

"You are right. I don't. But I do know this—we have been through heaven and hell, and I'm the luckiest man alive. You've given me love and the knowledge that we can be together beyond this life. Now that we stand at another crossroads, whatever happens, it won't be the end. If something happens to me now or in five or ten years, I need you to be strong and in your right mind. You are young, Florence. You shouldn't mourn for me for the rest of your life."

"Says the man who spent two decades grieving my death," I scoffed.

"True, but you know more than I did then. I wouldn't want you to be alone. I would . . ." he paused, the words catching in his throat. "I would like you to find someone to spend your days with. Maybe even have a family."

"Let me get this straight." I angled toward him. "You want me to have children with another man when you refuse to do the same?"

"If it will make you happy, then yes." His answer was brutal, but honest. "Promise me you'll remember this conversation."

It was déjà vu—the hopelessness of the moment when he left for his mission to France, leaving me at Keyhaven. Except this time, the stakes were higher. Alex was older, more than twenty years removed from active service. Would I lose him? Would I have to pass through the same sorrow he once felt for me?

I looked into his eyes and saw the anguish reflected there. None of this was fair or easy for either of us. Once again, I would try to be strong and let go of my fears, but inside, I knew I would wither.

"You will come back to me." I clung to his shirt placket with both hands. "Do you hear me, Mr. Sterling?"

"Promise me," he insisted.

"All right," I whispered.

Alex gathered me into his arms, my despondency fading with each kiss, with each gentle touch. It faded until, for that moment, it was defeated.

CHAPTER 7
~ HIDDEN ~

Dusk falls over the snowy fields. My teeth chatter as I stare at my nightgown. What am I doing out here? I need to go home. But where is home? I am lost—a ghost adrift in the dark.

"He is a little fragile but looks healthy," Dr. Jones's voice pierces the gloom.

Then, a black-cloaked figure materializes. I shriek. It hovers, its energy paralyzing me, as if claiming my soul. It moves. I am pulled after it.

We leave the fields and cross the forest. I know this path—I've walked it countless times. The Breamore Cemetery emerges. A gust of wind wrenches the gates open. I've visited often, but not like this. Not with this company.

Yet I follow, silent tombs watching as we pass. We stop at my grave. I understand now. My guide is Death. Has Death torn me from Alex's side? Will I be entombed?

The figure raises a hand, commanding the earth to tremble. Not my coffin—my son's—rises from the ground.

"No, no, no!" Tears scorch my eyes like acid. Death is cruel. Why torment me?

The tiny box creaks as it opens . . .

I bolted upright with a scream, the raw emotions following me into the waking world. Were my nightmares born of fear that Death would cross my path again? Was my yearning for children driving me to madness? Or was it something deeper—some hidden truth my subconscious wanted to reveal? Whatever the reason, I had to steady myself. The thought almost made me laugh—easier said than done—the agony of not having saved my child, of never having known him, pressing on my chest.

I reached across the bed. Alex's side was cold. He had stayed up again, preparing for his departure. It wouldn't be long now.

Things changed. The muteness of the radio felt strange. Typically, I would hear it from the hallway. However, Clarence was gone, and Zaira preferred silence over news of the war, especially of casualties. And with Will home, the Haywoods shared her preference. I entered the kitchen expecting to find no one, but the housekeeper sat at the worktable. The kettle rested on the range cooker, the flames glowing beneath it.

"Good morning, Mrs. Haywood."

"Good morning. Good morning," she responded absentmindedly, her attention on the papers before her.

"Is Martha around?"

She shook her head, still studying a page.

"Do you know where she is?" I pressed, eager to help the girl with house chores. Busyness, I found, was good therapy for the anxiety I couldn't control.

"Who?" Mrs. Haywood blinked up at me as if seeing me for the first time.

"Martha."

"Oh, yes, yes. I'm sorry. She's gone to fetch some herbs."

"I see."

Her gaze dropped again. "No, it can't come to this," she mumbled.

The kettle whistled sharply. When Mrs. Haywood showed no inclination to attend it—a strange lapse for someone so efficient—I grew alarmed. I switched off the burner, lifted the kettle, and set it aside.

"This can't be correct. What have I missed?" She scribbled numbers on the margins of a paper, adding and subtracting, erasing the sum, the cycle repeating.

I fetched two cups, poured the hot water, and dropped teabags into them. "Here, have some tea," I offered, handing her one.

"Thank you, Mrs. Sterling." She reached instinctively for the drink but quickly gathered her papers, turning them face down.

"What's the matter?" I laid a reassuring hand on her arm. "Do tell me."

"You must forgive me. Really, it's nothing." Coming out of the fog of her mind, her gaze focused, and she was present.

"Oh, there is something all right."

"I . . . I don't want to impose, Mrs. Sterling. Not again. You have more pressing matters than my difficulties."

"It's no trouble at all. Please, tell me—what is it?"

"It's the farm—our family legacy." She sighed, her expression grave. "We have worked so hard and have done mighty well with it—until now, that is. I can't bear to think what will happen if . . ."

"If what?"

"If we can't pay our creditors."

"You have creditors?" I was confused. According to Will, the farm was debt-free.

"We do, but Will doesn't know about it," she admitted quietly, as though confessing a sin, and unknowingly clarifying my confusion. "And I would like to keep it that way. There is no need to worry the lad when he has so much on his plate."

"Of course."

"You see, the inclement weather of the past year has wreaked havoc on the property. We had no choice but to acquire a few loans to keep it going. I'm afraid I've fallen behind on the payments, and the lenders are unforgiving. If I don't come up with the money, they'll seize the farm."

What was she speaking of? True, the storms had caused considerable damage, but I couldn't imagine anything so drastic as to sink a farm. Considering her anguish and the shame she must feel, I thought it best not to inquire further. Albeit something about her story troubled me, lingering like an itch at the back of my mind.

"Would you like our solicitor to look it over? Just to ensure the loan terms are fair?" I offered, gauging whether her creditors might be exploiting her.

"Oh no. I have reviewed the contracts many times. I assure you, all is in order from that angle."

"Right, then." I remained unconvinced. "Please, let me know if you change your mind. Is there anything else I might help you with?"

"Well . . . there is something." A blush crept up her cheeks, her embarrassment unmistakable. "You mustn't think me impudent, please."

"I shan't. Go on."

"I must catch up on the late payments." She intertwined her fingers nervously. "Could you possibly advance me three months of salary?"

"It can be arranged." I masked my shock. The Haywoods were well paid. Her request revealed just how strained their situation had become.

"Thank you, Mrs. Sterling. Truly. And thank you for not mentioning this to Will. As I said, he has enough to worry about. Nor to my husband, please. His pride has taken quite a blow as it is."

"You have my word."

"One last thing, if I may."

I nodded.

"Please keep in mind that all I do is for Will's sake." Her gaze held mine, and I saw something I had not seen there before—a connection between us, not that of employee and employer, but as one woman to another.

***

With a multitude of inquietudes vying for attention, I cut through the evergreens: the war, Clarence's departure, Zaira's broken heart, Alex's mission, Mrs. White's proximity, and Mrs. Haywood's financial dilemma.

I emerged from the wall of shrubbery into the Victory Garden. Instead of Mr. Haywood, I found Will on his knees, working the earth with a hand tool, his brow damp with effort.

"Good morning, Mrs. Sterling."

"Hello, Will." The scene brought the Haywood farm to mind, and guilt gnawed at me. He had no idea how dire their circumstances were.

When I lingered, he glanced up. "May I help you?"

"I am looking for your father. Do you know where he is?"

"Sorting seedlings in the greenhouse."

"Wonderful. I have a suggestion to run past him."

"The old man will be glad to hear it." Will's smile momentarily caught me off guard, it was disarmingly warm. "He is determined to grow everything and anything."

"The task is monumental, and he's handling it well. In fact, I'd like to expand planting into the west field and hope to convince him to keep the recruits who built the drying shed."

"The war is not looking good, is it?"

"I'm afraid not."

Will tossed the tool aside and dug into the clumps of earth with his bare hands. "With all this rain, you'd think the ground would be more forgiving, but no. I have to force it into shape."

"At least you know what to do."

"That couldn't be further from the truth." He chuckled. "I don't know what I'm doing half the time. But the old man taught me a few things, including that if I don't do a job right, he'll make me do it again. Believe me, I never start something I don't intend to finish, and I always do it right. I just needed a break from all that studying. Clears the head, you know." He brushed his hands against his trousers, smearing dirt as he stood.

"Studying?"

"The stack of documents the general gave me."

"Oh yes." I felt for him. "Quite the assignment."

"You can say that again. I see those papers in my dreams."

I laughed. "Good luck with it."

"Mrs. Sterling," he called as I turned to leave.

"Yes."

"So you know, I've heard about General Sterling my entire life. It's an honor to serve alongside him." His words warmed my heart. Knowing Alex would guard such a young life eased my worries about the mission.

"You are in good hands. I trust Alex with my soul." If Will only knew how literal those words were, he would never mistrust his superior. "Use your time wisely."

"I'll do my best."

———

I dressed for the day, with last night's dream tugging at my heart. It had been vivid—more memory than mere imagination. In the dream, I was trapped in a dark, airless space, a cage without doors or windows. Then, breaking the silence, came the cry of an infant—a primal, heart-wrenching sound that pierced my soul. I needed to reach him. I needed to calm his fears.

Without respite, I recalled yet another dream—my son dashing into the forest, always just out of reach. Each time I lost sight of him, he reappeared—taller, older, time stealing him from me. I gasped as the meaning of these visions clawed at me. What if my baby had somehow been taken from the grave? What if, like me, he didn't lie in the darkness of the earth?

No. My son is dead. But what if he isn't?

I paced the bedroom, consumed by the thought. The pull tore at my conscience and desires, so at odds I feared I might break. Frustrated, I stopped at the window. Sunshine bathed the gardens, its warmth soothing against my palm on the glass.

And then I knew.

After everything I'd survived—even a second chance at life—ignoring my instincts might be the real madness. Was it a foolish path? Certainly. And the most dreadful part would be convincing Alex.

———

"Good morning," Zaira greeted from the landing. Seeing a smile on her face, something so seldom since Clarence left, was wonderful.

"Good morning," I replied. "I got another hat catalog for you to look at."

"Oh, I would love that."

"I left it on the night table in my room."

"Thank you. I'll go grab it now."

"Do you know where Alex is?"

"I just saw them out in the fields."

"Them?"

"Mr. Sterling and Will." She climbed the first steps before pausing. "They are practicing archery."

"Archery?" I repeated incredulously. Alex had never shown the slightest interest in the sport.

"Yes, Florence, archery. And if I'm not mistaken, Will is teaching Mr. Sterling a thing or two." She said it so naturally that I couldn't help but laugh. "I'm sorry, I didn't mean to—"

"It's all right. I doubt Alex has ever touched a bow and arrow. Is it that pitiable?"

"Go see for yourself." She resumed her climb, leaving me smiling.

I found Alex and Will standing in front of a hay-bale target. The whole setup had an improvised charm. The twine was loosely wrapped, barely holding the bale intact, while tufts of grass jutted out in every direction, creating an untamed, uneven mess. Despite its ragged appearance, it served its purpose, judging by the arrows embedded in the target—or near it.

"Commander, this shot was mine," Alex argued.

"I must disagree, General." Will pointed to a mark farther from the center. "This one here was yours."

"You two seem to get along quite well," I said, amused.

"Come to join us, Mrs. Sterling?"

"Oh no. I'm hopeless at it."

"So is the general," Will teased, "but he's managed all right."

"You've won a battle, not the war, Commander." Alex shot Will a playful, dangerous look. "We'll play again later—under my rules."

"Fair enough." Will started to gather the scattered arrows.

"Shall we walk?" Alex laced my arm through his.

"Shouldn't you help him?" I motioned toward Will.

"He can manage."

"He'll think you are a sore loser."

Alex shook his head, mischief lighting his eyes. He enjoyed making Will do the work.

We strolled down the footpath, ancient trees towering above us.

"Did you win any of the games?"

"Not one. The little devil is good at it, but next time, we'll shoot rifles. He'll be my target."

I laughed. "Definitely a sore loser."

Alex grinned. Seeing him unbothered through defeat reminded me of the times I'd lost to him at Monopoly. It was good for him to know what it felt like. Really good. Will might be exactly what Alex needed.

"Will has an extraordinary future ahead of him," Alex remarked. "He'll do well in the Air Force."

"I think he wants to retire early."

"A shame, but understandable. Especially if he wants to start a family."

"That's true."

"He won't have trouble finding a wife. He's a well-rounded man."

We ventured deeper into the woods. The mood shifted with the fading light, the lively banter now replaced by reflective silence.

At last Alex said, "I leave in two days."

"That soon?"

"I want to get on with it, get it done. This is it. My last mission, Florence. I won't leave you again."

I stopped, turning to face him, my heart aching. "That's if you come back alive."

"I have every intention of doing so."

"Alex. There's something I need to ask of you."

"What is that?" His gaze locked onto mine with an intensity that made me question my plea. But if I lost him without knowing the truth, I would live forever in sorrow and uncertainty.

"Since I can't legally claim to be our son's mother, I would like you to request Scotland Yard to exhume his remains." My words came out swiftly. "A call to the inspector would suffice."

"Have you lost your mind?" he exclaimed in dismay.

"Alex, listen to me. What if our son isn't dead? What if something miraculous happened to him? You had my coffin dug up—why is this any different?"

"No, you listen," he said impatiently. "You came back to me. If it weren't for your reappearance, I'd never have dreamed of disturbing your resting place." It was a valid point.

"The problem is that I can't let it go. I need closure. After everything we've experienced, I can't stop believing that anything is possible."

"You had a mission, a choice to return and set things right. Our son is a different story. You and I have been graced with knowledge of the true nature of life and death. With what we know, can we not assume our son resides in a far better place?"

"Of course we can. But why does his memory haunt me? Why do I feel there is more to his death than we know?"

"Florence, he is gone. We must move on." He drew a long breath, exhaling slowly. "Besides, if we were ever to do something so unsettling, wouldn't it be better if I were here with you? Seeing him could backfire and disturb you more than the dreams already do." Was he leaving a door open for the future? I was about to ask when he spoke again. "But it's not the right thing to do. It simply isn't. We must let him rest in peace. Do you agree with anything I've said?"

"I . . ." Reason was on his side.

He extended his arms, and I stepped into his embrace. "I love you," he whispered.

"I love you too." Fearing that my insistence might drive a wedge between us, I relented. For now.

The fire in the hearth burned through the night as we shared our fears, our dreams, and the deepest recesses of our hearts. I clung to every moment—his voice, his lips brushing against mine, the caress of his hands—yet morning seemed to arrive within minutes.

At a tap on the door, I opened my eyes. Alex moved about the room, finishing his packing.

"General, the military car has arrived," Mrs. Haywood informed from the corridor. "The men are waiting in the sitting room."

"Keep them busy. Feed them breakfast or something, please." Alex stuffed a pair of boots into his suitcase. "I'll be down in a minute."

"Very well, sir."

I sat on the bed, struggling to hold back tears. *Will I ever see you again, Mr. Sterling? Is this it? It can't end like this.*

Will had said Adeline took half his heart. Alex was taking mine entirely. If this mission claimed his life and his heart stopped beating, I was certain mine would too.

Alex caught my gaze, and without a word, he descended beside me. Wrapping me in his arms, he held me tightly, my head resting against his chest. His shallow, uneven breaths betrayed his efforts to suppress his emotions.

Though I had told him countless times last night how much I loved him and would miss him, I longed to say it again. But as I opened my mouth, the words dissolved into harrowing sobs.

Alex buried his face in my neck, his voice trembling as he whispered, "I love you, Florence, more than you can ever imagine."

The Haywoods and I stepped out of the house into the courtyard. The morning was unnervingly still—no rustling wind in the branches, no chirping of birds in the trees. It was as if the world held its breath for this very inevitable moment.

The official car, with its driver and a second gentleman already in place, stood waiting—a sleek, black vehicle that evoked the image of a hearse— a comparison I didn't welcome but couldn't quite banish from my mind.

Alex and Will, both in uniform, loaded their luggage into the boot. Their faces revealed nothing—calm and composed, their feelings concealed behind the mask of duty. Whether they were apprehensive or resolute about their mission, no one would ever know.

The Haywoods bid their son farewell. I'd grown fond of Will, and seeing his parents hold him close, barely containing their emotions, cut through me. It also reminded me that I wasn't alone in this heartache. Others endured far worse than I could fathom—and I could fathom quite a lot. My self-pity felt small in comparison. If nothing else, I resolved to keep it hidden, at least outwardly.

"Mrs. Sterling, thank you for everything," Will said, and to my surprise, he pressed a kiss to my cheek.

"Take care of yourself, Will."

"I shall." He stepped back, a smile softening his features. "I'll see you soon."

Alex turned to me then, his hands taking mine. His touch, so familiar and grounding, made it harder to let him go. "Stay out of trouble, and please be careful. White could surface at any time. If she does, you know it will be to cause harm."

"I will."

"I'll come back to you."

"I'll be waiting." I offered a weak smile.

"But if I don't—"

"No." I shook my head. "Don't say it."

He said it anyway. "If I don't, Florence, move on with your life. Allow yourself to love again."

Tears welled in my eyes as I pulled him into a fierce embrace. I silenced him with one final kiss, pouring everything I couldn't put into words into that moment. When he pulled away, I saw his tears glimmering, though he blinked them back. Mine spilled freely down my cheeks.

Alex climbed into the back seat beside Will. The car eased forward, its tires crunching over the gravel. From London, they would sail to the United States—that was all I knew. The secrecy of their mission would shroud them until it was completed, leaving me with nothing but hope to hold onto.

"Come on, dear." Mr. Haywood reached for his wife's hand. "Let's go for a stroll."

Mrs. Haywood turned to me, her kind eyes misty as she patted them with a handkerchief. "Will you be all right?"

"I'll be all right."

They left me standing on the front steps, alone with the ache in my chest. I remained there for the longest time, staring at the spot where the car had disappeared into the morning sun.

———

I had to keep myself busy, or the void Alex left in me would consume me entirely. "*Stay out of trouble,*" he had advised. It wasn't in my nature. If Mrs. White was in the area, I would rather go to her before she found me. Hence, Zaira and I formulated a plan, not the most ingenious one, but sensible enough.

The walk to the Acker farm had been miserable, with an obnoxious wind kicking up dust that stung our eyes and tangled our hair. By the time we reached the gate and pushed through against the gusts, we looked worse for wear. We approached the house, and a well-presented man in his late sixties, in black trousers and a blue cardigan, answered our call.

"Ladies, may I help you?" His lively eyes stared at us expectantly. I sensed he didn't get many visitors.

"Good morning." Zaira flashed her most charming smile. "Mr. Acker?"

"That's correct. Miss . . . ?"

"My name is Alice Bates, and this is my sister, Lucy," Zaira replied smoothly. "We heard you have a cottage to let. We work nearby, so the location would be perfect."

I looked at her sideways. We hadn't discussed using false names, but it seemed a reasonable precaution.

"Oh, well," he said, patting his shiny, waxed hair. "I did, but it's been taken."

"Oh, no." Zaira faked disappointment. "That's just our luck."

"I'm sorry. I wish I had more than one to offer."

"If I may ask," I interjected, "how long is the lease for?"

"It's a month-to-month," he replied. "So, I suppose it could be available in the near future. Two bedrooms, one bathroom, and a spacious kitchen. If you'd like, I'd be happy to let you know."

"That's most kind," Zaira said. "Please do."

"Any chance we could look around?" I asked casually. "Just to get an idea in case it does work out."

"Well, Mrs. Burrell and her nephew left a while ago."

"Our luck continues to run its dismal course," I said, disappointed. We had come all this way, endured the biting wind and the gnawing uncertainty, only to leave with no answers and no resolution in sight.

"Do you think they'll mind terribly if we take a quick peek?" Zaira pressed, smiling again. "We might not get another chance to stop by."

"Well . . .." Mr. Acker scratched his head thoughtfully.

"It would truly help us decide if it's the right fit," she added.

"All right, I don't see why not. Come on, I'll show you."

"We can get a sense of whether it's her based on the belongings in the house," Zaira whispered, leaning closer to me.

I nodded. Mrs. Burrell and her nephew. If the woman was indeed Mrs. White, again I wondered, who the man might be. The question pounded in my head as Mr. Acker led us along a path that meandered through a wooded area.

"What was that?" Mr. Acker called over his shoulder.

"Oh, I was just thanking heaven the wind abated," Zaira lied.

The trees parted, revealing a clearing.

"There it is," he said. Set amid open fields where ponies roamed freely, a cottage with whitewashed walls and a thatched roof stood gracefully.

"It's lovely," Zaira admitted.

"Lovely indeed," I echoed.

"It's been in the family as long as I can remember," Mr. Acker said, a note of pride in his voice. "In fact, my wife and I lived there when we were first married. My parents stayed in the main house back then. Long time ago that was."

We toured the perimeter, our host speaking of the surrounding land, seasonal crops, and pastoral purposes. The peaceful environment was ideal for tenants. He then brought us to the front door and turned the knob, inviting us in.

"Take a look around."

Zaira and I moved swiftly, searching for anything that could confirm or refute Mrs. Burrell's identity.

"Oh, good storage space." Zaira inspected the kitchen cupboards. Mrs. White had distinct, expensive tastes that would stand out.

We passed through the smaller bedroom. A man's clothing hung on the back of a chair, the bed lay unmade, and a stack of newspapers sat on the nightstand. Nothing of interest here. I moved into the main bedroom and cast a glance over my shoulder at Mr. Acker. He lingered in the hallway, chatting with Zaira about property taxes.

Opening the armoire, I found a flamboyant collection of women's apparel—nothing Mrs. White would ever wear. If anything, she would have sneered at the fashion. My gaze shifted to the chiffonier, where two frames sat.

One held a photograph of a smiling couple, an older man with a hunched back and a gray-haired woman. The other featured a group of young people playing croquet. Nieces and nephews, perhaps? Surely the man who occupied the other bedroom was among them. Though I had no idea which one he might be, none of the faces were familiar.

I picked up the frame for a closer look, but the result was the same. Irritated, I set it back down. What was I doing rifling through these people's lives like a thief? This was wrong. We had to leave before the Burrells returned.

As I moved to the doorway, I glimpsed something at the edge of the pillow. Spots? No, a solid object. Jewelry? I stepped closer. A string of black beads—a rosary. The memory came rushing back: my fingers catching Mrs. White's rosary as we wrestled in the hallway at Oak's Place. The string had snapped, beads scattering as she fled into the night, a fugitive from the law.

"Are you done in there?" Zaira called.

I yanked my eyes from the rosary. It proved nothing. Rosaries were common these days—nearly everyone had one, whether for prayer or in solidarity with loved ones at war.

We thanked Mr. Acker profusely for his kindness, and Zaira gave him the number to reach us.

"Nah, no way the woman who lives there is Mrs. White," Zaira concluded as we left. "The place is too disorganized, and nothing matches her style."

"I agree." Could I ever trust my judgment again?

CHAPTER 8
~ FAR APART ~

Cruel time crawled along at a snail's pace while I had to keep pressing forward. My work with Mr. Haywood in the garden and my involvement with the Women's Institute volunteers on the herb-foraging project increased. For while the men fought on the frontlines, the nation's daily survival rested upon the shoulders of our women. Gone were the days of delicate dresses; most of us now donned trousers, ready to work in fields, farms, and orchards. Where we were once typists, clerks, or shop assistants, we now plowed the land, built fences and irrigation ditches, tended to crops and animals, and more.

After a long afternoon of taming the sprawling marrows—a wonderful problem to have—I was ready to collapse on the sofa when the phone rang.

"Hello?"

"Mrs. Sterling, this is General Frankfort."

"Thomas?" I blurted, abandoning formalities as a flurry of terrible scenarios involving Alex and Will raced through my mind.

"Hello, Florence."

"Did something happen to Alex?"

"No—no. Nothing of that sort."

"Will?"

"No. Relax. As far as I know, they're both fine."

"Thank heavens!"

"I'm ringing because I need your help. I'm in a rather rough spot."

Thomas in a rough spot? Rare. "Tell me. What is it?"

"The number of refugees has increased tenfold in the past month, and we're struggling to accommodate them. Just this week, a group of Jews reached our shores after escaping from Germany. They were on a prisoner train, being transported to . . ." Thomas hesitated.

"A labor camp?"

"You've heard about them, then?"

"Alex mentioned them."

"The train was bombed, and they made a run for it. Thankfully, good Samaritans helped them reach France, then England."

"That's a miracle," I said earnestly. German forces controlled France, and few ever escaped their grip.

"You can say that again, and, to tell you the truth, I'm seeing more and more miracles. I never thought the day would come when I wouldn't question things as much, when I would go with the flow. I suppose one lives and learns."

"In the end, it's all about where that flow takes you, isn't it? If it leads to a good outcome, so be it." I hoped he'd read between the lines and apply his newfound convictions to my likeness of the old Florence. "But tell me, how may I help you?"

"I'll be able to house the group in a matter of weeks. Until then, I have nowhere for them to go. Would you take them in? You can think it over and ring me back."

"I don't need to think about it. We'll gladly take them in. The house can accommodate a hundred people if necessary." History did repeat itself, and once again, our people would answer the call to help. I thought of the Great War and Hurst Castle. Catherine and her family had offered it as a hospital for convalescent soldiers.

"For now, I have eight. Three boys and five girls between the ages of six and sixteen. Two of the girls are siblings. None of the others are related. Most likely, their parents didn't make it out alive."

"They are children . . ." My heart ached for them—young, innocent souls torn from their families by the wickedness of men.

"You understand the implication in this, yes?"

"What do you mean?"

"Others might prefer to take in adults who can help with farm work."

"I'm not concerned about that. We have plenty to share, and I'll make sure these children are treated as children. If nothing else, I can give them a safe place where they can enjoy life and be happy. Do they speak English?"

"Enough to communicate. Florence, there is something you must prepare for." His tone grew somber. "You must be mentally ready to meet them. They've been to hell and back. Their scars run deep. Can you handle that?"

I couldn't say that my experiences in the Great War would be of help. Instead, I said, "Don't worry about that. I grew up an orphan in poverty. I've seen quite a bit, especially through the Depression in the States."

"Be that as it may, it might not be enough. Just remember to focus on their future, not their past. I'll bring them tomorrow afternoon."

"We'll be ready."

"Thank you, Florence. I'm indebted to you."

"I don't think so. Surely, Alex owes you a favor or two." I thought of all those years ago when Thomas had saved our lives in the forest and of the support he'd offered me in Keyhaven. The payment was overdue.

Punctuality was one of Thomas's greatest strengths. True to form, the refugees arrived the next day in a military truck. The Haywoods, Zaira, Martha, and I stood ready to welcome them.

"Good afternoon." Thomas jumped down from the passenger seat.

"It's good to see you again." I extended my hand, and he shook it firmly.

The driver lowered the tailgate and helped the passengers down. Thomas hadn't exaggerated—their condition was unlike anything I had witnessed before. My heart ached at the sight of their gaunt faces and the haunted, wary look in their eyes.

They huddled together in the courtyard, clutching at the clothes on their backs—the only possessions they had. Their garments provided upon arrival in England, hung loosely on their frames.

"Welcomed to our home. We are happy to have you here." I kept my emotions in check as I introduced the rest of us.

The response was a collective, faint, "Thank you."

The youngest, a boy Thomas had mentioned was six years old, peeked out from behind one of the girls. His wide, dark eyes were filled with curiosity. I smiled at him, and after a moment, he darted forward, pressing something into my hand—a yellow petal.

I tried to catch his eye to thank him, but his shyness won out, and he retreated behind his friend. When I smiled at her, she rewarded me with a tentative grin.

Mrs. Haywood came forward and hugged them as if they were her grandchildren. She then motioned for them to follow her and Mr. Haywood inside. We had scrubbed the guest wing from top to bottom. The fresh linens, the carefully arranged rugs, and the simple toys placed on the nightstands helped create a safe, welcoming space.

Furthermore, with plenty of bedrooms, we'd let them choose their own, hoping it would give them a sense of control and comfort in a world that had offered them little of either. Forti Radici would now be their sanctuary.

"I'd better see to the afternoon tea," Martha announced as she climbed the front steps. "I think we'll need more cakes than I planned."

I turned to Zaira. "We should give them a tour of the area as soon as they are feeling up to it. There are a few fun spots I think they'll enjoy."

"Oh, that's a wonderful idea!" Zaira lit up with enthusiasm. I could practically see the wheels turning in her head, already crafting plans.

"Will you join us for tea?" I asked Thomas and his comrade.

"It would be our pleasure," Thomas replied, "but would you take a walk with me first? I need to stretch my legs. It was a long ride."

"I'll show you to the sitting room," Zaira offered the other soldier.

"Thanks, ma'am," he responded, trailing her inside.

Thomas and I strolled to the rose garden, the sweet scent of flowers drifting through the air.

"Are you unwell?" Thomas broke the silence. "You are pale."

"I could never have imagined they would look so dispirited and worn down."

"I warned you."

"I know. I now understand, but don't fret. We'll take good care of them."

"Thank you." Thomas heaved a sigh. "I'm confident they'll eventually heal inside and out. They simply need time to do so."

"Time, yes. It controls everything and yet nothing." I thought about the past. "Doesn't it?"

Thomas halted mid-step and faced me. For that brief instant, it felt as though time ceased between us, our old friendship as strong as ever. Once again, war bound us together. Memories of collapsing into his arms at the loss of those left behind at Forti Radici flooded back. I could only hope this moment wasn't an omen of more heartbreak to come.

"How can this be? Florence, how can this be?" Was he speaking of the war or of me?

"War happens, Thomas." I recalled his words from long ago. "Without people like you, more lives would be taken, not just those of young men but women and children." My enigmatic answer straddled both subjects.

Recognizing the familiar phrasing, he finished the statement as he had a lifetime ago, "The cruelty would have no end." His eyes searched mine with unsettling intensity. "You have confirmed that which I see but sanity contradicts. You, Florence, are Florence." He shook his head, as if trying to dislodge the absurd notion. "No. It's delusional."

"Delusional or not, some truths are better left unsaid." The reality was too farfetched, too implausible for him to comprehend. Perhaps, with time, it would reveal itself in manageable fragments, easier to accept.

"You neither confirm nor deny it."

"Can you live with that?" I asked.

"I suppose I can . . . for the time being." He whistled, the sound low and resigned. "Like I said over the telephone, I'll go with the flow."

"Any news of Alex?"

"No," he answered.

"You'll let me know if you hear anything, won't you?"

"Of course, but you must try not to overstress. Alexander knows how to handle himself. Despite the challenges of his career, I only saw him broken once, and it had nothing to do with work."

"Tell me about it." Though I had a good idea of when that might have been, I wanted to hear Thomas's perspective.

"When you—" I suspected in the name of common sense, he corrected himself. "When his first wife passed away, those of us close to him thought he might die of sorrow. I confess I wasn't surprised when he went to war. What surprised me was that he returned. I didn't think he wanted to."

He was correct. Alex told me as much. Thankfully, death had eluded him.

"And when he did, he was, as expected, more disturbed than when he left. So, Catherine, a girl I was seeing at the time," Thomas said, and again, I suspected for the sake of clarity, "and I devised a plan to help him move on. She had a friend, Dorothy, who fancied Alexander."

"Did she, now?" I muttered. This was a story I hadn't heard before.

"We organized a get-together to introduce them."

"And Alex accepted?"

"It wasn't easy, let me tell you, but in the end he did. However, it didn't go as we'd hoped. In fact, it was a complete disaster." Thomas chuckled as if the memory amused him.

"Well, go on then."

"As the evening wore on, Alexander cleared the glasses from the sitting room and went to the kitchen. Dorothy followed him. I was elated —finally, some progress. But Catherine, observant as ever, noted his detachment. She said he was polite, but his heart wasn't in it. Still, when minutes passed, I thought maybe, just maybe, our plan was working. Then the arguing began."

"They argued?"

"Heck, yes. In an uncomfortable, sour moment, their voices rose to a fevered pitch, and their words multiplied. Catherine nudged me to intervene. I approached the kitchen, only to hear Alexander recommending Dorothy, in no uncertain terms, 'go to the devil.'"

Should I laugh or feel sorry for the girl? I couldn't decide.

"The next thing I knew," Thomas continued, "Dorothy stormed out of the kitchen, and out of the flat. Catherine ran after her, and I after Catherine. I took them both home and didn't speak of the incident again. Needless to say, we never tried setting him up with anyone after that."

"I don't blame you." Ironic how Alex encouraged me to date if tragedy ever struck, yet he had refused to do so himself, at least in that instance. I wish I knew what exactly transpired in that kitchen.

"Years passed," Thomas said. "Alexander moved to New York. Then I heard he remarried. I was happy for him and stunned all the same. When I saw you, I understood."

I seized the moment to steer the conversation away from myself to Catherine. "Tell me more about Catherine. What happened between you two?"

"Truthfully, I'm not sure." He shrugged, his expression neutral. "She moved up north, and our meetings became more and more sporadic until they stopped altogether. The last I heard, before I decided to move on, was that she was seeing someone else."

"I'm sorry."

"It's all right. It took a minute, but I found Mary. She's everything I could have hoped for, more than I deserve, really. She's perfect for me."

"Things have a way of working out in the end, don't they?"

"Apparently so, Florence. Apparently so."

I shifted, adjusting my pillow and tugging the covers tighter around me, but my thoughts refused to settle. Seeking relief, I cast my mind back to the afternoon: I had entered the library when the sound of laughter pulled me to the window. Peering outside, I saw our guests enjoying each other's company in the garden. The days had worked wonders for them. Their pallor had faded, color returning to their cheeks, as their physical and mental health continued to improve. Most remarkable of all was the light of hope that radiated from their faces.

Through a veil of tears, I watched two of the boys position

themselves to race. They exchanged a quick glance, and took off down the path. The boy trailing behind lost his footing and fell to the ground. Instead of surging forward to claim victory, the other boy turned back to help his friend. In that tender moment, kindness triumphed. Amid their struggles, they hadn't forgotten who they were or what love meant. There was much to be learn from these children—for starters, that focusing on others was a key to surviving life's harshest trials.

I rolled over again as my stomach rumbled, reminding me I'd barely eaten today. There might be leftovers in the kitchen—even a crust of bread would do. I threw my robe over my nightgown and padded down the hallway.

I descended the staircase, my hand gliding along the banister, when a memory surged: almost twenty years ago, heavy with child, I'd come down these very steps in search of a cup of milk. But that night, I found much more than milk—I stumbled upon the heart of a murderer.

I could still hear Mrs. White's chilling words as she conspired with Mr. Vines, "*If he is not with me, he might be better off alone . . . You know very well that I won't hesitate in removing any obstacles,*" she had said. True to her words, she had removed me. Again, I wondered if she had also removed my child? From suspecting that foul play might have been involved in his death to believing he might be alive lay a vast realm of unknowns—unknowns that deepened my belief that there could be more to his story.

I reached the landing and took the dark passage bordering the stairwell, my footsteps echoing in the hollow space. The air thickened, each breath feeling heavier, harder to draw in. Did something malevolent lurk just beyond my sight? I hurried to the switch at the end of the corridor.

The single bulb buzzed to life, light flooding the space. There was nothing here. Nothing but fear, mocking me for its hold. Still, the unease remained, as if the house carried remnants of Mrs. White's vile plans. Perhaps, in dredging up those memories, I had unleashed the energy of that fateful night. I could only hope she would never set foot in Forti Radici again.

Heaving a calming breath, I resumed my steps and crossed the double doors with carved flowers into the kitchen. Out of the corner of my eye, I saw a figure scurrying through the shadows into the larder. I flipped on the light and grabbed a rolling pin from the counter.

"Who's there?" I hated the fear in my voice. "Show yourself."

Silence.

I stepped inside the storage room and peered around in a frenzy. I noticed one thing out of place—a tiny foot sticking out from behind a shelf. I released the breath stuck in my throat and lowered my weapon.

"Good evening," I said gently. "Are you looking for something to eat? I sure am."

The little fellow who had given me the flower petal the day of their arrival peeked out from his hiding place. His eyes were wide and alert as he gave a cautious nod.

"Come on." I motioned for him to join me. "Let's find some treats. I'm sure Martha keeps plenty around."

For a long while, he stayed rooted to the spot.

"Come on," I repeated with a smile.

He sidestepped into the aisle, his movement careful as though unsure of what awaited him.

"Let's see." I scanned the top shelf. "No, nothing here."

He pointed to the fourth shelf from the bottom, the corners of his lips tugging in a shy smile.

Bending at the knee, I could see one tin of flour and another of bay leaves. The boy slipped closer and pushed the flour aside, revealing a jar filled with malted milk biscuits. Clearly, this wasn't his first outing to the larder.

"You like these?" I held up the jar.

He nodded eagerly.

"Right, then." I never would have guessed that a child would enjoy the malty flavor of the biscuits. "Let's bring them with us."

We settled at the table, and I handed him a biscuit.

"I'm Florence." I tapped my chest to reinforce my words. "What's your name?"

"Eldad," he responded through a mouthful of biscuit.

"That's a lovely name."

"Papa is gone." The boy shifted on his seat, his feet swinging in the air. "Evil men burn shop. Papa don't come out. They take us train."

The biscuit in my hand stilled, my appetite vanishing in an instant. It was clear he understood, in a way no child should, that his father would never return—not by choice, but by the cruelty of others. And although I longed to know what had happened to his mother, I couldn't bring myself to ask. Some truths were too painful to uncover and to relive.

"Would you like another biscuit?" I said instead.

"Yes, Florr—" His little tongue stumbled over the next consonant, unable to complete the word.

"It's all right." I smiled reassuringly. "Just call me Flor."

"Flor." He returned my smile, a little more confident now. "Big noise, big fire. Train stop, we run. Farms, more farms. Now here." He finished the story quickly, as though eager to unburden himself.

Thomas's account had been accurate. Bombs had struck the train, causing it to burst into flames. The chaos gave the prisoners their chance to escape, and heaven had blessed them with people who helped them cross two countries to safety. It was nothing short of extraordinary.

As Eldad devoured the rest of his treat, his gaze drifted to a point beyond my shoulder. I saw past the veneer of his composed expression to the anxiety simmering beneath. Love swelled in me for him, alongside an unyielding rage at the monsters who had caused such suffering.

"Would you like some water?" I offered, hoping to pull both of us to the present.

He shook his head, the light in his eyes dimming. "I miss Papa."

I extended my hand. To my surprise, he took it and climbed into my lap. I encircled him in my arms as he rested his head on my shoulder. Minutes ticked by. His breathing softened, his frame relaxed, and he drifted into sleep. I stayed as still as possible, not wanting to disturb him, but my mind churned. The Nazis' inhumanity was too surreal to grasp. How had the world allowed them to rise to power? Complacency and carelessness had blinded us while the enemy prepared to strike.

Eldad stirred, a soft groan escaping him as his head lolled back against my arm. His serene, angelic face pulled me from my dark thoughts. Somewhere in the woods, a rooster crowed, ushering in the new day. I pictured the bird perched on a fence, its red wattle swaying and its feathers gleaming in the early light.

With some effort, I stood, determined to carry Eldad to his bed where he could enjoy a few more hours of rest. I left the kitchen, and glanced at the boy in my arms. My world suddenly felt a little brighter, my burdens a little easier to bear. Would holding my son have felt like this? I believed it would have.

My baby. Just as daylight streamed through the corridors, my path became clear. There was one who knew more about my son than I did. One who had recently frequented my dreams—the one who had brought him into the world. Dr. Jones.

Was he still alive? Would he recognize me? And as Alex's second wife —supposedly uninvolved—would he even help me? I didn't have the answers, but I had to try.

CHAPTER 9
~ DR. JONES ~

A few telephone calls established that Dr. Jones was still alive, though from what I gathered, just barely. I kept my plans to myself, confiding only in Mr. Brown, though even he knew nothing of the visit's purpose. His role was simply to drive the Lagonda, lending the trip an air of formality. Older folks often appreciated such gestures, and I needed every advantage I could get.

Morning broke with pale, filtered light as dark clouds rolled over the countryside. Mr. Brown secured the Lagonda's roof, while I retrieved an umbrella from the boot and kept it by my side.

Thanks to Mr. Brown's engaging conversation, my nerves stayed at bay. He began by commenting on the erratic weather and his dislike of downpours, especially for the damage they could cause to vehicles. Then he launched into a monologue on the latest automobiles, detailing their features, performance, and price. While I appreciated his effort to keep me entertained, I feared I would learn more about the car industry in this one ride than I had in two lifetimes. It became clear why Alex enjoyed his company.

The Lagonda rolled into Breamore. The town lay as though death had beaten me here, leaving a stifling chill. Its brick homes stood in silence, their windows dark and unwelcoming. No pedestrians walked the streets, and the shops hadn't bothered to set out their goods for display.

We had advances only a few blocks when heaven unleashed the downpour. A gaggle of geese squawked and flapped their wings, scrambling for cover. Mr. Brown veered onto a narrow road, slowing the Lagonda to a crawl as the rain pelted the windshield, obscuring our view.

"It's really coming down," Mr. Brown rasped "but we are almost there."

My stomach twisted as my mind raced with the task ahead. What would Dr. Jones think of my unannounced visit? Would he discuss the affairs of the former Mrs. Sterling with me? Would he recognize me?

"This is it, Mrs. Sterling." Mr. Brown parked the car in front of an elegant house with a red-tiled roof. A tidy garden, bordered by a white gate, stretched toward the entrance.

"I won't be long."

"Take your time. I've got no complaints waiting here in my dry seat." He grinned, lighting a cigar.

Forgetting the umbrella, I dashed for the porch, my shoes splashing through puddles. I tapped lightly on the door, my pulse quickening as the seconds stretched. I knocked again, harder this time. Five, then ten seconds passed before footsteps shuffled inside.

The door parted, and a gray-haired woman appeared, her face framed by a pair of spectacles. The lenses were so thick I wondered if they improved or hindered her vision.

"May I help you?" She stared at me critically, leaving no doubt—she neither expected nor welcomed visitors.

"Good morning. I'm looking for Doctor Seldon Jones. Is he at home?"

"He is, but he isn't receiving visitors. May I schedule an appointment for you?" She was ready to shut the door.

"Would you please ask him? I've come a long way, despite my chauffeur's advice, I'm afraid." I motioned toward the car idling in the downpour, hoping to appeal to her sympathy. "Might Doctor Jones make an exception?"

She hesitated, just as a gust of wind swept rain into the doorway. "Come in, come in," she said in exasperation.

"Thank you, Mrs. . .?"

"Abbotts. I'm Seldon's sister."

"It's a pleasure to meet you, Mrs. Abbotts. I'm Mrs. Sterling. Alexander Sterling's wife."

"*The* General Sterling?" Her expression softened.

"Yes."

"You should have mentioned that from the start. Welcome to our humble abode, Mrs. Sterling. Please allow me." She helped me remove my coat, then hung it on a peg by the exit. "This way."

I followed her down a short passage, relieved that I'd made it this far. We entered the living room, where a fire crackled in the hearth, casting light over a burgundy Victorian sofa and a bookcase filled with medical tomes.

"This is lovely," I said.

"It's kind of you to say, darling. Of course, it's nothing compared to Forti Radici."

"You've visited the manor?"

"A few times, long ago. I used to bring fresh milk to Mrs. Allerton, you know."

Hearing Mrs. Allerton's name brought a smile to my lips. I missed her dearly.

"Oh, I'm sorry. You probably don't have the faintest idea who Mrs. Allerton is." Mrs. Abbotts misinterpreted my gesture. "You see, she was the housekeeper at Forti Radici ages ago. A wonderful lady—oh yes, truly remarkable. What happened there was horrid. Just thinking of it makes me ill."

I knew she referred to the attack and murder of my loved ones. And it occurred to me that she might know something about my death and my son. After all, the doctor's sister clearly had an excellent memory.

"I heard about the tragedy," I said softly. "I understand that my husband's first wife passed away shortly after."

"Oh, the poor thing. I didn't know her personally, but her loss devastated the town. It was as if the devil himself campaigned against the family."

"She died during childbirth, I'm told."

"That's correct. The baby died as well. My brother couldn't save either of them. It was a terrible blow. It took him some time to recover.

Anyhow, I'm glad the general rebuilt his life." She readjusted the spectacles on the bridge of her nose, signaling an end to the conversation. If she knew anything more, she wouldn't share it. "I'll check on Seldon. He's quite weary these days, and has lost most of his sight and hearing."

"I'm sorry to hear that." Though a little blindness might spare him the shock of seeing me.

"Please, do sit. It'll just take a moment." She marched out of the room.

I wandered to the hearth, grateful she hadn't asked why I wanted to see her brother. Surely, she would coax it out of him later.

I extended my hands toward the fire, praying that Dr. Jones might recall something—some overlooked detail that would either rekindle or extinguish—preferably the former—my hope that my son was still alive. I needed to know the truth to move forward.

Mrs. Abbotts returned sooner than expected. "Mrs. Sterling, it's your lucky day. He is awake and in good spirits."

"Wonderful."

I followed her to Dr. Jones's bedroom, where he lay motionless on the bed. The alert eyes, bountiful dark hair, and vibrant energy I remembered were gone. Memories of my interactions with him in my previous life flooded back. He had been there from the very beginning— witnessing my baby growing inside me, listening to his heartbeat week after week, month after month.

When the time came, he forbade me from riding horses, and in the final hours of my life, he worked tirelessly to save me and the baby. He had even defended me against Mrs. White's accusations that I'd caused the accident through carelessness.

"Seldon, dear, Mrs. Sterling is here," his sister informed, her voice raised. "I'll have her sit on your left side, all right?"

Mrs. Abbotts installed me in a threadbare chair, and I wondered how many hours she spent sitting here, caring for him.

As soon as she left, he spoke. "Mrs. Sterling, it's good of you to have come." The authoritative voice I remembered now emerged weak and slow.

"Thank you for allowing me to see you. I'm making inquiries on behalf of my husband, General Alexander Sterling."

"How is the general these days?"

"He's well enough to be involved in the war. He's away on an assignment."

"Ah, I wouldn't expect nothing less. When brave men are needed, they answer the call." His head turned to me in a slow, unsettling motion, his gaze burning into mine. "How may I help you?"

Guilt pricked me for not speaking openly to him, but I steadied myself and pressed on. "As you may have heard, Alex returned from America not long after his former housekeeper, Mrs. Deborah White, attempted to kill him."

"I did hear about that. I always suspected something was off about that woman. I never liked her—always hovering, always meddling in the Sterlings' affairs."

"She still is. The authorities tracked her to the New Forest, and I fear we haven't seen the last of her."

"Ahh." He watched me for a long, uncomfortable moment. "However, you haven't come to inform me of Mrs. White's deeds and whereabouts." His mind was sharp, his thoughts incisive.

Perfect.

I decided not to rush into the topic of the baby's birth and demise, letting the conversation unfold naturally. "The thing is, after dealing with her in New York, I've become curious about what happened to the late Mrs. Sterling. Alex told me about it, but I can't shake the feeling there's more to the story. I was hoping you could shed some light on the matter." I couldn't very well tell him she had thrown the snake into the stall, causing Sunny to injure me. Still, he might have suspected foul play, making this a good place to start.

"Do you fear for your life, Mrs. Sterling?"

"When dealing with an emotionally unstable person, anyone would. Both my husband and I want her behind bars. If there are additional crimes for which Mrs. White should be held accountable, I want to bring them to the authorities' attention."

"I see—well, Florence, the beautiful Florence. She was brave. She fought until the end. On the day of the accident, I was summoned to the house. The staff said the accident had just occurred, but my years of experience suggested otherwise. However, I saw no reason for them to lie, nor did I have time to dwell on it. The evidence showed that a horse had trampled her. Believe me, I did everything in my power to save mother and child, but the damage was irreversible.

"It was the most devastating case of my career. I wish I could have done more. If truth is what you seek, I must admit that countless times, I've wondered . . ." His voice trailed off.

"Wondered what?"

"Oh, so many things—chief among them the strange feeling that seized the room when Florence passed. Do you know what I mean, Mrs. Sterling?"

It dawned on me that this sensible, intelligent man, so familiar with death, must have felt the veil between worlds merging that day. Could he sense the connection I had to that moment? Did he recognize me?

"Do you?" he pressed.

"I'd like to think I do," I replied cautiously. "I've experienced my fair share of tragedy."

"An uncompromising answer." He chuckled softly. "Now, my dear Mrs. Sterling, we both know that even if Mrs. White had a hand in Florence's death, it's been far too long to prove anything. What is it you truly seek?"

As I braced to disclose my hopes and fears, I had the impression he'd already guessed the answer. "I'm here because I don't believe the Sterlings' son died that day. I'm here to find something—anything—that will confirm my suspicions and bring him back to m . . ." my voice wavered as I held back the word *me*, "his father."

"Ah, now we begin to understand each other." He pointed to a jug on the nightstand. "If you don't mind . . ."

"Of course." I poured water into a glass and helped him lift it to his lips. The moment's tenderness stirred my affection for my dear doctor.

"Thank you. That's enough." He closed his eyes and laced his fingers over his chest. "It was a forced, arduous delivery. When the boy finally made his appearance, I was relieved that his heart was strong, and he bore no signs of trauma. He was a beautiful baby.

"Until other arrangements could be made, our best option was to send him to the dispensary. The attending nurse there was equipped to ensure his well-being. I commissioned Mrs. White to bring him there— something I regret to this day."

"Why do you say that?"

"Because I fear she might have done something to the baby. When I called to inquire about him, the nurse informed me he was dead upon arrival."

Dead. My hopes waned. He'd confirmed Alex's account and my worst fears: if my son had died that day, it was possible Mrs. White had killed him en route to the dispensary. But just like my death, I had no way to prove it.

"That daunting possibility has haunted me ever since," he continued. "However, something else has puzzled me all these years, though at the time, it seemed insignificant."

"What is that?" I leaned forward, gripping the edge of the chair.

"The nurse also said that Mrs. White had already left the dispensary. Given the circumstances, I expected her to return to the manor immediately."

"She didn't?" Considering what she had done, she wouldn't have wasted a minute away from me. I might have been able to tell Alex the truth.

"She and the driver, Vines, I believe, took double the required driving time. I was beside myself. In such difficult circumstances, a doctor relies on the support of someone overseeing the patient's household. When she reappeared, I questioned her harshly. Unmoved by my frustration, she claimed they were delayed by a broken-down truck blocking the road. It was an unusual excuse. Surely there were ways to bypass the obstacle, but I had no time to investigate her lies. The general soon arrived from London, and then Florence was gone."

"Did you see the baby's remains?"

"No. When we took Florence's body to the parish, the boy had already been placed in a coffin. In those days, coffins were quickly sealed to prevent the spread of disease and so forth."

Like a lightning strike, it hit me. *"When we took your body to the church, his remains were already there,"* Alex's voice echoed in my head. I had assumed he had seen our son's body, but he hadn't. If no one had, then it was possible—he could have grown to adulthood. My emotions surged once more, hope rising with them. "Doctor, this is extremely important. Did Alex see the baby's body?"

"The general did not see it. As I said, the casket was closed when we arrived. The constable asked the general if he wanted to open it. Alexander refused. I was relieved. His grief was overwhelming, and seeing the little corpse would have sent him over the edge."

I recalled the cemetery scene Lucca had shown me during my journey back in time. While the mourners dispersed, Alex had knelt by my grave and our son's, inconsolable. He remained there for the longest time. When he finally walked away, I knew he'd left his heart at the burial site. The doctor was right—seeing his lifeless son would have been too much.

I let my thoughts tumble out. "Do you realize what you've just implied? If no one saw the remains, he could have survived. Mrs. White could have bribed the nurse to lie. She could have taken him elsewhere. And that's why she took so long to return. I must speak to the nurse. Do you know where she is now?"

"I'm sorry. She passed away years ago. Now, Mrs. Sterling, don't let your hopes run rampant. The cost of unfulfilled expectations is sorrow. I assure you, I questioned the nurse extensively. I believe she was truthful. The baby died of natural causes before reaching the dispensary."

I can't accept that. I simply can't.

"You must also consider the constable," Doctor Jones added. "He signed both death records. Before you ask, he's also dead. I once spoke to him about the case. He was a reserved man who disliked having his work scrutinized. He confirmed the baby's death and firmly stated that he wouldn't have signed the document otherwise."

"But did he see the body?"

"I assumed he did. By law, he should have."

"He *should* have," I emphasized, "but, Doctor, as you know, people in small towns often rely on trust."

"Are you suggesting he might have taken the nurse's word for it?"

"Precisely, Doctor, precisely."

"Hmm, it's an interesting thought. Improbable, but a thought nonetheless." Eyelids that had grown heavy slowly parted, his eyes beholding mine once again. "I'm afraid that's all I can recall. I'm sorry I can't be of more help."

"You have been more than gracious. Thank you."

"It was my pleasure, Mrs. Sterling. And if I may say so, it's admirable that you're investigating the past for the general's sake, considering this all happened so long ago—even before you were born." His fading sight may have limited him, but the rumors about my supposed age clearly hadn't escaped him.

"Once again, thank you. I'll take my leave now." I attempted to rise, but he grasped my hand.

"Mrs. Sterling, few people understand the complexities of life and death. Most want to believe in an afterlife, but so few *know*. Don't let yourself be consumed by what you can't accept. Instead, find peace in what you know and in what you've been given."

His statement stunned me. Though improbable, again, he spoke as if he knew who I truly was. Perhaps it was simply that, in his final days, he understood the futility of chasing a past that would never return. The problem was that I had emerged from that very past, and because of that, nothing seemed impossible.

There was one way to clarify the confusion. I had to see my son's remains, which I now had growing reason to question if they existed. While Alex might be right that no miracle had saved the baby, he could still be alive if Mrs. White had placed him with another family.

If that were the case, the lengthy drive suggested they might have taken the baby far—perhaps even beyond the boundaries of the New Forest. Such an act was within her capability. However, it contradicted the claims of those who supposedly saw the body—unless, of course, she had bribed them. Still, the Sterlings were a prominent family in the area. If Mrs. White had given my son away, the recipients would almost certainly have suspected whose child he was. That they, too, might have been willing accomplices in her crime seemed utterly implausible.

Amid the conundrum, one thing was clear: I still didn't know the truth. "I can't accept what I don't know. I must know," I said.

"Then I wish you the best in your quest."

"I hope our paths will cross again someday. Goodbye for now."

"They will. Perhaps not in this life, but they will . . ."

CHAPTER 10
~ DEADLY COMPLICATIONS ~

The morning stroll lasted longer than I had anticipated. This early in the day, my mind was clearer, my thoughts more focused and precise. Nevertheless, I had no idea how to solve my problem. Since my visit to Dr. Jones, I'd seriously considered exhuming my child. There had to be a way to do it, preferably without running afoul of the law. Despite my determination, the numerous calls I made confirmed the legal course would lead to a dead end. Worse still, each time I hung up, I was tempted to falsify Alex's signature giving me permission to unearth the truth. But I wouldn't cross that line.

"Flor! Flor!" Eldad dashed down the path, my heart warming at the sight of him. Our lives were like tree roots—twisting and turning through the soil, finding ways around the obstacles in our path. And our relationship—like shoots breaking free into the light, it steadily grew stronger. Day after day, I found joy in our late-night snacks and newly established reading routine in the library. He was an enthusiastic learner, and I, an eager teacher.

I knelt on the ground, reaching out to embrace him. "Hey, little fellow. How are you today?"

"Good. We playing on rose garden."

His English improved by the day, but he still had much to learn. "We *are* playing *in* the rose garden," I corrected.

His lips curled into a smile. "We are playing in the rose garden. Friends and me."

"*My* friends and *I*."

"That's right, Flor."

"Let's practice saying my name. Flor-ence. Try it."

"Florr . . . ce."

"Try again. Flor-en-ce."

"Florr . . . ence."

"Perfect, Eldad. Perfect."

We strolled to the house, his small hand in mine.

"Go back with my friends," he said at the door.

I checked my watch. "Remind them to come inside soon for math time." Finding a tutor proved a challenge. The remote location didn't help, and most candidates preferred not to stay overnight. For now, Zaira and I took turns teaching the children the basic subjects—a rewarding endeavor we embraced wholeheartedly. "The lessons must be fun," Zaira had said. "Otherwise, they'll grow tired of us."

"I will." Eldad skipped away, humming a happy tune. I couldn't help but wonder if he'd had siblings and how much he remembered of them. Perhaps, once the wounds healed, he would share more.

I stepped into the foyer and peeled off my scarf and hat.

Mrs. Haywood popped out of the drawing room. "Mrs. Sterling, may I have a word?"

One glance told me she was in a cloudy mood. "Well, of course."

We moved into the room, and I paused in front of the French window that overlooked the garden, where the children played.

"You've grown fond of them," Mrs. Haywood remarked, "especially of the little lad."

"I'm afraid I have. He is a wonderful child. They all are."

"It will be difficult to let them go," she noted.

"Let them go?"

"Yes, when the government relocates them."

"I hope that doesn't happen anytime soon." Even though I knew it was inevitable, I preferred not to dwell on it. "What was it you wanted to speak to me about?"

"There isn't a comfortable way to say this . . . Please don't think poorly of me." She fidgeted with a button on her cardigan.

"You know I wouldn't."

"I . . . I need another advance. Two months' worth, to be exact. Some urgent bills have come up, and I must settle them immediately."

In her eyes, I detected a distress deeper than I'd ever seen before, and an uneasy feeling crept over me. Her troubles seemed to reach beyond the farm's finances. What could she possibly be entangled in?

"Is there anything else I should be aware of?" I finally asked.

"No. I'm not asking for a gift," she answered, her tone growing defensive, "just an advance."

"I'll do it this one last time." My tone was definitive, as I feared she wasn't being truthful.

"Much obliged, Mrs. Sterling."

"Please remember that our solicitor is at your disposal. He might identify solutions we haven't considered. Perhaps cutting back on spending or even renting out part of your land?" I reiterated the proposal I'd made when she first mentioned her financial struggles.

"You must think us utterly incompetent," she snapped. "Rest assured, we have considered every possible solution."

"Right, then." I could see her resolve was unyielding, and my curiosity only deepened. "I'll have the bank prepare the note for you."

"I thank you again, Mrs. Sterling. I'd better see to the dinner menu." With that, she withdrew.

As her footsteps faded into the distance, another set approached.

Zaira soon entered, her arms laden with books. She deposited them on the game table, ready for her lesson. "What's gotten into Mrs. Haywood? I passed her in the corridor. She's in quite a sour mood."

"She's probably overstressed about Will and keeping up with their farm," I said, offering a half-truth. It wasn't my place to disclose the housekeeper's personal challenges.

"Hmm." Zaira studied me for a moment. "And how about you? Anything out of the ordinary happening?"

"I don't think so. Why?"

"You know you can trust me." She smiled broadly, almost conspiratorially.

"What has gotten into you?" I raised an eyebrow.

"Well, these days . . . you know, with the guests . . . the children running around . . ." She floundered in a sea of nonsensical words, trying to articulate her point.

"For goodness' sake, Zaira—what are you alluding to?"

"Since we are friends, I assumed you would tell me the news."

"What news?"

"That you're in the family way."

My jaw dropped.

"Aren't you?" She looked baffled.

"No! What on earth possessed you to think that?"

"Isn't that why you visited the doctor?"

"Oh, my. I can't believe how quickly gossip travels." I settled on the settee, disappointed her suspicions weren't correct. "No, that's not why I visited him. Besides, he doesn't practice anymore." Before she could ask, I related the story. "Doctor Jones attended the late Mrs. Sterling. I wanted to speak to him about Alex's son."

She perched herself on the edge of the table. "Why?"

"This might sound deranged, but after all Mrs. White has done, I've started to wonder if there was foul play surrounding the baby's death."

"Goodness gracious, Florence! Are you saying she may have dispatched the child?"

"Either that, or she hid him somewhere." I explained what I'd learned from Dr. Jones—the peculiarities involving Mrs. White, the nurse, the constable, and the unsettling fact that Alex never saw the baby's body.

"Wait, if they offered for Mr. Sterling to see the body," Zaira reflected, "it must have been there. It must have. The constable would have checked. Don't you agree?"

"It could be either way. There are too many unknowns. Still, I can't shake the feeling that something is terribly off, and I want to know what that is. Of course, complicating matters, both the nurse and the constable are dead."

"Regardless of what's been said, the idea that the boy survived is farfetched. Mrs. White is insane. I'm not disputing that. But why would she make the baby disappear? That's beyond evil, even for her. On the other hand, if she had a hand in his death, after all these years, there is no way to find out." Zaira sat down beside me. "You know, Mrs. White's escape from justice and Mr. Sterling's departure might be playing with your emotions. And," she looked at me sideways, "maybe even your attachment to little Eldad. You are too invested."

It was interesting that both she and Mrs. Haywood had mentioned him. Indeed, I was invested. I loved the child. However, Zaira's assessment of my emotions missed the mark. After all, she knew nothing of Mrs. White's culpability in harming a pregnant woman—or in my death. If Mrs. White hadn't cared for the child before he was born, why would she afterward? My truth was both a blessing and a burden—too extraordinary to believe.

The sound of the front door bursting open reached our ears, followed by the children's laughter ringing through the halls. In that moment, like a star piercing the night sky, clarity struck. I knew exactly what to do.

"Zaira." I seized her hand. "I must do something, and I'd like your help."

"You know you can count on me."

I pray you'll feel the same after you hear me out. "There's one way to know if Alex's son is alive. We need to look inside his casket."

Zaira went as white as a sheet, her mouth opening as if to speak, only to close it again.

"And since I don't have Alex's permission," I went on, "I'm going to persuade someone to help me."

"And if that doesn't work?" she stuttered.

"Well then, I'll bribe him."

"And . . . who might that be?"

"Mr. Morris, the cemetery keeper."

———

All day, I stressed about things I could and couldn't control, the latter most exhausting. I missed Alex more than usual. I wondered where he was and if he was safe. Simultaneously, I fretted over the Haywoods' financial ordeal. These hardworking people had spent their lives planning for their future, and now that it had arrived, they deserved the retirement they had worked so hard to achieve.

I crawled under the covers, hoping to stave off the headache pressing behind my temples, but my mind refused to settle. Inevitably, it turned to my plans to disturb my son's grave.

"Don't let your hopes run rampant. The cost of unfulfilled expectations is sorrow. I assure you I questioned the nurse extensively. I believe she was truthful. The baby died of natural causes before reaching the dispensary," Dr. Jones's advice looped through my head.

What if I was wrong? Disturbing the grave would haunt me forever, a shadow of shame darkening every glance I shared with Alex. Doubt chipped away at my convictions. *All this thanks to that woman.* Mrs. White's evil seeds continued to bear their bitter fruit. And precisely because of that, I had to put an end to the speculations. Tomorrow, I would visit the cemetery.

I fumbled for the aspirin and water on the night table, gulped them down, and redirected my thoughts to happier times. As my body relaxed into the mattress, the tension eased, and I drifted into sleep.

I peer out the window into the woods. The sky fades into darkness, and shadows stretch and twist through the trees, transforming the familiar landscape into something eerie. From within the gloom, a man emerges. I recognize his brown eyes and confident posture—yet his gaze carries an intense warning. A sense of wrongness grips me, a primal alarm whispering that something terrible has happened—or is about to.

"Lucca . . ."

"Florence, wake up!" his voice roared in my head. "Wake up!"

Lucca! I gasped for air but found none.

"Fight, Florence, fight!"

Fight what? What is this pressure? I came to, a scream lodged in my throat. Someone was pressing a pillow over my face. Panic surged as I flailed, clawing desperately for anything to push it away. My hands found the attacker's arms, nails scraping against unyielding fabric that rendered my efforts futile. The pressure intensified, cutting off my air. My chest burned, my head spun, and the world around me began to dissolve. Darkness crept in as consciousness slipped further away.

"Don't give up!" Lucca's voice cut through the haze, infusing me with a burst of energy. "Fight!"

As if yanked upward by unseen hands, I shot upright, shoving the assailant off me. I rolled off the bed, hitting the floor with a heavy thud. Instinctively, I flipped on the lamp. Light poured into the room, revealing my deadly enemy. She stood at the foot of the bed, the only barrier between us. Her gray hair was thinner than I remembered, but her catlike eyes were unchanged—still burning with murderous intent. Momentarily, I stood dumbfounded—here was the woman who held the answers to the questions that tormented my soul. Yet I knew with utter certainty that the truth would never escape her lips.

"I see you are thrilled to see me again," she said, her voice dripping with mockery.

How in the world had she gotten in the house? Once again, she had taken me by surprise, exploiting my vulnerability. I had no weapon to defend myself. Not even screaming would help. My bedroom lay out of earshot of the others. "How dare you come in here?" I sputtered, struggling to mask how shaken I was.

"I could say the same to you—admirable how you've managed to worm your way into Mr. Sterling's life. You are a parasite I intend to remove. Never again will you stand in my way, you rotten creature." She inched closer.

"What else do you want from us? You have already taken enough." My hands fisted, readying for impact.

"It's not what I have taken, but what I have not taken, that will hurt you most."

"What are you talking about?" *Was it my child?*

"Wouldn't you like to know?" She chuckled darkly. "You have meddled in Mr. Sterling's life long enough. You—the usurper—a mere imposter, lucky enough to resemble the deceased. I must admit, you've masterfully exploited the circumstances to your advantage. Credit where it's due."

"I *look* like the deceased because I *am* the deceased!" I sputtered, my only weapon was the truth and the belief that I could win this fight.

Her confident demeanor faltered—her eyes widened, and her lips parted in surprise. She took a step back, as if distance could shield her from the implication in my words.

"I am the Florence Contini you trapped in Sunny's stall with the snake, the same woman you laughed at when I screamed in terror for my baby's life." Gaining confidence, I stepped forward. "You have much to account for."

"Enough nonsense! Enough!" She pulled out a pocketknife, its blade catching bits of light.

"How many times do you plan to kill me?" I yelled, uselessly trying to delay the inevitable.

"As many as necessary." She lunged at me like a jaguar out of a tree.

I reached for the nearest object—the jewelry box on the nightstand—and swung it wildly, deflecting the knife as it sliced through the air, its cold steel seeking the warmth of my blood. To my horror, she pressed closer, her resolve unwavering. Tightening my grip, I swung again with all my strength. The bronze lock connected with the side of her head with a sickening thud. The knife slipped from her grasp, clattering to the floor as she stumbled backward.

In a heartbeat, I kicked the knife under the bed, out of reach. A sharp sting drew my gaze to my forearm; blood trickled from where the blade had grazed the skin.

Recovering with unnerving speed, Mrs. White seized the footrest and charged like a trained assassin. With blind rage, she slammed into me, knocking me to the floor. I threw up my hands to shield my head, bracing for another blow. But to my relief, she abandoned the attack and bolted for the door. The jewelry box must have struck her harder than I'd realized.

Pressing a hand to my wound, I scrambled to my feet and chased after her, flipping on light switches as I went. On the fourth step of the staircase, I spotted a drop of blood—then another, and another. She was injured too.

The front door stood wide open, a cold breeze sweeping through the foyer. Plunging into the night after her would be reckless. Instead, I locked and bolted the door. Then, a thought hit me: *What if she's still inside? What if she wants me to think she's gone?*

The children.

I needed to make sure they were safe. I needed help.

Grabbing a five-arm candlestick for protection, I sprinted through the hallways, my eyes darting into every shadow for signs of danger. Urgency dripped from my voice as I roused the household. Together, we checked on the children. They were safe——peacefully asleep in their beds. Once reassured, we combed through every corner, leaving no closet unopened and no attic unsearched. By dawn, we were certain: she was gone.

Zaira and I convened in the kitchen as the adrenaline slowly ebbed from our veins. I sat at the table, unwrapping the makeshift bandage from my arm to replace it with something cleaner.

"That wretched woman!" Zaira rumbled from the stove, slamming the kettle onto the burner. "Thank heavens she didn't do more harm."

"How did she get in? The Haywoods are careful to lock up the house every night." My voice shook with anger and exhaustion.

Had someone let her in? Did she know Alex was gone? She wouldn't have come armed with just a knife otherwise. But how did she know? The staff understood the importance of keeping everything private for Alex's safety. Martha crossed my mind. She was from Salisbury—the last place Mrs. White had been spotted. Could they know each other? Was Martha feeding her information? I dismissed the idea almost immediately. Martha came from a respected family, boasted impeccable references, and, aside from her occasional bouts of boredom, seemed entirely trustworthy.

I groaned inwardly. Because of Mrs. White, I was starting to see enemies where there were none.

"I wouldn't be surprised if they missed a door. There are quite a few, you know," Zaira reflected.

"And Mrs. White happened to find it? What are the odds?"

"It's possible."

"I'm not so sure. I don't picture her hopping from door to door. She is not one to waste time."

"Let's not jump to conclusions," Zaira said, rummaging through the cupboard. "Where is the coffee?"

"We might be out. Check the shelves."

"For Pete's sake—what in the world?" Zaira called out from the larder.

I hurried over, my breath catching as I took in the scene. Several floorboards had been removed, revealing the entrance to the old tunnel. *I should have known.*

"What is this?" Zaira leaned over to peer into the dark hole.

A spot full of memories. The recollection of the German attack came swiftly: Colonel Swinger's arrival with news of their impending approach, the shattering of windows into a million pieces, the flight through the tunnel into the forest.

"Are you all right? You look flushed, as though you're about to explode." Zaira placed a steadying hand on my shoulder. "Do you need to sit down?"

"I'm fine." Now that the danger—from the past and from the night's events—had passed, I could feel again. And I was filled with smoldering anger at the abhorrent woman. "This is the entrance to a tunnel that exits on the south lawn. Alex told me about it," a half-truth.

Of course, Mrs. White had lived in Forti Radici and was familiar with the escape route. It seemed no one had let her in after all. Even so, it didn't explain how she had known that Alex was away.

"By the time the constable shows up, Mrs. White will be far away," Zaira lamented.

"If she went this way, though, it might explain how she got in. We must seal it at once."

CHAPTER 11
~ UNFORESEEN ~

The coming and going of the local police and Scotland Yard delayed my plans to visit the cemetery. Chief Inspector Overton—a clean-shaven man with curly brown hair who stubbornly wore his trench coat despite the warm weather—established that Mrs. White had entered the house through the tunnel and exited through the main door.

"We've been following her tracks but never saw this coming." The inspector alluded to last night's intrusion. "It was unpredictable—and I don't like unpredictable."

"I feared it was possible but never truly believed it would happen. Inspector, you must find her," I pleaded.

"We'll do our best. I'll ring you if anything comes up."

"Please do."

"Now, you must heed my advice and lie low. In fact, stay out of sight. She knows the household will be on high alert, so I doubt she'll return here. To be sure, I'll have the constable increase their patrols in the area." With that, the inspector departed, taking Mrs. White's knife as evidence —along with my request to look into Martha's background, just in case.

Through the window, I watched the police car drive away, its silhouette framed by verdant trees and a clear blue sky—a peaceful scene that contrasted with the turmoil roiling inside me.

"It's not what I have taken, but what I have not taken, that will hurt you

most," Mrs. White had threatened. The odious woman took a twisted delight in inflicting physical and mental anguish.

I glanced at my wristwatch. I still had time.

Minutes later, I sat behind the Lagonda's steering wheel with Zaira in the passenger seat.

"There is still time to reconsider." Zaira wrung her hands anxiously. "This could be dangerous in more ways than one. We'll be pushing the boundaries of the dead by disturbing their rest—and defying the inspector's advice for you to lie low. Mrs. White could be watching your every move."

"She won't hang around waiting to be apprehended. She'll go into hiding like before. I must say that if I had any doubts about doing this, her attack removed them. She could've done anything with the baby. For Alex's sake, I need to know he rests in peace."

"Well, that's the thing," Zaira shot back, her voice tightening. "Mr. Sterling will be enraged when he finds out. It's a tremendous desecration of his son's grave. It could destroy your marriage. Have you thought about that?" Her words hit harder than I expected, but she didn't know the truth—he was my child too.

"I have, but I'm not planning to tell him anytime soon. Unless, of course, we find no corpse."

"And if that's the case, how will you find out what happened to the child? Mrs. White will remain silent, even if she's facing the gallows."

"I haven't thought that far ahead."

Zaira gave me a sharp glance, her lips pressed in a tight line.

"I'm sorry for dragging you into this. If you'd rather not be involved, I understand. You can wait for me in the car."

"Too late for that," she retorted. "I'm too curious to jump ship now."

I floored the gas pedal, eager to reach our destination. For the rest of the ride, I mentally rehearsed my conversation with the cemetery keeper.

Aside from a middle-aged woman arranging flowers on a freshly dug grave, the cemetery was deserted.

"The fewer people we encounter, the better," Zaira remarked, veering onto the first path off the main entrance.

"We should have brought flowers," I muttered.

"Now you think about it."

"You didn't think about it either."

"No. I do not like graveyards or anything that makes me think about them." Zaira's gaze flickered from one headstone to the next.

"I don't mind coming here. It's peaceful."

"I can think of a million other peaceful places."

Thank goodness she had no idea how often I visited. But would her perspective change if someone dear to her heart were buried here—someone like Clarence? I pushed the thought away, hoping she'd never have to know that pain.

We cleared the corner of a mausoleum with an angel clutching a sword at its entrance. Up ahead, in the oldest section of the yard, I spotted the caretaker hunched over, shoveling weeds.

"That's Mr. Morris."

"He looks creepy," Zaira assessed. "Are you sure he's alive?"

I smiled. The first time I encountered him, I'd wondered as much. "Last I checked."

"You still haven't told me how you know him."

"Oh, just by chance. I stop by on occasion to let Betsy rest."

Our approach brought Mr. Morris's work to a halt. He removed his hat and ran the back of his hand across his forehead. "Good day, ladies. May I help you find someone?"

"Good afternoon, Mr. Morris. Actually, we were looking for you."

"For me?" He rested his hands on the shovel handle, studying us.

"Do you remember me?" I asked.

"How can I forget?" he mumbled. "You are Mrs. Sterling, all right."

"It's nice to see you again." I smiled, concealing my hesitation. Now that I was here, I feared saying the wrong thing and offending him. My intentions, while questionable and unorthodox, weren't malicious. I hoped to convey as much.

"How may I assist you?"

"Do you recall what you told me about the late Mrs. Sterling's grave? About Scotland Yard?"

Zaira gazed at me with curiosity. No doubt she'd ask later. I'd have to come up with an explanation—one that didn't involve Alex digging up my remains, thinking I was his deceased wife.

"I do. Why?" His eyes narrowed.

"Because there are rumors the general's baby didn't die, that it was all a lie, and his coffin is empty. We suspect it was part of a vile scheme to separate the child from his father."

"You don't say!" he exclaimed. "That's serious business."

"The worst is that the general is away on military assignment, not knowing if this is true. And as you know, Scotland Yard can be a bit sticky to work with. They complicate matters more often than not." I would appeal to his pride to win him over. "They undermine the locals' abilities to solve their own problems." I watched as my reasoning unlocked something in his brain.

"That's exactly what I've always said. They think they're the sublime capos, but all they do is step on people's toes."

I inched closer and lowered my voice. "Here is the thing—I want to help the general find the truth, but I'd like to do it discreetly, without involving the authorities. It wouldn't cause any harm . . . just a quick look. The general would be forever grateful." He observed me with a blank expression as I concluded. "The problem is, I don't know how to go about it."

"It's a risky business, indeed, very risky." He cleared his throat. "I'm sorry, miss, but you understand that you can't go about digging up the dead. I'd have to report you. Patrons are only permitted to clean the tombs and bring flowers."

Did he misunderstand my intentions, or was he cleverly playing along? I suspected the latter. It was time to be direct. "No, I can't dig up a grave, but you can."

"I can, but it doesn't mean I will. I could be dismissed from my post. I've been here ages, miss. Worse yet, if I did, the missus would wring my neck like a goose. Too many mouths to feed at home, you understand."

"How many children do you have?" Zaira asked, shifting anxiously from one foot to the other.

"Six little ones."

"Quite the brood," Zaira muttered.

"Miss," Mr. Morris squinted at her, scrutinizing her closely, "do I know you?"

"I don't think so." She looked away to avoid his probing gaze.

"Hmm."

"Mr. Morris." I construed my next words carefully. "Please don't take offense, but with the war and all, wouldn't it be helpful to have extra cash in hand?"

Zaira eyed the shovel in his hand and retreated a few steps, as if bracing herself to run. Persuasion had failed; we were now venturing into criminal territory—bribery. I half-expected him to swing the tool at us.

"Indeed, these are hard times," he admitted, the shovel still.

"If anything goes awry, I'll take full responsibility," I assured. "What do you say? One quick look could put a million worries to rest. Just one look."

"I'm sorry." Mr. Morris turned away and, muttering something about what the world had come to, resumed his work.

"Come on, let's go before he calls the police," Zaira whispered urgently.

"Mr. Morris," I called in a last-ditch effort.

He ignored me.

Stung by failure, I followed Zaira as she took a shortcut through the mausoleums, her legs pumping toward the exit.

"For goodness's sake, Zaira, slow down." I hustled to catch up.

"This was a terrible idea," she hissed. "What if he tells Mr. Sterling? I might end up without a post and you without a husband."

"Nonsense," I said, though she might not be far from the truth.

Suddenly, a figure burst from behind one of the structures, collapsing with Zaira. She let out a startled squeal, her hands striking the man's chest and shoving him backward.

"Mr. Morris! What the devil are you doing?" I snapped. "You scared us stiff!"

"I . . ." he stuttered, regaining his balance. "I was trying to catch you before you left."

"Why?" Zaira demanded, still shaking.

"I'm keeping guard tonight."

"And?" Zaira growled.

"Come back after dusk. Just you two. No witnesses."

"You'll help us?" I questioned, hardly believing his change of heart.

He nodded. "I'll be at the back gate."

"When alms are too generous even a saint grows distrustful," Zaira challenged.

"Well, you know what they say," Mr. Morris countered. "A wise man should have money in his head, not in his heart. In my case, I'd rather have it in my pocket. My *brood* could use new shoes. Bring the money, and don't forget—come alone."

"Hello?" I said into the receiver.

"Hello. Is this Miss Bates?"

"Miss Bates?"

"The lady who inquired about my cottage? This is Mr. Acker."

"Oh, yes, yes. This is she." I silently cursed my inability to remember my fabrications. It would be easier if I simply told the truth.

"Lucy or Alice?"

Darn. Who was I? "Lucy!" I responded a bit too enthusiastically, glad I had remembered.

"Miss Lucy, I rang to let you know the cottage is available. Mrs. Burrell and her nephew left this morning."

"Oh. I didn't think they would leave this soon."

"Neither did I. She had a family emergency up north. In her haste, the poor woman slipped in the bathtub and cut her head." Mr. Acker was quite the chatterer today.

"Oh my. Is she all right?"

"Well enough to get on the road without delay," he retorted. "She's sporting quite a patch but insisted she didn't need stitches."

I had to lie again to maintain my story. "I appreciate the call, but I'm afraid my sister and I have committed to another place."

"It's fully furnished. Apart from your clothing, you won't have to bring anything," he said encouragingly. "The furniture, bedding, ice box . . . even the picture frames are included. Did I mention that before?"

"I don't think so."

"Well, if you change your mind, let me know."

"Wait. Mr. Acker—"

"Yes."

"Did you say the picture frames come with it?" My stomach knotted.

"Yes."

"They weren't Mrs. Burrell's, then?" I had to be sure.

"No."

"And the photos—weren't they of Mrs. Burrell and her nephew?"

"Oh no. I suppose she didn't plan on staying long enough to switch the photographs. They belong to the previous tenant."

"I see." I considered the implication. "Mr. Acker, out of pure curiosity, did Mrs. Burrell injure the right or left side of her head?"

He paused, likely wondering about my odd question. "The right side."

"How unfortunate. Well, thank you, Mr. Acker. I'll ring back if the other place falls through."

"Please do."

I stumbled to the sofa—the photos in the frames weren't of Mrs. Burrell. She'd been just injured. She'd left in a rush. I had seen the rosary at the cottage. I'd struck the right side of her head with the jewelry box. Mrs. Burrell and Mrs. White were one and the same. The knot in my stomach tightened so hard I could barely breathe. She'd made a fool of me again.

"*You have meddled in Mr. Sterling's life long enough*," she had said. If she wanted something buried in the past and had discovered my visit to Dr. Jones, her brazen attack made more sense.

If I had called Inspector Overton the day I visited the cottage, she would be behind bars and wouldn't have had the satisfaction of assaulting me. Instead, courtesy of my foolishness, she remained in the wind. It had been easy to discard the only clue, the rosary, when there was so much that pointed away from her. If only I had asked Mr. Acker a few more questions. If I had waited for Mrs. Burrell to return. *If I had*— the saddest words. Yet no amount of guilt could change the past.

Now, to my shame, I would relay the information to the inspector, though it might be too little, too late. She was too clever to leave obvious traces, but she wasn't perfect. Hopefully, the next time she made a mistake, the authorities—or I—would not dismiss it.

When the appointed hour arrived, my heart pounded with a rhythm I hadn't felt in years. What if the coffin was empty? What if my son was alive somewhere? Alex and I would move heaven and earth to find him. True, I would come in as his stepmother. But that would be enough.

However, the probability of encountering his remains sent me into a frenzy—it would forever haunt me. Every moment with Alex would be tainted by the memory of my decision.

The telephone rang from the far end of the library. I answered it, every nerve on edge, as if I had already broken the law and the police were already at my door. "Hello."

"Mrs. Sterling?"

"Yes. This is she."

"I'm glad to find you at home," said the woman. "I'm afraid I have sad news, but I thought you'd like to know."

"Who is this?"

"Mrs. Abbotts, dear. Doctor Jones's sister."

"Mrs. Abbotts—what's happened?"

"Seldon passed away this morning."

"Oh no." Grief clawed at me, feeling his absence and the severed connection to my previous life. "I'm so sorry. He was an extraordinary man."

"He truly was. He lived a wonderful life. There is much consolation in that."

"It must be hard for you." I remembered the worn bedside chair. Would she still sit there thinking of him, unable to let go? "How are you holding up?"

"Oh, I already miss him dearly. My days will be frightfully lonely."

"We didn't have much time to chat when I visited." Acquainted with death's loneliness and the sustaining power of friends, I invited, "You must come for tea sometime."

"Sounds wonderful, dear. Once the dust settles, I shall."

"When is the funeral?"

"Tomorrow afternoon."

"I'll be there."

"I'll ring you once I know the details. Please relay the news to the general."

"I will as soon as I can. He is still away with the military."

"I trust he is safe?"

"As far as I know."

"Well, dear, until tomorrow."

"Until then."

I could hardly believe Dr. Jones's passing. Death kept crossing my path, a shadow I couldn't escape.

A disturbance drew my attention to the doorway. I shrieked. A woman shrouded in black, her face hidden behind a veil, stood as if she had just emerged from a long-buried crypt.

"Don't fret. It's just me." Zaira lifted the tulle off her face.

"You turned my blood to ice!" My hand flew to my chest, my heartbeat hammering against my ribs. "Why in the name of all the saints in heaven are you dressed like that?"

"For no other reason other than to avoid detection."

"Honestly, you have the most fascinating ideas." The veil was a bit too much.

"Mock all you want, but there is always someone watching. A busybody with nothing to do but look for something to gossip about. Now, we don't want that, do we?"

"No, we don't."

"Well then," she said, eyeing my light-colored dress, "go change into something more suitable."

"All right—don't get worked up." I moved to the door. "I won't be long."

"Should I get Mr. Brown?"

"No. I'll drive. He left the car up front. I told him we were visiting someone in the village."

"At this hour? Did he believe you?"

"Don't know." I shrugged. "At any rate, he didn't question it. Oh, before I forget—Doctor Jones's sister telephoned. He passed away this morning."

"You don't say!"

"I'm afraid so."

"That's just our luck," she retorted.

"And why is that?"

"His spirit may roam the cemetery. And I must add—he may be angry at us for what we are about to do."

"Don't be absurd." I waved her off, though her comment lingered in my mind.

We left the car under the willow trees near the main entrance. As Zaira and I crossed the deserted street, I searched for the moon. It was hidden behind a layer of clouds, plunging the night into darkness so deep that we could see only a few feet ahead.

"Mr. Morris said to meet him at the back," I recalled. "Come on."

We skirted the brick fence toward the far side of the property.

"This wall must have cost a fortune," Zaira muttered.

"Do you think it was built to keep people out or to keep something in?" I honestly wondered.

"Let's not find out," Zaira said with a shiver.

I quickened my pace, scanning the shifting shadows. A chilling sense of unseen eyes tracking our every step settled over me. Though I had encountered the otherworldly—having seen and spoken with my deceased brother—this felt different. This energy pulsed with dread, a warning against what lay ahead. We were about to disturb something that demanded respect. I could only hope we'd leave unscathed. We hurried the final stretch, half walking, half trotting, until Mr. Morris's silhouette emerged from the gloom.

"There he is," I said.

"Wait!" Zaira grabbed my arm. "He is not alone."

I squinted into the darkness. "You are right."

"This could go horribly wrong. Think about it. We are in a graveyard, out of earshot from anyone, with two complete strangers. If Mr. Morris can add two and two, he's already figured out no one knows we're here. And if that's not enough to make your skin crawl, you are carrying a wad of cash."

"You're overthinking it." I tried to sound calm despite my doubts. "He's probably brought a helper."

"Helper or not, I don't trust him."

"If it makes you feel better, we can hide the cash," I offered. "We'll give it to him on our way out."

"It doesn't make me feel better, but fine," she grumbled.

Concealed by the night, I buried the envelope under a layer of leaves against the wall. "Remember, it's below the third figure—there, the gargoyle."

"Why do people even make those grotesque things?" Zaira muttered, glaring at the statue.

"And why put them in graveyards?" I added. "Come on, let's go."

"Just in case." With one graceful movement, Zaira picked up a rock and slipped it into her pocket. "A little more leverage. One wrong move, and I'll beat them silly."

Any other time, I might have laughed. Tonight, I prayed we wouldn't need the weapon. My thoughts drifted to the self-defense tips the nuns had taught at Higher Grounds. "*Go for the vulnerable areas,*" Sister Callahan had instructed with a grin. "*Between the legs is a perfectly good spot. The eyes are next. If you've got nothing sharp to stick in them, your fingers will have to do.*" I smiled inwardly. When it came to the girls' safety, she didn't fool around.

"Good evening, ladies," the caretaker greeted.

"Good evening," Zaira and I responded, our voices a bit too forced.

"Welcome to the cemetery—a whole different world at night." He chuckled unnervingly. "This is Frank, my lad. He'll be helping me tonight."

The moon peeked out from the clouds, illuminating Frank's young, tense face. He couldn't have been older than fourteen. Clearly, he didn't want to be here any more than we did.

"See, nothing other than an innocent helper," I whispered to Zaira, though minutes ago, I hadn't been so confident.

Zaira grunted in response.

Mr. Morris surveyed Zaira's appearance with a smirk. "Miss, are you here to unbury the dead or to bury yourself?"

His joke hung awkwardly in the air. After all, just the other day, he had said, "*Not that anyone with half a brain would wander in at night.*" I realized that it was too soon to feel safe.

"That's in poor taste," Zaira snapped, her hand darting to her pocket and the rock.

"Ah, don't get agitated," the caretaker said, laughing it off. "Let's get on with it."

We trailed behind as the men led the way toward the Sterlings' burial spot.

"I must warn you," Mr. Morris called over his shoulder. We aren't the only ones moving about the grounds."

"What do you mean?" Zaira asked.

"At night, the dead stir. Ignore them, and they'll ignore you."

Was he joking again? I glanced at Zaira. She moved like a robot, mechanically, rigidly. I owed her.

"Come on, Pa," Frank said, walking briskly to take the lead. "Let's hurry."

We wound our way through the graveyard, careful not to tread on the sacred resting spaces. A low hooting drew my attention to the beech tree. I could just make out the shape of an owl in the dappled moonlight, perched on a lower branch, its talons gripping the wood with intensity. Its wide eyes gleamed in the obscurity as its head tilted toward the moon. At the trudging of our feet on the dry twigs, the bird turned in our direction.

We passed under the tree, and I could have sworn its gaze was fixed on me as it emitted a string of bold sounds. A shiver ran through me as I glanced over my shoulder. The owl was behind us now—still watching.

About fifty yards ahead, the Sterling tombs loomed. My tomb, with my name. This was the worst time for Zaira to discover the former Mrs. Sterling's given name. She wasn't prepared to learn it. I wasn't prepared to explain it. Gratefully, the darkness favored me on this point. I had to be extra careful.

"Here we are," Mr. Morris announced.

I positioned myself to obscure the headstone bearing my name, steering Zaira's attention toward the child's grave instead.

Mr. Morris rounded a grave guarded by chains and came back with a lamp. He produced a match and lit it. Frank hustled to a nearby angel statue. From behind its massive pedestal, he retrieved two shovels and several other tools. The men set to work, shoveling away the soil.

"Good thing this one doesn't have a cement cover," Mr. Morris pointed out. "It would be nearly impossible to do this otherwise." The grave featured a magnificent headstone but lacked any covering across its length. The size of the coffin was also convenient. One man could tackle the task alone, but with two, the work would go fairly fast.

"Imagine that—a million concrete pieces scattered everywhere," Zaira said. "Concealing our crime would prove far more difficult."

Crime. Guilt stabbed my heart, but the need for truth overrode it. Still, with each scoop of soil removed, the magnitude of my decision pressed on me like a ton of bricks.

"Put some muscle into it," the caretaker urged his son.

"Wait, Pa, we are digging a bigger hole than necessary." Frank stepped back to catch his breath and survey their progress.

"It's the perfect size," his father assured.

"The coffin isn't that big, is it?" Frank questioned.

"No, it isn't." Mr. Morris frowned. "But once we reach it, there needs to be enough space for you to jump in and secure it so we can pull it up."

"Me?" Frank's voice rose in alarm.

"Let's put it this way," his father replied, his patience thinning. "If I go down, I might not be able to climb back out—and that wouldn't be good, now, would it?"

Without another word, Frank resumed digging as the minutes dragged on. My legs began to strain from the long standing, and just then, a gust of wind gathered the clouds in its grip and swept them away. The full moon appeared above us, its light bathing everything within reach.

"Oh, good . . . good," Zaira muttered.

"Good indeed," I echoed. The added clarity was comforting.

Abruptly, Zaira squealed—her previous relief shortly-lived.

"What is it?" I stammered, my eyes flickering with anxiety.

The men stiffened; their shovels suspended midair.

"There—do you see that?" With a trembling hand, Zaira pointed to a mausoleum on the other side of the path.

"See what?" I could see nothing.

"There!" Zaira insisted.

"You don't see her?" Mr. Morris sounded surprised and maybe even amused.

Frank turned away as if avoiding what apparently was there. "Come on, Pa, let's get this done. I want to get out of here."

"Easy now. Don't make a fuss," Mr. Morris advised. "She's harmless."

"Until she isn't anymore." Zaira laced her arm through mine, her body shaking violently.

"Who?" I pressed.

"Lady Catherine," Mr. Morris said.

"What?" I was confused.

"A ghost," Frank clarified.

I squinted into the gloom and gasped. The air sliced down my throat, icy and sharp. There she was—a black figure with a pale face and long dark hair, floating silently between the mausoleum columns. "Goodness gracious!"

"You see her now?" Zaira's arm gripped mine so hard I thought she would break my bones.

"I do."

"The ghost of Lady Catherina di Leccio. One of the oldest souls on these grounds. She comes out every night." Unconcerned, Mr. Morris went back to digging.

"There she goes now," Frank observed.

She slipped away, a dark cloud traversing the headstones.

"Where is she going?" Zaira asked, and I got the feeling that, like me, she was relieved the specter moved away from us.

"To the beach," Frank answered.

"To the beach?" I wondered.

"The tale is that her lover sailed from Hurst Castle and drowned in the sea," Mr. Morris said. "She spent her life pacing the shoreline, waiting for him."

"So she's still waiting for him?" I assumed.

"That's right. Every night, she goes to the water, then comes back at dawn to the confinement of her existence."

The sadness of the tale hung in the air, a poignant reminder that not all burdens were shed in death.

Zaira's gaze darted from one tomb to the next, her body rigid, poised to flee at the slightest movement. "There could be more . . . they could be anywhere," she stammered with barely contained fear.

"No need to fret, miss," Mr. Morris assured. "Rarely do others come out on a full moon."

"Is that supposed to be comforting?" Zaira questioned.

"It's all right." I wrapped my arm around her shoulders, drawing her close. "Just focus on the lamp."

The men continued their work with determined focus. Before long, Frank was waist-deep in the excavation, his figure partially obscured by the loose soil piling up around him.

"We are close, really close . . ." I whispered.

"Good. Good." Zaira inhaled deeply.

"Ah, there you are!" Mr. Morris exclaimed. The shovel finally hit wood. "Careful now . . ." He handed Frank a cord. "Tie this around it to keep it together."

Frank did as told, supporting the bottom as Mr. Morris hoisted the coffin out of the darkness of the earth. Once they set it on the ground, Mr. Morris helped his son climb out.

I fell to my knees and pressed my palm on the tiny box, brushing it off with a sweeping motion.

"Please, Mrs. Sterling, move back. We must be extremely cautious,"

Mr. Morris warned. "If we break the frame, we can damage the remains —and we mustn't alter them in any way."

"Amen," Zaira agreed.

I scooted back but remained on my knees. Fueled by anticipation, sadness, and even rage at having to do this.

Wielding a heavy tool, I wasn't familiar with, the caretaker loosened the nails. Under the careful pressure of his hands, the brittle wood screeched but held its form.

Another blast of wind blew through the graveyard, knocking the lamp over. Zaira seized it at once. The light flickered more in her unsteady hand than it had in the wind.

"Are you all right?" I looked up at her.

"I'm ch-chilled to the b-bone," she stuttered.

"Are you ready?" Mr. Morris asked.

"Go on." My emotions finally took over, and tears flooded my eyes. This moment, no matter the outcome, would change me forever.

He gently pried open the lid and stood aside.

Zaira shrieked and dropped the lamp.

"It can't be!" I cried in bewilderment.

A tiny skeleton lay within the shadows of the coffin.

CHAPTER 12

~ HAUNTED ~

Morning found me awake, heartbroken and horrified by what I had done. Every time I drifted into sleep, the image of the tiny skeleton flashed through my mind, jolting me awake. I should have listened to Alex, to the doctor, to Zaira. But 'I should have' were the saddest words. I couldn't turn back time. The shame of disturbing my son's remains would haunt me for the rest of my days. Not to mention the unanswered question: Had he died of natural causes or had Mrs. White killed him? I'd never know.

A tap on the door broke my thoughts. I grabbed my watch from the nightstand—nine o'clock. I'd lingered in bed longer than usual, but honestly, I had little energy or desire to face the day. Succumbing to self-pity was more appealing.

The knock came again.

I sat up. "Come in."

The doorknob rattled, but the door didn't budge.

I forgot I'd locked it, a habit I'd picked up courtesy of Mrs. White's shenanigans. "Give me a second."

I threw on my robe, turned the key, and pulled open the door.

Eldad stood in the corridor, his bright eyes staring up at me.

My frustration and despair vanished in an instant. I smiled. "Good morning."

"I've been waiting to gather vegetables with you. Why are you taking so long?"

"Oh, I'm so sorry. I forgot about it."

"Hurry, then. Mrs. Haywood won't let me go by myself. She says she doesn't want raw *courgette* in her soup." He shrugged. "I don't know what she means."

I suppressed a laugh. "I'll get ready and meet you in the library in ten minutes. All right?"

With a grin, he skipped down the corridor, happily sliding his thumbs up and down his suspenders.

I watched him go. He was a gift from heaven.

The sound pierces my ears, jarring me awake. As the haze of sleep dissipates, it becomes clear: the bells of the Breamore church pealing through the night. I know it's too far from the manor to hear it. Yet, its sharp, insistent chime demands that I answer its call.

I spring out of bed, trudge down the staircase, and cross moonlit fields. Then I plunge into the pitch-black woods. The ground is sodden, my feet sink with every step. Branches scratch and tear at my skin. I lift my arms to shield myself, but the forest fights back; here and there, its thorns draw blood. Still, I press on.

At last, I break through the trees. It has taken me years to reach this place. Years.

The moonlight highlights the church; the bells continue to ring. I push through the door, and the sound ceases, the summons complete. The pews, organ, and lectern are gone, the hall empty. Ancient chandeliers spill their light onto a rising mist.

I step farther in and gasp at the blood, and filth on my white nightgown. I am battered and worn. Then, like a storm lifting, the mist swirls around me. When it clears, I am transformed—my wounds healed, my skin unblemished. My gown gleams with a brilliance I have never known, as if imbued with divine light.

At the end of the hall, a young man emerges. With a breathtaking smile, he shortens the distance. We throw our arms around each other.

"It's all right. I'm all right," he says. It's as if we've never been apart. Serenity washes over me, and my heart fills with the eternal love that binds mother and son. "Welcome home, Mum! We are together at last!"

I woke with a muffled cry. The dream was still vivid, but my son's face had been erased from my recollection.

Dr. Jones's funeral was well attended, a testament to the countless lives he'd touched and blessed. I was fortunate to have known him and benefitted from his wisdom. Wherever his spirit currently resided, I prayed he'd never learn of my folly at the cemetery that night—a night I did my best to forget. Thankfully, Zaira hadn't brought it up. While silence wouldn't erase my wrongdoing, it gave me space to process it and, hopefully, forgive myself.

After a night of wrestling with these thoughts, I joined the Women's Institute volunteers. Gathering at dawn, the group broke from its routine by mending mountains of men's clothing to send back to the army. I hadn't sewn for ages, so despite the thimble on my thumb, I managed to accumulate more than my share of puncture wounds. Thus, immersed in serving and the sting of needles, the day passed in a blur.

By the time Mrs. Martindale, the group's supervisor, dropped me off at home, the sun had slipped below the horizon. "If I'm not mistaken, that's Doctor Wales's car." She pulled up behind a gray vehicle parked in the courtyard. "Is someone unwell?"

"Not that I'm aware of." My mind raced as I stepped out of the car. I did not like illness. It was unpredictable and vengeful. "Thanks for the ride, Mrs. Martindale. I'll see you next week."

I dashed straight to the kitchen in search of information.

Zaira looked up at me from the range cooker, her face tight with worry. "Thank goodness you are home. I was about to ring the institute."

"What's happened? Is the doctor here?"

"Yes. We called him this afternoon." Zaira poured steaming water into the coffee pot. "Rose and Mary developed high fevers and are struggling to breathe. They are quite sick."

"With what?"

"Diphtheria," she informed somberly. "The doctor has isolated them in the far bedroom of the wing. He's also brought in a couple of nurses to help and laid out strict rules to prevent the spread of the disease. So, don't even think about checking on the girls."

No. Not the children. I went numb. Memories of New York's diphtheria outbreak flooded back—the brutal disease attacked the upper respiratory tract with a randomness as merciless as it was unpredictable. Three of my classmates at Higher Grounds and several nuns had been struck by it; some were bedridden for weeks, while others lost their lives. To make matters worse, scientists were close—but not close enough—to finalizing a vaccine.

"How are the girls doing now?" My heart ached for them.

"Last I heard, not great."

"How did they get it?"

"Mr. Haywood is convinced it came from the folks who come for produce," she answered.

"It's possible, especially when the children haven't been to town much."

Zaira placed the coffee pot and sugar dish on a tray. "For the doctor and nurses."

"Please, let him know I'd like to speak to him."

With a nod, Zaira left. I dropped into a chair, the wheels in my head turning. How else could I help the girls?

I paced the drawing room. What could be taking the doctor so long?

"Florence! Florence!" Eldad burst into the room.

I knelt, and he ran into my outstretched arms. It felt wonderfully good to see him. Every moment we spent together mended the fractured pieces of my heart a little more. "How are you today?"

"Good." He stepped back, twisting a lock of my hair around his fingers. "How are you?"

"Better now."

"You were gone all day."

"I helped the ladies in town to mend the soldiers' clothing. What did you do?"

"Well, I played with my friends, helped Martha cook a fruitcake, and finished the homework that Zaira gave me."

"A busy day, I see." I ruffled his hair. "I must say, your English is almost perfect."

"Thank you." He beamed with pride. "When are going to read?"

"When are *we* going to read?'" I corrected.

He frowned. "You said my English is perfect."

"No, I said almost perfect," I teased. "Tell me, which book do you have in mind?"

Before Eldad could answer, Dr. Wales appeared at the open door, tapping lightly to announce his presence. Standing six feet tall with piercing green eyes, a navy suit, and a radiant smile, the man was stunning.

"Please, come in," I invited.

"He helps my friends." Eldad pointed at him.

I gently lowered his hand. "Yes, he does. Now, be a dear and run along to your room and get ready for bed. We'll read after I chat with the doctor. Yes?"

"All right." Though reluctant, Eldad kissed my cheek, and off he went.

"Mrs. Sterling, it's a pleasure to meet you. I'm Doctor Wales." He extended his hand, holding mine for a moment too long. When he made a move to kiss it, I pulled back. "I've heard much about you. You hail from New York? I've never been there—but no doubt, it's beautiful— beautiful indeed." His tone hinted at familiarity, and I sensed at once he was unattached—a man in need of proper boundaries and restraint.

"I do. Please have a seat." I gestured toward the sofa, resolving to keep our interaction professional.

"I prefer to stand."

"How are the girls?" I remained on my feet as well.

"Not well, I'm afraid." The sparkle in his eyes dimmed, replaced by a serious expression. "If there is no improvement within a few hours, I'll have no choice but to insert intubation tubes to keep their airways open."

Intubation sounded brutal. "There must be something more we can do. Should we take them to London?"

"I don't see why we would. Rest assured, I'm administering the latest treatments available. It's a matter of time now—to see how well their bodies respond to the medicine." He strode to the window, his gaze pensive as he stared beyond the glass. "Besides, the hospitals in London are bursting at the seams with injured soldiers. Transporting them would expose others to the bacteria, which spreads aggressively fast."

His assessment, sound and measured, quelled my doubts about his competence. I felt a growing sense of trust in his care for the children.

Still gazing into the darkened garden, he continued, "There is something you should keep in mind . . ."

"Tell me." I joined him at the window.

"Diphtheria can be lethal even for the healthiest among us," he said. "The girls have been through significant physical trauma. While they've regained some health recently, there are lingering signs of osteomalacia —weak bones that cascade into other complications. The next forty-eight hours are the most critical."

The unsaid verdict—their bodies might not have what it took to win this battle. How would the close-knit group react if we lost the girls? After so much loss, this felt like an injustice past bearing.

"I'll pray for a miracle," I said.

"Pray hard."

The pitter-patter of small feet I'd come to cherish echoed through the halls of Forti Radici. "Come, come, Florence." Eldad tugged at my hand, his excitement pulling me along. A pair of field glasses dangled from his neck, oversized and comically out of place on his small frame.

The morning air lay still, broken only by the occasional trill of birdsong as the sun climbed. We passed the evergreens and came to an ancient yew, the oldest tree on the grounds. Its gnarled branches spread outward from its massive trunk, reaching skyward in a display of resilience.

Eldad raised the glasses to his eyes, scanning the branches. After a moment, he climbed. "Come up here—look."

Careful not to damage the yew, I followed him, stepping onto the thickest branches until I reached his perch.

"There." He pointed to a crook in the tree. Nestled in the hollow lay a nest, woven from twigs and leaves. Inside, a cluster of speckled eggs rested like precious jewels. "The mother bird is going to have babies," Eldad whispered with awe.

"Have you seen her?" I feared she would abandon the nest if threatened by our presence.

"Yes, from down there. That's why I bring Mr. Haywood's glasses. I never climb up here when she's around. Papa taught me not to disturb nests when we went birdwatching back home." I detected sadness in his voice. Though a naturally cheerful child, Eldad often seemed haunted by his past.

"I think these are hawfinch eggs," I noted, hoping to redirect his focus. "You know, the orangey-brown birds with the bulky heads. They are very pretty."

"They have black around their eyes."

"That's right."

"Let's go down. She'll be back soon," he said, already climbing down with careful movements.

We retreated to a grassy patch, far enough to avoid disturbing the mother bird's return.

Eldad flopped onto the grass, peering back at the yew through his glasses. "I miss Rose and Mary," he said softly. "They must be terribly bored, locked in their room all day."

"Doctor Wales is taking good care of them. You'll see—they'll be out here playing before you know it." I was hopeful. Though their progress was slow, the last twenty-four hours had been steady enough to stave off the need for a breathing tube—for now. By tomorrow, we would know whether they triumph over the illness or succumb to it.

"I'll show them the nest."

"They'll love that."

The worry over the girls bore down on me, even as I reeled from my trials: the guilt of unburying my son, the constant fear for Alex's safety, and the anger at Mrs. White—an untouchable threat. I couldn't fathom her audacity in breaking into the house. She deserved nothing less than a cell to rot in.

I turned to brighter thoughts. Eldad and I hardly separated these days. Through our friendship, we discovered that sorrow and joy could coexist, like sunshine piercing through the clouds even while the rain fell.

The night stretched on, time stalling beneath the hours of darkness. The Haywoods, Zaira, Martha, and I gathered in the kitchen. Spoken and silent prayers, words of encouragement, and a constant flow of coffee helped us endure it.

When dawn finally broke, I could wait no longer. I trudged up the stairs to the west wing, heart pounding. Doctor Wales had expressly forbidden it, but I had to know.

Outside the girls' bedroom, I hesitated, paralyzed by the fear of what I might find. I bowed my head and whispered what must have been my thousandth prayer of the past hours. Steeling myself, I reached for the doorknob. Before I could turn it, the door swung inward.

Dr. Wales stepped into the hallway, his shoulders slumped, his eyes rimmed with fatigue.

Assuming the worst, I blurted, "Please, don't tell—"

"None of that," he interrupted gently. "I'm just bone-tired. The girls fought hard and won. They'll be all right."

"Thank you—thank you." The tension and sleepless hours crashed over me at once. A muffled cry of relief escaped, and without thinking, I hugged him.

His arms tightened around me, a warm embrace reminding me how starved I was for care. I'd spent so long being strong for others that I'd forgotten that I, too, needed kindness and comfort.

"I'll stay through the day to ensure there are no setbacks," he said.

"I appreciate that." I stepped back, my gratitude evident in my smile.

Martha came around the corner just then. "Doctor Wales, breakfast is ready—porridge, sausage, and eggs with spinach—just the way you like it," she announced with a twinkle in her eyes.

"I better share the good news with the others," I decided at once. "Thanks again, doctor." I smiled at Martha as I walked past her. Her attraction to him was undeniable. I wondered if he reciprocated it.

I stretched out on the sofa. Even when It had been a rewarding day. At last, we'd harvested a significant amount of foxglove, dried it, and delivered it to London for medicinal use. I was proud to have contributed to a project that would bless many lives.

I was drifting off into sleep when the telephone's ring jolted me from the sofa. I reached for the receiver, my nerves already fraying. What kind of news would this call bring?

"Hello?"

"Good evening, Florence. Thomas here."

"Thomas, hello." My heart skipped a beat. "Please tell me you have good news."

"Yes and no." He cleared his throat, a sound I had come to dread. "I suppose it's all relative."

"Tell me." I sank into a chair, bracing for the blow.

"Good news first. Alexander and Haywood have been cleared, so I can tell you they've arrived safely in the States."

"That's wonderful, Thomas! Truly wonderful!" I let out a long, relieved sigh. "When will they head back?"

"My guess is a week or two. For security reasons, we don't get many updates. But don't worry, I'll let you know if I hear anything. Will you relay the news to the Haywoods?"

"Of course, as soon as we hang up."

"Right, then." His tone shifted, becoming more formal. "Now, about the other matter."

"It's the children, isn't it?"

"Yes. I know you've grown fond of them, but the laws are clear, and we are bound to follow them. The paperwork is complete, and the assigned families are eager to welcome them. I know these folks personally. The children will be in excellent hands. You can even visit them if you'd like."

The news overshadowed my previous elation. Life, it seemed, never gave without demanding something in return. "I didn't think it would happen this soon."

"I didn't think it would take this long."

"Did you manage to arrange what we discussed last time?" After nearly losing Rose and Mary, I had pleaded with Thomas to keep the two sisters together, and, if possible, to group the other three girls and the two older boys. This way the transition would be less painful.

"I did as you asked. Furthermore, they'll be in the same vicinity so they can see each other regularly. Now, about the youngest boy—"

"Wait." I cut him off, the idea finally forming into words. "I'd like to become Eldad's legal guardian."

"Florence—"

"Please, hear me out. He's too young to be sent to a farm or anywhere else. He needs stability and care, and I can give him that. There's no reason to uproot him again."

"It's not that simple. There are legal hurdles."

"There must be something you can do. Please."

"And Alexander? Have you considered what he might think?"

"He'll be thrilled," I said, though I knew Thomas had a point—I was acting unilaterally. But I trusted that Alex would support my decision.

Silence stretched, thick with unspoken deliberation.

"I can't promise anything," Thomas said at last. "But give me a few days."

"Take as long as you need." I dreaded having my hopes shattered again, for I couldn't imagine a future without Eldad.

CHAPTER 13
~ SCARS OF WAR ~

We bid our friends farewell that morning. These remarkable children had bravely recovered from their traumatic past, their resilience awe-inspiring. Amid great adversity, they had clung to life, to their goodness, to the hope of a brighter day. Indeed, even after my two life experiences, my progress felt infinitesimal compared to theirs.

I would miss them—all except for one. Eldad remained at the manor. Thomas had arranged it, and Eldad shouted for joy when I asked if he would like to stay. The only pending detail was a trip to London. To obtain official custody, I needed to complete the paperwork in person.

I readjusted my apron and headed outside. Martha would be on my case if I didn't return soon with the thyme for supper. The plot of land, populated with vegetables and herbs, stretched out before me.

The Haywoods were here, assessing the weeds on the pathways.

"They'll be the death of me," Mr. Haywood grumbled.

"Don't be so dramatic," Mrs. Haywood calmy advised.

The groundskeeper waved a dismissive hand at his wife's comment.

"Even with the weeds, this garden is remarkable. You have done an extraordinary job," I said to both.

"That's kind of you to say, dear." Mrs. Haywood smiled.

Mr. Haywood didn't respond, but his eyes shone with pride.

"Mrs. Haywood, before I forget—I'll be moving Eldad to a bedroom close to mine."

"Very well. I'll bring you fresh linens."

"Thank you."

"If I may say—what you do for the boy is a blessed deed. You will be rewarded with unimaginable happiness." The kindness in her words was clear, but I sensed something more—an unspoken depth behind them.

The groundskeeper yanked another invasive plant by its root, hurled it into the wheelbarrow along with the rake, and departed with a stiff nod.

"Is he all right?" I watched him trot away, wondering why he'd retreated so hastily

"Don't mind him. Old Haywood is used to his ways. Always moving, always busy."

I had never thought of her husband that way. He was hardworking but also a well-centered, well-mannered man. Had my mention of the boy stirred something in him? Longing for his son, perhaps?

"What about the blue room down the corridor from yours?" Mrs. Haywood reverted to our previous conversation. "It's always sunny, and there is plenty of room for the little fellow to enjoy himself."

"That's the one I had in mind. I may order a few things for it. There aren't many toys or children's furniture in this house."

"Will is a talented woodworker. He could build a rocking horse for the little one."

Will. His name brought to memory his earnest character and sweet smile. "Have you heard anything from him?"

"Only what you told me—that he's coming home. Every morning, I tell myself that today is the day, but it never is."

"I feel the same about Alex. But really, it shouldn't be long now."

Zaira popped into the yard, her steps urgent. "This just arrived in the post." She waved a telegram.

Mrs. Haywood and I exchanged apprehensive glances. Did it concern the men we loved?

"It's from Clarence!" Zaira exclaimed.

"Tell us he is all right," I said, my heart missing a beat.

"Now, girl, do tell us," Mrs. Haywood pressed.

"Well, he is not dead. He's been injured in action and sent back to London for treatment," Zaira sputtered. "He's scheduled for surgery on his shoulder tomorrow."

"Oh, good," Mrs. Haywood said. "If it's just his shoulder that needs the knife, he'll be up and running in no time."

"I'm so glad he's safe." I considered Clarence part of our family—not only for his pleasant disposition but because he meant so much to Zaira. "You must go to him at once."

"Yes, that will cheer him up all right." Mrs. Haywood nodded approvingly.

Zaira lit up like Piccadilly Street during the holiday season. "You think so?"

"Of course. Mr. Brown will drive you to the train station, and you can stay at Alex's flat in London." The neighborhood had thus far been spared from the bombings. It would be perfect for her stay.

"I'll help you pack," Mrs. Haywood offered.

"Thank you both." Zaira embraced us briefly and hurried into the house with Mrs. Haywood on her heels.

I smiled, elated for my friend's happy day. Hopefully, mine would come soon.

Thomas was on the phone again. This time, I knew it wasn't good. I could feel it in my bones.

"It's Alex, isn't it?" I muttered into the receiver.

"I'm afraid so."

"He is not dead." My free hand gripped the edge of the table. "Please, don't tell me that."

"No, I can't say he's dead. However, I can't say he's alive either. We don't know."

"What do you mean you don't know? What happened to him?"

"Please, Florence, take a breath. Calm down."

"Seriously?" I let out a sarcastic laugh.

"Yes. Seriously," Thomas replied sternly, his tone bringing me back to my senses.

"I'm sorry. Go on." I drew a long breath.

"Alexander and Commander Haywood were on their way home, but there was an incident—an unusual and completely unexpected one.

For security reasons, they were required to sail on different vessels. One of them boarded a passenger ship, the other a merchant vessel. The passenger ship was attacked and sunk. Some were killed or lost at sea. I don't know which ship Alexander was on."

"What you are saying is that either Alex or Will is dead, and you don't know which." I felt as if the ceiling had collapsed, burying me ten feet underground. If it was Alex, I would be utterly lost and devastated. If it was Will, the Haywoods would. And, of course, I would grieve him too. He was young and intelligent, with so much to experience and enjoy in life. Winning, this time, seemed out of reach.

"Until we have more information, we don't know who or even if one of them died," Thomas said diplomatically. "There are some survivors. I'm still waiting to hear from the medical ship that rescued them."

I could be many things, but I wasn't a fool. If Alex had survived the wreck but wasn't quickly recovered, he couldn't have lasted long in the icy ocean. The same was true for Will. Yet, *some survivors* awakened a spirit of hope, and I clung to it steadfastly. Thomas was right—until I had proof otherwise, they were alive.

"I'm doing all in my power to find out more. You'll know as soon as I do," Thomas assured.

"Please do. Ring anytime, day or night."

"Will you relay the information to the Haywoods?"

"I will. Thank you, Thomas." The idea of telling the Haywoods terrified me. The news would strike them like a deadly bullet.

I walked out of the office with a heavy heart. Mrs. Haywood appeared at the end of the corridor, holding a vase of flowers and a soft smile—a smile I was about to erase.

"Oh dear, you look grim," she noticed. "Are you unwell?"

I made up my mind. Until I actually knew what had happened, I wouldn't burden her or Mr. Haywood. "I think I overdid the horseback riding today. My entire body hurts." It did, but not because of the horse.

She observed me curiously. Did she suspect my lie?

"I'll lie down for a while," I said hastily. If I didn't escape her presence, I would crumble to the ground in tears.

"Let me know if you need anything," she offered.

I avoided her gaze and hurried past her.

The joyous laughter of the couple filled the foyer and drifted into the library. I hurried to greet them, and in that fleeting moment, life felt bearable.

Zaira glowed with happiness. Clarence, aside from the crutch under his left arm and his apparent exhaustion, looked quite content.

"Welcome home, Clarence." I embraced him, then Zaira. "It's wonderful to have you back. We did our best to care for the horses, but I'm afraid they don't like us as much as they like you."

"Oh, Mrs. Sterling, I doubt that. But I've missed them terribly."

"Bring them a treat now and then, but no work until you've fully recovered."

"Yes, ma'am."

"Don't worry, Florence," Zaira said. "I'll make sure he follows the doctor's instructions. And truly, thank you for letting me stay in the flat in London. The city is in chaos. The bomb sirens go off when you least expect them. All one can do is run for cover like a headless chicken. It's terrifying, but I always felt safe in the flat, and being so close to the hospital was a blessing."

"I'm glad it worked out. Now, don't let me keep you. Mrs. Haywood and Martha have cooked up a storm in anticipation of your arrival. They are eager to see you."

"That's thoughtful of them." Clarence grinned. "I've been dreaming of their cooking since I left."

"He thought the army food was dreadful—until he tasted the hospital's," Zaira teased, laughing.

"Go on, then. Enjoy the feast."

"Thank you, Mrs. Sterling." Clarence shifted on his crutch and started toward the kitchen.

"I'm truly happy for you," I whispered to Zaira as she walked past me.

"Thank you." She beamed with joy.

I climbed the stairs to my bedroom seeking solitude. The conversation I'd had with Alex by the stream replayed in my mind. He'd been adamant that, if he didn't survive the mission, I should remarry and start a family. At the time, the idea had been so alien, but now, with the responsibility of raising Eldad, it pressed me to reconsider. But I simply couldn't. After risking my eternity to have a second chance with him, I couldn't accept a life without him. The possibility of not seeing him again, of not feeling his warmth or hearing his voice, was maddening. I dropped onto the bed and wept bitterly.

The grounds were soaked in sunlight, the stone statues gleaming like Roman gods amid autumn's tapestry of reds, yellows, and oranges.

"Florence, Florence!" Eldad called from the French window. "Come see the book Mr. Haywood brought me from town."

I joined him inside. We sat on the sofa, flipping through the pages of a beautifully illustrated volume about the horses and ponies of the New Forest.

"This pony is called a Shetland." I pointed to an image.

"He's chubby." Eldad giggled, crisscrossing his legs.

"Chubby and lovely, isn't he?"

"Mm-hm."

"This one is a workhorse. His breed is called Clydesdale."

"He looks strong." Eldad turned the page, his eyes bright with curiosity. "Wow, I love this one."

"You know what he's called?"

He shook his head. "No, tell me."

"It's one of Britain's best—the English thoroughbred."

"Can we get one?"

"Umm . . . we'll have to ask Alex when he gets home."

"And if he says no?"

"We'll have to find a way to change his heart." I smiled.

"We'll cook a delicious supper for him," Eldad decided. "Martha says the way to a man's heart is through his stomach."

I burst out laughing. Nothing went unheard by the boy. His sweet spirit and amenable character never failed to uplift me. I then recalled the exuberant meals Martha had prepared for Doctor Wales—she certainly had a soft spot for him.

"Why are you laughing?" Eldad asked innocently.

"No reason." I swallowed hard, regaining my composure. "Oh, look, here is a white pony."

He took over the book, tracing the text with his finger, he read the animal's description. "He's about my size."

"Not quite, but he's the perfect size for you to ride alone." Until now, Eldad had only ridden with me. "Would you like to learn to ride a pony?"

"Me? Can I?" His gaze filled with a look of wonder.

"Most certainly. We'll have to find a pony first, but it shouldn't be too difficult."

"I can't wait!"

"Florence!" Zaira's voice interrupted. "Where are you?"

"In the sitting room." I turned toward the threshold. "What's the matter?"

"There is a military truck approaching," she wheezed, out of breath.

"Stay with Eldad." I dashed into the corridor and out the front door.

The vehicle traveled fast, dust and pebbles rising in its wake. Could it possibly be that Alex was home? Or were they here to notify me of his passing? The truck came to a sudden stop, its doors flying open. I couldn't breathe, my heart beating out of rhythm.

Thomas jumped out. "Good afternoon, Florence."

A second man leaped out. *Will.*

My eyes remained on the vehicle, praying for one more passenger. Not today. The only man still in the cabin was the driver. Will had made it home, and I was grateful for that, but Alex wasn't here. My mind and heart went numb. I couldn't think, couldn't feel.

"Mrs. Sterling." Will nodded softly, his eyes on the ground.

"Welcome home, Will," I said quietly, though I truly meant it.

"Thank you."

I found Thomas's gaze. "Alex?"

"We still don't know. Commander Haywood confirmed Alexander was aboard the ship that went under. That's all we know with certainty. The medical ship was rerouted for safety reasons, and it hasn't arrived yet."

"I'm deeply sorry, Mrs. Sterling," Will's voice cracked. "I wish there was something I could have done."

I opened my mouth to respond, but my voice was lost, buried beneath the awful possibility of a life without Alex.

"Don't lose hope." Thomas placed a hand on my shoulder, conveying his love and sympathy.

Fighting back tears, I looked up at Thomas. Just like in the past, his unwavering friendship was a stabilizing force. Even when the world felt colorless and muted, drowned in sorrow, I stuttered, "I won't—not until he comes home, dead or alive." I knew then that, like the ghost of Lady Catherine di Leccio, I would forever wait for Alex, the anchor in my life.

CHAPTER 14
~ EMBRACING HOPE ~

For Eldad's sake, I swallowed my pain and put on a brave face.

"Martha makes the best marmalade," he said between bites of toast.

"Indeed, she does." The late berries from the garden had been used to the very last.

"I'm here to steal Eldad." Zaira stepped into the breakfast room. "Mrs. Haywood and I will take his measurements. He's growing at light speed." She playfully tousled his hair.

"Can we do it later?" Eldad implored.

"Absolutely not. Mrs. Haywood will fuss for days if we make her wait." Zaira held out her hand.

"Behave, or Mrs. Haywood will poke you with the needle," I teased.

"Nah." He laughed, taking Zaira's hand as they left the room.

I gathered the dishes and brought them to the kitchen. Armed with a luffa sponge, a testimony that nothing went to waste, I scrubbed the plates. The sound of the water, the smell of soap, and the texture of the sponge in my hands transported me to Oak's Place, where I used to help Zaira in the kitchen. Memories of Alex roaming the house, close but never daring to approach me, rushed back. That strange, magnetic pull between us felt incomprehensible then but undeniable. Ours had been a surreal trajectory. We were bound to be together. It couldn't end like this.

All of a sudden, the walls felt stifling. Turning off the tap, I sought escape.

I saddled Betsy, and we galloped across the fields, the morning air brushing against my skin. It was freeing, a fleeting reprieve. When her initial burst of energy dwindled, she skirted the tree line and slowed to a trot, then to a walk. "That was a wonderful ride, wasn't it?" I patted her crest, and tilted my head back, soaking in the sunshine.

It wasn't to last. Betsy began to stomp, tossing her head nervously.

"Whoa! What is it, girl?" I glanced over my shoulder and froze. A rider approached, his posture and silhouette eerily like Alex's. I blinked, my breath catching.

The rider came level with us. "Good morning, Mrs. Sterling."

"Will—good morning."

"It's beautiful out here. May I join you?"

"Certainly," I answered, though I feared I would be morose company. "Do you always ride like that?"

"Like what?" He smirked.

"Like a soul haunted by the devil."

He chuckled. "No, just when I'm in a hurry."

"In a hurry for what?"

"To catch up with you, of course. I've been meaning to tell you about my trip with the general."

"Oh." My unease grew. This might not be the right time, but knowing was better than wondering. "Let's find a place for the horses to rest. Shall we?"

We rode on in silence, Will looking as though he wanted to speak but holding back. Cutting through the woods, we reached a sunny clearing where heath bedstraw and tormentil grew in abundance. Ignoring my pulling on the reins, Betsy eagerly began to graze.

"All right, girl. You win." I dismounted. "This will do."

Will joined me, letting his horse roam. "I'm sorry the general is not back yet."

"Me too."

"May I share a few things?"

"Please." I folded my arms, bracing myself.

"Before boarding the ship in London, General Sterling ordered me to stay true to the mission regardless of any difficulties we might encounter —even if it meant leaving him behind. He said a nation is more important than one man. I'll never forget that."

It was the kind of sentiment my father, General Marcus Contini, would have spoken. He, too, was loyal to the end.

"Thankfully, we made it to New York without incident. I couldn't believe how beautiful the city was—buzzing with life and no signs of war anywhere. To be honest, it wasn't easy to leave. I'd have much rather stayed."

New York. I missed it. "I can understand that." My thoughts wandered to the hellish aerial raids and the gnawing uncertainty that shadowed England's future.

"From New York, we went to Washington, D.C., for a week of grueling meetings—one after another, day in and day out. Afterward, we had a few days to spare before our return, so the general took me to the monastery. Sister Dolores was delighted to see him."

"You met Granny? That's wonderful." I perched on a fallen tree, with memories of my dear granny warming me.

"Oh yes. She inspected me like a soldier assessing a minefield. In the end, I think I passed muster." Will chuckled, settling on the grass across from me.

"I can't believe she didn't call me. I'd have loved to know you two were there." The idea of Alex visiting Granny comforted me, allowing me to imagine him on a simple business trip rather than lost—or worse.

"The general asked her not to call. Security reasons, he said."

Security reasons. How I hated those words. "How is she?" Remorse pinched at me for not having called *her* lately. I missed her, but I knew she would hear the sadness in my voice. I didn't want to burden her with problems she couldn't solve.

"Engaged in lots of charity projects, I think she said."

"That sounds like her." I pictured Granny in her black habit and shiny spectacles, bustling between the monastery and the parish, tackling a million tasks with Friar Thompson by her side. She was never idle.

"We also visited Oak's Place."

"You did?" Alex would have loved to see Mr. Snider again. "Tell me, how is Mr. Snider?"

"He seemed well. Busy chopping wood, from what I saw."

I laughed, the heaviness in my chest lifting momentarily. "He's quite good at that." I imagined Mr. Snider in his straw hat and worn overalls, an axe swinging in rhythm with his steady strength.

"Certainly is."

"I'm glad you visited Western New York. Much different from the city but beautiful in its own quiet way."

"So true." Will leaned back, gazing at the clear sky. "The general told me all about how you two met."

He did?

"He truly loves you, Mrs. Sterling. You were meant for each other. Listening to him made me think of Adeline, and how our lives might've been if we'd had a chance. I guess I'll never know."

"Perhaps after this life?" I wanted to offer him hope, but the words felt shallow, even to me.

"Perhaps."

The question swirling in my mind finally escaped. "Tell me about the return trip."

Will straightened, brought his knees to his chest, and wrapped his arms around them. "The day we were to depart, we learned that our names had been compromised, and we were ordered to travel separately. As you know, I was assigned to a merchant ship, which sailed first. I was in the command room when the captain received a report that a German sub had been spotted near the passenger liner. Everyone knew it was bad news. Not long after, we heard a torpedo had struck the ship, and all communication was lost. They had rafts, but the attack happened so unexpectedly—I doubt they had time to do much." His gaze locked on mine, his voice somber. "Heavens, I wish we could have helped, but we were too far away and had to remain on course. Duty can be cruel."

I was acquainted with that side of *duty*. "But a medical ship was sent, right?"

"That's right, but it took time to reach the accident."

"Thank you for being honest with me and not trying to minimize the truth." I rose. "Though it hurts like hell, I'd rather know."

"I would too." He stood, brushing broken twigs and dead leaves from his trousers.

"We should head back before Betsy eats the whole forest." The ground beneath her was already stripped bare as she continued to graze undisturbed.

"Mrs. Sterling," Will took my hand in both of his, "as grim as it sounds, the general is a tough man. If anyone can survive this, it's him."

"I pray that's the case. Let's go home."

Winter was on the verge of overpowering autumn. I tightened my scarf around my neck, bracing against the chill. After a fruitless search for Eldad indoors, I ventured outside, Inspector Overton's recent call echoing in my mind.

"Martha," he had said, "aside from her twice-a-week rendezvous with Doctor Wales from midnight to five in the morning at the inn in town, she's clean as a whistle." I was relieved—thrilled, even—that Martha appeared to have no connection with Mrs. White. It was one less thing to weigh on my mind. However, the revelation about her relationship with the doctor, stunned me.

As far as I knew, no one in the household had the faintest idea that Martha was slipping out into the night. What else, I wondered, might be unfolding unnoticed under my roof? But it was clear the women of Forti Radici were blessed with the men they loved by their side—all except for me.

Zaira burst into the path with a confused look on her face and a wicker basket in hand. Oblivious to my presence a few steps behind, she murmured, "That's odd. Quite odd."

"What is?" I caught up with her.

"Oh—my!" She flinched, caught off guard. "Where did you come from?"

"Sorry. I'm looking for Eldad. He seems to have vanished off the face of the earth."

"He's in the old cottage with Commander Haywood."

"He is?"

"Yes. The commander bundled him up, and they went off searching for materials to build something—I couldn't tell you what."

"I see."

"I'm going to fetch some vegetables." Zaira motioned to the basket. "With Mrs. Haywood under the weather, Martha and I are pulling double duty."

"I asked Martha to assign me more chores. She hasn't yet."

"Don't worry, I'll remind her." Zaira smirked.

"You haven't answered my question."

"What question?"

"A minute ago, you said something was odd."

"Oh, that." She sighed. "It's Mrs. Haywood. She's been unnerving me."

"How so?" As far as I knew, the housekeeper had been confined to her quarters. Dr. Wales diagnosed her with pneumonia and prescribed strong medicine and a good dose of rest.

"She called me in to speak to her."

"And?"

Zaira's hazel eyes darted around, scanning for any unwelcome listeners. Finding none, she dropped her voice to a whisper. "You aren't going to believe this."

"Believe what?"

"She asked me for a loan."

"Wait—what?" I blinked, needing a moment to process her words. Mrs. Haywood had already received a substantial advance from me. Now I was certain something was terribly wrong with her finances.

"I know. It's odd."

"Did she say what the money was for? Is it for the farm?" I asked.

"She said it's for overdue expenses but didn't go into detail. Now, how many expenses can they have? I mean, their daily needs are covered by their jobs, aren't they?"

"They are."

"At any rate, I was so flustered by the whole thing that I didn't dare pry. Seriously, though, I can't believe she came to me before going to you, her employer. I find it quite strange."

"Hmm." Guilt crept in as I refrained from revealing that Mrs. Haywood had already approached me for money. For now, I decided to keep that to myself. "Did you lend her the money?"

Zaira pursed her lips and nodded. "I'll leave you here unless you want to help me pick vegetables."

"I'd better check on Eldad."

Zaira took the path to the garden, and I hurried through the cluster of birch trees to the cottage—an ancient building with cob walls and a thatched roof. Once, it housed the groundskeepers. Now, it served as a storage space for relics, including the broken furniture from the German attack. Memories upon memories lay within its walls. One of my favorites lifted my spirits as I approached.

Alex and my father left for London early in the week. While I paced the garden, I remembered one of my mother's paintings was kept in the cottage, waiting to be sent to London for restoration. Turning the knob, I let myself in.

It didn't take long to sift through the clutter on the main floor. No success. I climbed the stairs to the loft, where a stack of paintings rested against the wall. I slid my hand across the top of the first frame, dust particles swirled in the sunlight streaming through the window. My nose pinched, my eyes watered, and my lungs protested. I fumbled with the window latch. As the glass swung open, fresh air flooded the space. I drew a cleansing breath and returned to my task.

"Aha. There you are." Near the back, I found the one I sought. My mother stared back at me from the painting, serene and radiant. She sat by the stream in the woods—the very stream where I spent much of my time. Her red dress contrasted with her dark hair, and breathtaking smile. Surrounded by nature's greenery and a clouded sky, she looked dazzling. I sighed, longing for the impossible—a chance to have known her.

Two arms wrapped around me from behind, and I jolted. Alex's

*laughter followed, warm and familiar. I loved his laugh. I spun within his
embrace. His eyes met mine, brimming with a love that left me weak in the
knees.*

*He lowered his head, his lips brushing mine. "What are you doing out
here? Looking for trouble?"*

"No, but I think I found it anyway."

He chuckled. "I'm no trouble—unless you want me to be."

"Hmm . . . tempting."

*His lips captured mine with an intensity and desire that made my
insides melt like morning dew in the sun. I returned his kiss, lost in the
moment, wishing it could stretch into eternity.*

*Alex drew back, raking a hand through his hair as he took a steadying
breath. "I mustn't lose my head, or your father will send me to the gallows
—as if I weren't already in enough trouble."*

"What do you mean?"

*"I escaped work after the morning meetings. I couldn't wait any longer
to see you. General Contini will not be pleased."*

*I couldn't help but smile, thrilled by his audacity. My father was as
methodical as he was strict, and Alex's actions wouldn't go unnoticed. "I
can put in a word for you if you'd like."*

*"Nah, I'll be all right. It's worth it." He removed his coat and rolled up
the sleeves of his shirt. "It's hot in here."*

*"Indeed, it is," I murmured. He was insanely attractive, and I still could
hardly believe I was the woman who'd won his heart.*

My reverie of the past evaporated as I entered the cottage. Its
wooden shutters stood open, welcoming the afternoon sunlight. Bathed
in a fine mist of sawdust, Will and Eldad sat at the table, carving a block
of wood.

Zaira hadn't exaggerated. Will had layered the boy. Eldad wore a
heavy coat, a wool hat tugged low over his eyes, and a matching scarf
wrapped around his neck. By contrast, Will was dressed in a cream-
colored, long-sleeved shirt tucked neatly into dark trousers. He was
strikingly handsome, his well-defined physique hinting at a rigorous
exercise routine. Yet, what stood out even more was his kindness and

patience with Eldad. It spoke volumes about his character. The Haywoods had clearly raised him well.

"Welcome to our shop, Mrs. Sterling," Will greeted.

"Florence, come see what we are making!" Eldad exclaimed joyfully. "It's a rocking horse for my room."

"I hope this is all right. My mother suggested Eldad and I build something together."

"It's frightfully kind of you," I replied. "I see you have captured Eldad's interest—and made an admirer of him."

The boy looked up at me, wrinkling his nose in confusion. I would explain the compliment later.

"I'm having as much fun as he is, maybe more." Will picked up a wood-carving tool and started along the edge of what I suspected would become the horse's tail. "I miss those days, you know, when life was simple."

Simple. The word struck a chord. A simple life sounded heavenly—a dream, and an unattainable one at that.

Clouds must have gathered; the room dimmed, and the air grew noticeably cooler.

"Why don't you bring your project to the house?" I suggested with a shiver. "You'll be more comfortable there."

"I like it here." Eldad said. "It's fun."

"I'm afraid you'll catch a cold," I argued. "Besides, it'll be dark soon."

"Nah, I'll be fine." Eldad pulled at his scarf, tightening it around his neck. "We'll be fine, right, Will?"

I held Will's gaze, seeking an ally.

"The missus is right about the lighting," Will said gently. "And we still have a ways to go. Let's move to the house."

That was all Eldad needed to hear. If the suggestion came from his newfound friend, he couldn't object. He began gathering the tools while Will packed the wood pieces and supplies into a box. In minutes, we exited the cottage, the boy dashing ahead.

"No news about the general?" Will asked in a caring tone.

"I'm afraid not." Through the trees to our left, I spotted Mr. Haywood pushing a wheelbarrow full of firewood. The sight reminded me of their precarious situation. It might already be too late to intervene, but I couldn't shake the suspicion that the problem went beyond financial mismanagement—and that it was only going to worsen. Their son needed to know. "Will. May I discuss something with you?"

"Sounds serious." He glanced at me curiously, slowing his steps.

"Forgive me for meddling in your family's affairs, but please know that I genuinely wish to help."

"I'm listening."

"I learned from Mrs. Haywood that your farm has accrued substantial debt. Your parents have spent their salary well into the future. I believed the situation was under control until just now. Your mother has asked Zaira for more money."

Will halted, his grip on the box loosened. For a moment, I thought he might drop it. "None of this makes sense."

"I'm sorry. I'm just telling you what I know. I offered professional assistance, but your mother turned it down."

"I don't know what to say." He looked shaken—almost sickly. "I was sure the farm was debt-free, and my parents were close to retiring. I've been giving them as much of my military salary as I can."

"Mrs. Haywood blamed the situation on the recent heavy rains and high winds," I offered.

"I don't buy that. We've had worse weather before and managed just fine. Wait, there was a property line dispute with a neighbor recently. I believed it was resolved, but maybe not. Maybe they're engaged in a costly legal battle."

"If that's the case, please consider accepting the help I offered your mother. Our solicitors will be happy to help."

"I appreciate that," he said. "But first I must have a chat with my parents."

"May I suggest waiting until your mother feels better? One or two more days won't make much difference."

"Let's hope not."

Thomas was on the line again. Would he extinguish every ray of hope I had left? The thought was soul-crushing, even before I'd heard a word from him.

"Good morning, Thomas."

"Florence, as much as you surely dread my calls, I dislike making them—nothing personal. I'm starting to feel like the bearer of nothing but bad news," he began, his tone apologetic as if he'd read my mind. "That said, I have good news and not-so-good news. Which would you like first?"

"The good news." *Oh, please let Alex be alive.*

"The boy's papers are ready for you to sign."

"Oh, that's wonderful." Knowing Eldad would officially be part of our family filled me with joy. As long as he was happy with us—and unless his birth family ever came searching—I wouldn't let anyone take him away.

"However, as I mentioned," Thomas continued. "The civil office is a mess, and no business is allowed outside its quarters. You'll have to come to London."

"I'll come at once. This afternoon."

"Are you sure? It can wait a few days."

"No. I want to finalize it."

"Very well. Ask for Miss Andrews. She's handling the paperwork. I'll ring her to let her know you're coming."

"Thank you."

"Florence, London is not what it used to be. Be cautious, and whatever you do, don't come alone."

"I'll ask Mr. Brown to drive me. The Lagonda is fast, and he knows the city well."

"Now for the unpleasant news." He paused, as though searching for the right words. "There isn't an easy way to say this, so I'll just say it. The hospital ship arrived last night, and Alexander wasn't on the list of survivors. He wasn't among the recovered bodies either. I checked myself."

Lost at sea. The words were like a blade to my heart. "He is dead, isn't he?"

"I'm sorry. It sure looks that way."

My chest felt like it would split in two, the pain inside clawing to break free. However, if I was to survive this, I had to cling to something, so I said, "Be that as it may, I won't give up on him until I see his body, until I say my final goodbyes."

"Florence, I promise you, we won't stop searching."

"Please, Thomas, I beg you—find him."

"You have my word."

I replaced the receiver and stumbled to the garden.

Dead. How could my dear Alex be dead? The ache in my chest, like a raging demon, threatened to shatter me. I couldn't breathe, I couldn't speak, it hurt too much. The only consolation was my task ahead to protect Eldad's future.

***

Despite the string of pedestrians here and there, the city was grave, particularly in this quarter: debris from recent bombings had left a layer of ashes and fear. Blackout curtains veiled every window, following strict regulations to obscure the Luftwaffe's view of the city at night. Shops, many already abandoned, bore forlorn *Closed* signs.

"This breaks my heart," I murmured.

Mr. Brown maneuvered the Lagonda onto a multi-lane street. "As sad as it is, it's nothing compared to what's been done to other parts of the nation. Take Southampton, for example, utterly devastating."

We passed through several intersections, the murky atmosphere tightening its grip—like the darkness of hell, it was not merely the absence of light and life but a living void, pulsing with despair.

"The civil office is just ahead," he announced.

"The gray building, right?"

"That's the one. I can't park on this street. I'll go around the corner and wait for you there."

"That's perfect. Thank you."

The Lagonda idled as I stepped out, pulling the collar of my overcoat tight against the chill. I moved quickly across the pavement and into the building. A guard in a blue uniform approached with a no-nonsense air, his voice clipped as he asked my business. His eyes betrayed a weariness that mirrored the city's soul. I thought of Adele, the woman in town, who had described them: *"They're a peculiar bunch—quite traumatized by the bombings."* This man, like so many others, lived with the constant fear of death and destruction over his head, literally.

I answered his question as efficiently as I could.

"If you'll follow me, please." He escorted me to the lift.

We exited on the second floor, navigating a hall filled with desks and overworked staff. At the third desk on the first row, he introduced me to Miss Andrews, a young woman with a pointy nose and black, curly hair. She scrutinized me from head to toe, then gave an enigmatic smile. Was it approval?

The guard left. Miss Andrews gestured for me to sit as she opened a drawer and shuffled through an astonishing number of documents. Our nation was not only defending itself but also working tirelessly to aid those seeking refuge.

"Here it is." She placed Eldad's folder on the desk. "We'll go over this briefly—just a formality, you understand." Her practiced speed suggested she had done this countless times. She summarized the obligations I was taking on, including a one-year probationary clause. The well-being of the adopted children, both physical and emotional, was paramount.

"What happens after a year?" I dared to interrupt her rapid monologue.

"That depends on how well the year goes. Our department will conduct periodic check-ins on the boy's welfare. But, surely, Mrs. Sterling, you have nothing to worry about."

"Of course not."

"If all goes well, you will become his legal guardian. Unless, of course, a surviving member of his family claims him."

"What would happen then?"

"You must keep in mind," she lowered her chin and observed me intently, "that's highly unlikely."

"Unlikely, but not impossible."

"In that case, you would have to relinquish all rights."

"I understand." As much as I loved Eldad, reuniting him with his family was the only greater joy I could imagine.

Miss Andrews finished outlining my duties before sliding the folder toward me. "If you would, please sign here." She pointed to a line at the bottom of the page.

With a rush of elation, I signed. She followed suit, then stamped the document twice for good measure. Oh, how I loved the sound of the stamps—it meant finality.

The chaos came at once—a rumbling in the sky accompanied by distant blasts, the wail of sirens, the furniture rattling out of place.

"Air raid!" Miss Andrews yelled. "To the underground station!"

An air raid? The Luftwaffe rarely attacked during the day—too risky, too costly. But here we were, under siege.

Panic swept through the hall like wildfire. People scrambled for the lift and staircases. I grabbed the folder, shoved it into my handbag, and joined the frenzied mass fleeing downward.

I struggled to keep my feet but made it down the first flight of steps. Would I survive the second? It hadn't occurred to me that, in moments of desperation, people could prove more dangerous than bombs.

A burly man elbowed past me, jabbing my ribs in his haste.

"There is no need to be such a beast!" I cried out angrily.

He kept going, this time, shoving an elderly woman aside. She crumpled onto the steps, clutching her side in pain. The stampede would crush her.

I pushed through to her, hooking my arm around hers. "Come on, we can do this. Just a few more steps."

She leaned into my support and managed to steady herself.

"Six, five," I counted to keep our nerves in check. "Almost there. Four, three."

We made it to the ground floor and spilled out with the crowd into the street. She thanked me and joined the stream of people heading toward the underground. I turned in the opposite direction, desperate to find Mr. Brown.

Then came the sound that froze me—the grinding roar of airplane engines overhead, where the Luftwaffe's wings stretched across the heavens, and hell rained down. I dove behind a magazine kiosk, knowing it offered little protection. Bombs descended in a continuous round, accompanied by the staccato firing of guns. In its wake, everything shook, exploded, fell.

The first contingent of enemy planes vanished, but there was no respite. I darted around a corner just as the second wave came into view.

Explosions erupted, louder, closer. Shrapnel tore through the air, striking indiscriminately. A fragment hurled me into the rubble. Pain seared through me as I fought to stay conscious, watching flames lick the sky. My gaze followed them to the gray-white smoke veiling the city in doom.

Then everything went dark.

CHAPTER 15
~ SHADOWS OF A LIVING PAST ~

The absence of physical sensation unsettled me. How could I suddenly feel nothing when, moments ago, I'd been consumed by pain? My body felt weightless, unconfined. I surveyed the destruction around me with an almost unnatural clarity—colors sharper, shapes more distinct, distances precise—as if the world had snapped into focus like never before. I had felt this way when Lucca took me back in time, when my spirit left my body in the monastery. I raised my hands. They were translucent, confirming my fear. I was in my spirit body, but this time, my brother hadn't caused the phenomenon.

Was I dead?

A torrent of thoughts surged through me, more terrifying than the air raid itself: What would happen to Eldad if I were gone? If Alex was still alive, how would he manage without me? And if he wasn't, would I find him in this other plane? Was Mr. Brown safe? What was I supposed to do now?

Find my body. That was the only way to be sure. I raced, my heart heavy with sorrow as I passed the injured, writhing in agony amid the ruins. I could do nothing for them. I had no physical form, no way to intervene.

I came to a pile of bricks and twisted metal. There—fingers

protruded from the debris. I looked closer. A man's hand. The sight churned my stomach, but I had to keep searching. Beyond the vestiges of a green-and-white awning, my gaze fell upon a lifeless figure in a burgundy dress and overcoat.

I fell beside her—beside me.

My ethereal hand hovered over the flesh one, but the disconnection was absolute. An impenetrable wall separated my spirit from my body. No matter how hard I tried, I couldn't breach it. I couldn't return to the mortal world. The realization left me utterly alone and lost.

"Mrs. Sterling, it's good to see you again." The voice was pleasant, soothing.

I whirled to see its owner and was rendered speechless. He was younger than when I last saw him, his countenance aglow with wisdom and joy. Any lingering doubts about my disembodiment were now gone. He was here, speaking to me. And he was dead.

"Doctor Jones . . ." Was he here to reprimand me for unearthing my son's remains? I assumed my mistakes would trail me into the next world, where I would be left to unravel them.

"You are perplexed, Florence, but I assure you all is well."

"Are you here to take me into the next life?"

"None of the sort. Do you remember the last time we spoke?"

"The circumstances were . . . different," I reflected.

"I was old and crippled then." He chuckled.

"That's not what I meant."

"I know, but I was. Being younger and free to move, even if in this spiritual form, is a gift. But enough of that. As I told you before, my thoughts have always wandered back to *your* case."

"*My case?*"

"Yes, Florence, your case. I know who you really are."

"I'm glad you do. I'm sorry I didn't tell you the truth."

"When you came to me that day, my mortal body was near its end, but my spirit hovered in the space between realms. In that heightened state, I recognized you the moment you walked in, but not understanding the phenomenon of your existence, I dared not tell you.

However, I wanted to help, but I lacked the answers you sought—the same answers I had failed to uncover in life.

"I somewhat discouraged you from your quest because I feared you'd waste your life chasing shadows. Yet, ironically, I couldn't abandon my own suspicions. They followed me here, to this sphere. And I've learned the truth about your child's fate. There was indeed foul play."

"You know?" Would I finally know the full story?

"I do. I've been granted the knowledge because I played a role in his birth. However, I still don't know the truth about your accident. That's why I'm here—to give you the piece of the puzzle you're missing and to receive the one I'm missing from you. Only then can I finally find peace."

His words struck a chord deep within me. Life, in its infinite wisdom, had orchestrated this meeting to mend both our souls.

"You first," he urged.

"Mrs. White was infatuated with Alex. So much so that she wanted to eliminate me. On the day of the accident, she followed me into the stable. I was with Sunny in her stall when she threw a snake at our feet." Even after so many years, the memory carried a profound sadness. "I turned to protect the baby while Sunny, panicked, kicked at the striking snake. Her hooves hit my back. Before I lost consciousness, I heard Mr. Vines yelling at her. If not for him, she would have left me to die there." An awareness hit me. "And now thinking back, I'm convinced that's precisely what she intended. By the time I was found, my baby and I would have been beyond saving."

"Oh, that explains my suspicion that your accident happened much earlier than when I was called to the house. She must have taken her time transporting you inside." Shock filled the doctor's eyes. "Deborah White will not escape justice. Sooner or later, it will catch up with her. Her soul will find no peace until she accounts for her wicked deeds."

Her wicked deeds. "Please, tell me about my son."

"You must see for yourself. We are going to take a short journey into the past."

"The past?" I had walked its corridors before. It held truths veiled by time but never erased.

"Because this matter is eternally linked to you, you must live through it. It's both a reward and a price you must pay. You'll see, feel, and understand things as they were and are. And you'll be bound to your baby by the same love you would have developed had you raised him. But I must warn you the truth can be painful. Furthermore, you'll be held accountable for the knowledge you acquire and the feelings you develop from it. Can you handle that?"

The truth was the truth, and there was no moving forward without it. "I can."

"Well then." Excitement flickered in his eyes. "Unless I'm terribly mistaken, you're already familiar with time travel. Am I correct?"

"You are." I cast my mind back to Lucca's instructions. "But it's been a while."

"Time is of the essence. You must return quickly, or you risk losing your connection to your physical body permanently. In other words, you may die in the mortal realm. Also, remember that in this sphere, you will neither be seen nor heard. We may observe, but we are not part of it. You will be a silent witness."

A ghost, drifting through time. Nothing new. "Let's go."

He took my hand, and instantly, we stood at Forti Radici.

The bright day was etched into my soul forever, for it had changed me to the core. This was the day I became a mother.

Dr. Jones and I stood on the front drive as the scene unfolded. Mr. Vines burst through the door. Looking grim, he stumbled to the Silver Ghost. He turned the key, and the engine sputtered to life. Then Mrs. White emerged, carrying my child in her arms.

"My son . . ." My pulse quickened as I tried to move closer. Dr. Jones stopped me.

"You mustn't disturb the elements," he warned. "Doing so will pull you back to your physical body."

That was enough to keep me still.

Mrs. White entered the car, and it sped away.

Dr. Jones reached for my hand. We were now outside the town's dispensary. Like a specter from another dimension, the Silver Ghost rolled down the deserted road toward us.

A cry of anguish split the air.

"What is that?" I turned toward the woods.

"It's the sound of a mother's heart breaking. Come with me."

We skirted the dispensary as the cries grew louder. A dark-haired woman emerged from the trees, clutching a bundle in her arms. She ran to the entrance and pounded on the door in desperation.

Silver arrived, and Mrs. White stepped out, holding my baby close. A muffled sound came from within the blanket—he was alive.

"He did not die on his way here." He was so close, yet impossibly far. My heart longed to comfort him, to hold him, to answer his soft cries.

The distressed woman turned to face the newcomer. "Mrs. White, is that you? Please, help me! I beg of you. The nurse must be out—the door is locked!"

"What's the matter, Agnes? Why are you here?" Mrs. White said.

Agnes? I took a long look at the woman. The past two decades had not been kind to Mrs. Haywood. Here, her skin was supple, her cheeks high, her posture straight.

It might have been a mercy from heaven that brought them so near, but the women edged closer and closer until they were just inches from me. Being taller than both, I had a clear view of the infants. The blanket swaddling my baby concealed his face, so I turned to the child in Mrs. Haywood's arms—and recoiled. The tiny body was gray and still, resembling a marble sculpture.

"Mrs. White, my tragedy is too painful to bear. Last night, I noticed something wrong with Will."

Will? I shot an inquiring look at Dr. Jones. He motioned for me to keep listening.

"He wasn't his usual self. He fussed all night and well into the day," Mrs. Haywood sobbed. "When he finally fell asleep, I did too. I awoke to total silence, no more crying, no heavy breathing, just dreadful silence." She couldn't speak anymore, an unchecked stream of tears coursing down her cheeks.

"Come now, Mrs. Haywood, try to calm yourself," Mrs. White encouraged, swaying my son, who whimpered and wriggled in his blanket.

"I can't bear this. I waited a lifetime to have a child, and now he is gone. This is going to kill me and my poor husband."

"Where is he?"

"He's gone to collect his brother's body. He was killed in the war. As if that wasn't atrocious enough, we'll now have to bury our son too." Mrs. Haywood let out another mournful sob.

Tragedy upon tragedy. I felt for the Haywoods.

Like the flip of a switch, Mrs. White's demeanor changed. "Come, come now." She maneuvered Mrs. Haywood to the trees and away from the dispensary. "Listen carefully. This baby in my arms just lost his mother, and his father is missing in action, most likely dead."

Liar! I wasn't dead. I was severely injured, thanks to you. And Alex was very much alive and on his way home.

"I came here to leave him with the nurse, but I doubt he'll survive without a mother to nurture him." Mrs. White lowered her voice, assuming a compassionate tone. "But even if he did, he'd be put up for adoption, which would initiate the endless and costly process of unnecessary paperwork. Think about it—you'll go home to bury your child and lament what could have been, and this baby most likely won't make it. Instead of losing two precious souls, however, we can use this opportunity to save one." She pulled back the blanket, revealing my son. "Look at him."

Mrs. Haywood leaned closer, her features softening at his sight.

My precious child. At last, I saw him. He was so peaceful and perfect, his tiny fingers curled into soft fists, his light skin and dark hair resembling his father. I extended my hand but stopped before I touched him. His eyelids parted, and his brown eyes met mine. In that instant, Dr. Jones's prediction came to pass. An incomprehensible depth of feeling flooded through me. This love was stronger than life or death and would have developed over the years had we not been separated. The eternal bond between mother and son had been restored.

"Whose child is this?" Mrs. Haywood asked.

"It's better you don't know," Mrs. White replied smoothly. "Here, hold him." The women exchanged babies.

My son whimpered again as Mrs. Haywood cradled him with the tenderness of a mother. "Hush, hush, little one. You'll be all right."

"Let's forget this meeting took place. You never came here with a dead child. I did. Raise him as your own and never tell a soul. You must take the secret to your grave."

Mrs. Haywood nodded, her arms tightening around my son.

Mrs. White smiled, a wicked gesture. She reveled in the power of keeping our son's existence a secret, a sinister satisfaction that gave her control over Alex's life. Meanwhile, he drowned in sorrow. Alone and vulnerable, he was easier for her to manipulate. *"It's not what I have taken, but what I have not taken, that will hurt you most,"* she had said. At last, I understood.

"Have Mr. Vines drive you a few blocks away to avoid curious eyes. I'll wait for the nurse and inform her of his passing as though he were the child I carried here." Mrs. White glanced at the lifeless infant in her arms. "Once everything is settled, we'll take you to your house."

Of course. A child was deceased upon arrival at the dispensary, only it wasn't my child.

Mrs. Haywood headed to the Silver Ghost.

"Agnes—wait. What about your husband? Surely, he'll recognize the difference between the babes."

"Don't worry about him" Mrs. Haywood replied, her voice trembling but resolute. "Babies change rapidly, you know, and men don't notice these things the way women do. I'll emphasize that Will has been sick and lost weight."

Lost weight. Of course. Mrs. Haywood's son, Will, had been a little older than mine. Hence, the date on his birth record didn't align, and the Haywoods were listed as his parents. Will, the one I knew, was *my* son.

In a split second, my son, the women, and the Silver Ghost disappeared, and I stood staring at the silent road.

"Mrs. Sterling, how do you feel?" Dr. Jones placed a hand on my shoulder. I had forgotten his presence.

"Feeling?" I repeated numbly. "I don't know."

"You are processing the truth. That's natural. Now, if I may, I'd like you to consider that your son might have died under the nurse's care. Agnes Haywood might have saved his life so he could grow into a man."

"I guess we'll never know." But I did know that justice had interfered when Alex came across the Haywoods and hired them on the spot. And certainly, our pull to return to Breamore had been guided by something far deeper—our connection to Will. The dreams, his sweet familiarity, and the curiosity I'd felt toward him all made sense now. No wonder I mistook him for Alex when I first saw him. Other than his bright eyes, which he clearly inherited from his uncle Lucca, he was the shadow of his father. Of course, I had questioned his supposed death. The truth had guided me all along, just as it had in the past. "There is so much to take in," I said, overwhelmed.

The doctor extended his hand. I grasped it, and the scenery shifted. We were back to the present, at the bombing site. Mere seconds had passed here. My physical body still lay amid the rubble, awaiting my return.

"I know my son. The Haywoods work at our house. Since we came back to England, he's been near us."

"That's an advantage," Dr. Jones said. "Now, while I don't know how you'll proceed, remember to be fair with the knowledge you have gained and to bestow mercy upon others as life has bestowed it upon you. And one more thing—you had a dream about your son. You met him at the parish."

"How do you know?" I thought back on the way the Breamore church bells summoned me there, and after a painful journey, I'd found my grown son awaiting me.

"When we transition permanently into this sphere, we become aware of many things. Now, I want you to remember that your dream is a living dream."

"A living dream? What does that mean?"

"It's a dream tied to life itself. Often, it carries through into the hereafter. When the light seems to have gone from your soul, you must remember the dream." His words were a riddle.

"I don't understand."

"In time, you will." He smiled warmly. "Goodbye, my dear Mrs. Sterling."

"Thank you," I whispered, gratitude heavy in my heart. "Thank you for everything."

Some unseen force propelled me to my motionless body, and intense pain seized me the moment I reentered it. I struggled to breathe, acrid smoke burning my lungs. Sirens blared in the distance. My vision blurred, and I slipped into unconsciousness.

CHAPTER 16
~ LIVING TRUTH ~

I awoke in a grand hall lined with rows of beds. Groans of patients, the clatter of medicine carts, and hurried footsteps of nurses echoed off the high ceilings and bare walls, a cacophony of distress.

A sharp throb pulsed in my head. My arms ached, stinging with each movement. I sat up on the cot and saw the bruises mottling my skin. I reached up, and my fingers brushed against a bandage wrapped around my forehead. I remembered—the explosion, the force of the blow, my spirit leaving and reentering my body. Miraculously, I had survived with only cuts and contusions. Nothing broken.

"Doctor Jones . . ." I murmured. "William." The truth hit me, poignant and undeniable. I couldn't stay here. I had to speak to Will. I swung my legs over the edge of the bed, but I froze before my feet reached the floor. Truth was both friend and enemy. How could I tell Will that I was his mother? I was his age, younger in fact. He would never understand.

I stood. On the chair beside me sat my handbag. At the civil office, I'd slung the strap over my shoulder and across my body, Eldad's papers were inside. Next to it, my overcoat lay in shreds, having protected me from worse injuries. I grabbed both.

A low groan, followed by a string of curses, pulled my attention two beds down. A man thrashed against the thin blanket, causing it to slip to the floor. His bandaged stump, where his right leg had once been, now lay exposed. My breath caught, a wave of nausea tightening my throat— the fabric was soaked in blood.

Where was the nurse? I neared the man, retrieved the blanket, and spread it over him. At the motion, pain radiating from my legs, clawing up my spine. "Sir, I'll find the nurse for you. Just hold on."

He grunted in response, his jaw clenched against the suffering.

I moved into the aisle and waved at a brunette woman in a white uniform tending to a patient at the far end. "Ma'am, this man needs help."

"Why are you out of bed?" She hurried to meet me, her expression stern. "You should be resting."

"Me? I'm fine." I signaled toward the injured man. "He's not. He needs fresh bandages."

"I'll check on him, but please, you must return to bed."

"I need to call home." I was desperate to find out if Mr. Brown had called, if he was all right.

"Have it your way." She shook her head at my supposed foolishness, and quickly busied herself with the patient.

The nurses' station was bound to have a telephone. I focused on the exit, counting the beds as I passed them, each one bringing me closer to freedom. Twelve, ten, eight. Almost there. Seven. I stopped midstride, not believing my eyes. But I would have recognized that profile anywhere. My chest swelled with euphoria, drowning out my aches and exhaustion. I rushed to his side.

My dear Alex lay on the cot, his features softened in sleep, his breath steady. Tears blurred my vision as I stood over him, aching to touch him —to prove he was real. But fear held me back, as if the slightest contact would shatter the moment, dissolving him like a dream upon waking.

"Miss, what in the world are you doing?" the same nurse asked impatiently. "Move on."

"This is my husband," I choked out, emotion thick in my throat. "I've been looking for him."

"Your husband?" The nurse's skepticism was evident as she glanced from Alex to me. Picking up the chart at the foot of his bed, she read aloud, "Matthew Oakley, *forty years of age*, from Leeds?"

True, this man was a bit older than I was, but, "Matthew Oakley? His name is not Matthew Oakley. He is not forty, and he is not from Leeds. This man is General Alexander Sterling from Breamore, my husband."

"If the chart says he is Matthew Oakley, he is." The nurse sighed with exasperation. The medical personnel, already at their wits' end with the influx of injured, need not be bothered by a delusional woman, but I wasn't delusional. "I suggest you return to your bed. Your concussion might be worse than we thought."

"Nonsense!" I stood my ground, my resolve hardening. "You've made a mistake. Here, I can prove it." I extracted a photograph from my handbag, creased but intact. "This is Alex."

The nurse frowned as she studied the picture, then glanced back at Alex. "Hmm. There's been a serious mistake."

"That's an understatement."

"I don't understand how this happened." She flipped through his chart carefully examining each line.

"When did he arrive?"

"Last night."

Thomas mentioned that the medical ship arrived last night.

"And he didn't say his name? Has he been unconscious all this time?"

"He's on heavy medication. He could very well sleep until morning. I understand he survived a shipwreck. However, a piece of metal perforated his side and lodged under his rib cage. The procedure to remove it went well, and he should recover fully."

With a silent prayer of gratitude, I pulled a chair from the neighbor, who also lay dormant, and settled beside Alex. "Has no one inquired after Matthew Oakley?" I wondered aloud. "I mean, his family would've discovered the misunderstanding."

"Leeds—it might take them a while to get here, if they were even notified. The past day was quite chaotic, and it only got worse with the air raid. Now, if you'll excuse me, I must see to this error." She scribbled a few notes on the chart and walked away with urgency, leaving me to my thoughts.

Who was Matthew Oakley? How had the hospital confused him with Alex?

Since the nurse's prediction was proving accurate, and Alex might not wake up until morning, I went in search of a telephone. From the nurses' room, I called Thomas and left him a message about Alex. Then, after several tries, the operator connected me with Forti Radici.

"Oh my, Florence, where have you been? We heard about the air raid and were worried sick about you and Mr. Brown." Zaira's voice crackled with concern on the other end.

"Mr. Brown—he hasn't called?"

"No. We haven't heard from him."

Fear rippled through me. I was the reason he came to London, why his life was placed in danger. *Oh, heaven, let him be safe.* I briefly explained how Mr. Brown and I had been separated and how I later found Alex.

"I can't believe it! It's wonderful, but, seriously, what are the odds?" Zaira exclaimed.

"I know—I know. It is hard to believe." And she knew nothing of the transcendental day. "How are things at home?" I thought of Will.

"I'm afraid Mrs. Haywood is not getting any better. She's had a rough day. Doctor Wales is here and, for now, has no plans to leave."

"How is Will handling it?"

"You know military men. He's keeping a stoic façade, but I can tell he's quite distressed."

"I can imagine." He had already lost Adeline, and now this. "Please, Zaira, do all you can to help Mrs. Haywood." If Mr. Haywood knew nothing about his son's true identity, which I found hard to believe, but possible—then Mrs. Haywood was the only person on earth apart from Mrs. White who could tell Will the truth.

"That goes without saying."

"Thanks, Zaira. We'll be home as soon as we can."

I returned the receiver to its cradle just as a tired-looking doctor with a gray mustache walked in.

"Is there a list of names of those injured during the air raid?" I asked, though he didn't seem eager to talk.

"There is, but some lacked identification. If they passed, there is no way of knowing who they are right away. Are you looking for someone in particular?"

"My friend, Albert Brown. He was waiting for me outside the civil office when the bombing started."

"Let's see." From a stack of folders on the cluttered desk, he pulled a paper and traced the writing with his finger. "No, no Browns here."

"Hmm."

"Would you like to check the deceased? He might be among them," he suggested, his tone matter-of-fact.

"I . . ." I hadn't considered examining corpses, but it was the logical next step. "I think so."

"Follow me."

We descended a set of concrete steps to the underground floor. Three things hit me as we crossed the landing into a cavernous space—the cold, the dark, and the silence. Then, of course, came the scent of decay. The doctor flipped a switch, and a few lightbulbs buzzed to life, casting weak, uneven light across the room.

On the floor lay several inert bodies under white sheets. My heart sank to my stomach. These were sons, daughters, husbands, and wives—real people with dreams and hopes. Someone would miss them dearly. A thought struck me: the dead would also miss their kin.

The lights flickered, and out of the corner of my eye, I saw shadows dancing on the wall. My gaze snapped to them, gooseflesh prickling my arms. There was nothing there but plaster and paint. Still, I sensed the presence of others. Spirits who might be in shock at their newly disembodied states and who might linger until their loved ones offered a final farewell. Death was heart-rending, but when premature, its agony and sorrow could be staggering.

"These are the males." The doctor veered to the group of bodies on the left, bringing me to the present task. "Are you ready?"

"As much as I'll ever be."

He studied me for a second or two, his eyes on the bandage wrapped around my head. "You aren't going to pass out on me, are you?"

"I have no intention of doing so." I must have looked worse than I thought. "It's dreadfully cold, that's all. Please go on."

He leaned over and uncovered the first body. I shook my head. It wasn't Mr. Brown. One by one, he lifted the sheets, each time met with my negative response, until we reached the third body before the last. The sight of short legs, thick arms, and a potbelly took me aback. My hand flew to my mouth, stifling the scream rising in my throat.

The doctor pulled down the sheet, and I released the breath I hadn't realized I was holding. Mr. Brown was not among the dead.

With its windows shrouded in black fabric and its lights strategically dimmed, the hospital had disappeared into the night.

Alex still slept. I caressed his face, but he didn't stir. I sat in the chair, took his hand, and rested my head on the mattress.

As the ward quieted, I drifted into sleep, interrupted every few minutes by the images of the corpses in the underground morgue—startling white faces, eternally frozen in the shock of sudden death.

"I thought I would never see you again." A hand brushed through my hair accompanied the familiar voice.

I raised my head and met the blue eyes that I loved. "Alex . . ." I leapt from the chair and kissed his cheek, then his lips.

"Don't stop. Keep kissing me," he said when I pulled away. "I can't believe I'm here with you."

I kissed him again before sitting back down, not wanting to overwhelm him. "I've missed you so much."

"What happened to you?" His gaze moved between the bandages on my head and the cuts on my arms.

"I was caught in the air raid."

"Another raid?" He glanced at the daylight slipping past the edges of the curtains. "Who told you I was here?"

"I didn't know you were here."

"You didn't?"

"No. I knew you were in the wreck, but Thomas said you weren't aboard the medical ship. In fact, according to the hospital, you are still not here. They think you are Matthew Oakley from Leeds."

"For heaven's sake! How?" His expression darkened for a moment, then cleared. "Oh, I see."

"You know?"

"Yes." Alex shifted slightly, wincing at the movement. "When the torpedo hit the ship, all hell broke loose. I was helping people into lifeboats when the explosions started. One blast threw me overboard, and something from the wreckage pierced my side." His hand went to his ribs.

"It was a piece of metal, surgically removed."

He pulled open the hospital gown to reveal the wrapping around his chest. "I hope they didn't butcher me," he joked.

"You shouldn't complain." I smiled.

"I know, but I will." He smiled back. "When I flew off the ship, I thought I was dead. The water felt like a million knives as it sucked me under. I struggled to surface, and when I did, I found myself surrounded by debris—and bodies. My head was foggy, my limbs ready to give out. Even in the worst battles, I had never felt so helpless—for it was my body that fought against me. I feared I would fall asleep and never wake up. Worse, I feared I would never see you again in this life."

"Thank heavens that's not the case." Tears stung my eyes as I pressed his hand to my cheek, his warmth grounding me.

"Then I saw a man go under, and something in me snapped. I found the strength to pull him onto a teak plank. His name was Matthew Oakley. Before he passed, he asked me to deliver his pocket watch, an heirloom from his father and grandfather, to his son. His name is engraved on it. I had it in my pocket."

"Oh . . . that's how your name was switched with his."

"I'm afraid so," Alex said. "You know, as I watched him die, I promised myself I would fulfill his last wish. That promise kept me awake. Thankfully, it wasn't long before a lifeboat spotted me. Next thing I remember, we were in London, but I was in and out of consciousness."

"You have been under heavy sedation."

"Well, I'm done with that. I want to get out of here. I want to go home."

Home.

"Alex, I . . ." There was so much I needed to tell him.

"You haven't told me why you came to London." He raised an eyebrow. "You were supposed to stay out of trouble."

Any other time, I would have waited until he was stronger before breaking the news. But some of it was too urgent, too important, to delay.

"I came to adopt a child."

"I might still have seawater in my ears. What did you say?"

"I better start at the beginning."

I recounted the events selectively. There would be a better time for full disclosure if necessary. The outing to the cottage outside town in search of Mrs. White tumbled from my lips first. I then told him about the refugees, diphtheria, Mrs. White's attack, my visit to Dr. Jones, and the doctor's subsequent death. I hesitated before revealing my trip to the cemetery to unearth our son's coffin.

"You did what?" Disbelief, grief, and anger tightened every muscle in his face.

"Please, hear me out. Please." I rushed to explain, knowing my actions, while startling, were justified. Otherwise, as Zaira had warned, I might end up without a husband.

I described the events at the civil office, the air raid, and finally, what I'd learned during my trip back in time: the unplanned meeting between Mrs. White and Mrs. Haywood at the dispensary, the lies, and the swapping of babies. I ended with Mrs. Haywood's fragile health.

"Will . . . if it weren't for our surreal past experiences, I wouldn't believe it." Alex's voice was soft, his eyes distant. "But I should have known. He is so much like me."

"A daredevil, pigheaded, and handsome?"

"Don't forget intelligent." He faked a smile. "Tell me he is back home."

"Yes. He is safe with the Haywoods."

"We need to speak to Mrs. Haywood before it's too late. She can tell Will the truth," Alex said.

"We can't tell him I am his mother, at least not for now."

"But we can tell him I'm his father."

CHAPTER 17
~ CONFESSIONS ~

No force in heaven or earth could keep Alex in the hospital.

"I've been through worse. I can handle a little scratch," he said, as anxious as I was to see Will and to clarify his lineage.

Alex arranged a ride home, knowing the train would take too long and be too exhausting. Though my aches were far less severe than his, I still felt considerable discomfort. One of Thomas's men, a reserved fellow with intelligent eyes and a square face, came to fetch us. We settled into the back seat, and after a brief exchange with the driver, we fell into silence. I rested my head on Alex's shoulder and slept for most of the journey.

With a yawn, I straightened and realized we were in Breamore. Night had fallen, and the town rested under a serene hush. The chaos and fear of London were behind us, but the emotions simmering in us were almost palpable. I could feel the storm of anger and regret within Alex—years of stolen love, missed milestones, and lost unity with Will pressed upon his heart.

"Florence, I'm sorry," Alex said, leaning close.

"For what?"

"For being selfish about your desire for a family." He lowered his voice. "I was afraid of losing you in childbirth. I thought only of myself. I let those fears hold me back until I was in the water, wondering if I'd survive. As I encouraged Oakley to fight for his life, to think about his wife, he taught me an unforgettable lesson.

"He said that his time had come but he knew his *children* would carry her through the difficult days ahead. I understood then. I'm not immortal. Sooner or later, I'm going to die, and, given my age, I'll probably go first. I don't want to leave you by yourself. We'll have as many children as your heart desires." Alex put his arm around my shoulders, bringing me into his embrace. "Besides, I'd love and enjoy them too."

"Well . . . we have a head start. We already have two."

"Good thing, too. I might be a bit old to chase after little feet," he said, but I saw the warmth in his gaze, the fondness for the thought.

"Don't you worry. I've heard that people rejuvenate when they become parents." I stole a quick kiss.

"Hmm. We'll see about that."

The car pulled into Forti Radici's courtyard.

"Come in and have a cup of coffee before you head back to London," Alex offered the driver.

"Thank you, sir. I'd like that."

Martha met us in the foyer. After a heartfelt welcome, she turned to the driver. "Please, this way. I'll show you to the kitchen."

From the end of the corridor, Zaira appeared, her voice bright with delight. "Welcome home!"

We embraced briefly.

"Florence, you look beaten, disheveled, and in need of a bath and fresh clothes," she observed with her usual bluntness, almost making me laugh. "You told me about the air raid, but I didn't think you were right in the middle of it! I mean, I thought you were taken to the hospital just as a precaution, not as an emergency." True, I had omitted the details of how I'd arrived there.

"Don't fret. It's not as bad as it looks. I was caught in some debris and flying objects, that's all."

"That's all?" She stared at me with horrified eyes. "Well, at any rate, I'm thrilled you are in one piece." With a sigh, she turned to Alex.

"Welcome home, Mr. Sterling! We were all ecstatic to hear you were safe and coming home."

"That's kind. I appreciate your concern."

"You'll be happy to know that Mr. Brown returned earlier today."

"That's wonderful news!" Relief washed over me.

"Wonderful indeed," Alex echoed.

"He said his cigars might have saved his life," Zaira continued. "He drove to a shop just beyond the bombing zone to buy a pack right before it all started. He tried to ring us but couldn't get through. So he stayed to help clear the streets, caught a few hours of sleep at a shelter, and then made his way back."

"With the Lagonda?" Alex loved the car.

"Yes. It got away with a nice coat of grime, but other than that, it fared better than Florence." Zaira smiled. Poor Mr. Brown—ever so particular about cars—the filth on the Lagonda from the bombing likely distressed him more than the attack itself.

"Good to hear." Alex smiled back.

"How is Mrs. Haywood?" I couldn't wait another second.

"Not well. The poor thing has had an awful day."

"Let's go see her," Alex said.

"You should wait," Zaira suggested. "She's just fallen asleep. Mr. Haywood and the nurse are looking after her. The doctor will be back in the morning."

"And Will?" Alex asked.

"He left a little while ago."

"He left? Why?" I was surprised he had left Mrs. Haywood's side.

"Honestly, I don't know," Zaira answered. "He suddenly took off. It was rather odd. And if I may say so, he wasn't in the best of moods."

"Hmm." Alex rubbed his chin thoughtfully. "Interesting."

"Eldad. Is he in bed?" The thought of the boy steadied my emotions.

"I tucked him in not long ago. He spent most of the afternoon outside and was completely worn out. He did ask about you—three times, in fact. He wasn't happy with me putting him to bed two nights in a row."

My heart warmed at her words. "All right. I won't bother him. I'll introduce him to Alex in the morning."

"Zaira," Alex said, "please let Mr. Haywood know that if he needs anything or if there are any changes with Mrs. Haywood during the night, he should send for us, no matter the hour."

"Of course, sir."

"Let's get cleaned up and get some rest." Alex grabbed my hand, and we crossed the foyer to the staircase.

Where could Will have gone?

A rap on the door jolted me awake. I sat up in bed as Alex rolled onto his side with a groan. We'd slept in. The anxiety of the previous day, along with the urgency to speak to the housekeeper and see Will, came back like the crack of a whip. Still, the silent night reassured me that nothing had taken a turn for the worse.

Another tap. The doorknob rattled, the door opened, and Eldad came running in with a book in hand.

"I was waiting for you downstairs, but you are taking too long." He was about to climb into the bed when he froze, his eyes widening as he stared at Alex. "Who is that?"

"Alex," I said. "Remember, I told you about him. He just got back from his trip to America."

"Oh." Eldad eyed the stranger warily before crawling in beside me.

"Good morning," Alex said warmly. "What do you have there?"

"A book," Eldad answered innocently, turning it over in his hands, nervously.

"What is it called?"

"*The Adventures of Molly the Cow.*"

"Ah. One of my favorites." Alex winked at me.

I narrowed my eyes at him, quite sure he'd never read it. "How are you feeling?"

"I've been better, but it's bearable."

"Would you like some medicine?" I offered.

"Maybe later."

"I'll give you some anyway. It's easier to stay ahead of the pain than to battle it once it takes hold."

"Florence is stern today," Eldad mumbled.

Alex's eyebrows shot up and a smile crossed his eyes.

"*Stern*? Where did you learn that word?" I asked.

"I heard it from Martha."

"You did?"

"Mm-hmm. She said it to Zaira," Eldad explained. "She said women have to be stern with men."

Alex laughed but immediately winced as his wound protested. "I'll need medicine after all."

"Martha also said that women are always right," Eldad added matter-of-factly.

Alex pulled me closer and whispered, "I don't think we are clever enough to raise this child."

It was my turn to laugh.

"Can we read now?" the boy asked, looking up at me expectantly.

"Bring the book over here," Alex encouraged.

Eldad climbed over me and handed Alex *The Adventures of Molly The Cow.*

"I'll read with him while you get ready. We better check on Mrs. Haywood," Alex said.

I left the bed.

"'Molly was white with black spots and a jolly personality.'" Eldad's voice rang through the room, brimming with excitement. "Your turn."

"'She liked to dash through the fields and race the other cows,'" Alex read.

I knew then that a long-lasting, loving relationship had just been born.

Mrs. Haywood lay motionless on the bed, her face ghastly and still. In my journey back in time, I had seen her young and vibrant—a striking contrast to the frail woman before me. Mr. Haywood sat beside her as a young blonde nurse, moving with quick efficiency, checked on the patient.

"Good morning, Mrs. Sterling. General, it's wonderful to have you with us again," Mr. Haywood greeted.

I responded with a soft smile, noticing how spent the man looked.

Alex nodded stiffly and addressed the nurse. "Please give us a moment."

"Certainly, sir." She gathered the soiled towels from the floor and left the room.

"How is Mrs. Haywood doing?" I asked.

"About the same. Thankfully, she rested better last night," Mr. Haywood replied.

"I'm glad to hear that."

"Agnes, the Sterlings are here." Mr. Haywood held his wife's hand.

Mrs. Haywood stirred, releasing a few disgruntled sounds before her eyelids fluttered open.

"We are here to speak with you about my son," Alex announced.

Mrs. Haywood's gaze fell on Alex like a hawk on its prey.

"Forgive me, but who are you speaking about?" Mr. Haywood's question sounded innocent enough, but there was a subtle unease in his voice that gave me pause.

"The one who supposedly passed away twenty-three years ago on his way to the dispensary," Alex said. "I have reason to believe your wife has information about him."

"I don't understand . . . we weren't even here back then," the groundskeeper said defensively.

"No, but your acquaintance, Deborah White, was," Alex countered.

"What does she have to do with us?" Mr. Haywood countered back.

"What would you like to know, General?" Mrs. Haywood intervened in a tremulous voice.

"The truth," Alex said bluntly.

"I knew this day would come," Mrs. Haywood said, resignation edged into every word.

"Oh no, Agnes." Mr. Haywood turned ashen, as if he had seen a ghost —one from his past at that. "I've feared this all along."

"It's all right, dear. I can't take this secret to the grave. It's been a blessing as much as a burden," the housekeeper admitted. "General, I will tell you what happened to your wonderful lad."

I perched on the chair across from the groundskeeper, my heart pounding. Alex remained on his feet, his hands clenched at his sides.

"Haywood and I had longed for a child our entire lives," the tale spilled from the housekeeper's lips in a slow cadence. "Then the miracle came, but it was short-lived. Our baby passed away days after birth. When I took him to the dispensary, Mrs. White happened to be there. I was drowning in grief, and when she told me the baby that she had with her was an orphan, I didn't question it. She proposed we exchange the boys and that I return to my life as if it had never happened. I agreed. She was persuasive, preying on my loss, but that doesn't excuse what I did.

"As the days went on, the nudging that Mrs. White hadn't been honest tortured me. Then I heard about your tragedy, General, and suspected Will was your son. But by then, it was too late. I couldn't give him up or the opportunity to be a mother. I'm so sorry, Peter. I couldn't bear to fail you, to fail us, by not giving you an heir."

"Oh Agnes, I'm as guilty as you are. I suspected the truth from the start. When I returned from my trip, I recognized the baby wasn't the same, but you were so happy. I didn't have the heart to confront it. I wanted him just as much as you did." Mr. Haywood's composure crumpled as he glanced at Alex. "What have we done?"

"We have loved Will as our own," Mrs. Haywood responded. "We have cherished every second with him and gave him all we could."

"That doesn't make it right," Alex said. "You robbed him of his right to grow up with me. You took from me his companionship and love. By exchanging babies, you traded your darkest days for my brightest ones. You took away the only thing I had left after my wife died. She gave her life fighting to save him, to bring him into this world. How could you do something so cruel?"

"I don't expect you ever to forgive me," Mrs. Haywood said. "And believe me, I wasn't as happy as you might think. Over the years, his appearance and character became a constant reminder that he wasn't ours. Then when he longed to explore beyond the farm, we knew we needed money. We couldn't secure a post anywhere, so I took the chance and came here for work. After all, you were leaving the country. The income was enough to keep Will in school and the farm afloat.

"Of course, Mrs. White didn't want Will or me anywhere near you, so she tried to send us away. Then I met you and knew without a shadow of a doubt you were Will's father. He is your carbon copy." A fit of coughing seized her, cutting her words. Her husband helped her to sit up, gently patting her back until the discomfort passed.

I stood beside Alex, a whirlwind of emotions raging inside me. Indignation clawed its way to the surface, but Dr. Jones's advice echoed in my mind. *"Remember to be fair with the knowledge you have gained and to bestow mercy upon others as life has bestowed it upon you."* I inhaled deeply, willing the anger in my chest away. Her crime, though inexcusable, was born of desperation—and desperation breeds deeds otherwise unthinkable. It would take time to come to terms with her actions, but life had happened to us both.

Mrs. Haywood gathered herself. "I can't tell you how unrelenting my remorse has been. Many times, I considered telling Will the truth, but I feared he would despise me."

The Count of Monte Cristo. How had I have not seen it before? *"It's too tragic. Too much anger and revenge . . . I'd prefer it if the story focused more on Edmond's growth and the rewards he gained from his ordeal . . . rather than dwelling on vengeance,"* Mrs. Haywood once said, speaking of Will—not Edmond Dantès.

"Will you tell him now?" Alex asked.

She nodded. "There is something else you should know."

I held my breath, dreading what came next.

"Go on," Alex prompted.

Mr. Haywood clasped his wife's hand, a quiet show of support.

"Mrs. White came to me some time ago, threatening to reveal Will's identity. I worried that, as atrocious as the truth is, she would make it worse. I feared she would place all the blame on me. And how could I refute her when I had kept silent this long? Will wouldn't have believed me."

"Where is White now?" Alex's shoulders stiffened.

"That I don't know." Tears edged Mrs. Haywood's eyes. "We met in random places of her choice. She had the upper hand, and I became a slave to her extortion."

"Extortion?" I repeated, the reason behind the housekeeper's financial strain now clear. "She's been taking money from you, hasn't she?"

"Money?" Mr. Haywood's voice carried disbelief. It was clear this was news to him. "Agnes, is that true?"

"I'm sorry, Peter. I have been such a fool. Our savings are gone, and bills have accumulated. Will, somehow, found out about it." Her eyes flicked briefly to mine, the message unmistakable. She knew I'd told him, and I sensed she also knew I'd gone through his military file. She had been the shadow watching me from the hallway. "We spoke about it yesterday. I still couldn't tell him the truth. And when you don't tell the truth, you lie.

"I told him I pitied Mrs. White and had loaned her money. I said that she'd threatened to tell the Sterlings that I'd helped her if I stopped providing financial aid. Will became enraged, and rightly so. He worried about his career and friendship with you, General. He reminded me how she tried to kill you and steal your fortune. And, of course, he's also aware of the assault on Mrs. Sterling, of which I had no idea beforehand. I swear I had nothing to do with it."

I believed her.

"Foolish woman, indeed," Mr. Haywood lamented with a loving undercurrent. "Why didn't you come to me? We could have face it together."

Mrs. Haywood pressed her lips into a thin line as her tears spilled over now.

"Where is Will?" Alex inched toward the door, ready to go find him.

The Haywoods exchanged puzzled glances.

"He is in the house, isn't he?" Mr. Haywood said.

"No, he left last night," Alex answered.

"No!" Mrs. Haywood exclaimed, her hands clutching the bed linens. "He's gone to find her."

"To find White?" The idea rattled me to my bones. I did not want Will anywhere near that woman.

"Where? Tell us." Alex demanded.

"Will knows I was supposed to meet her at Bristol station today at noon. I told her this would be the last time I would help her. She knew I was done."

"The train station?" I said, my mind racing.

"Yes, the train station," Mrs. Haywood sobbed.

"That's quite a ride from here." Alex checked his watch.

"With the police on her heels and no more money from the Haywoods, she's going to flee the country. That's why she chose Bristol," I reasoned.

"Let's go." Alex headed for the door.

"I'll come with you," Mr. Haywood offered, rising from his seat.

"No, dear." Mrs. Haywood held on to his hand. "You'll only slow them down."

Mr. Haywood hesitated, glancing between us and his wife, torn.

"Stay with your wife." Alex stepped into the corridor. "We'll handle this."

"Don't worry," I added. "We'll find him."

"I now know that whatever happens, my son will be all right, and that's all that matters." Mrs. Haywood sighed wearily, her shoulders slumping as she closed her eyes.

I couldn't imagine the guilt and crippling anxiety she must have felt.

CHAPTER 18
~ COLLIDING ~

Alex alerted Inspector Overton, and we left the house. I feared this drive might be the longest of my life. We crossed into the neighboring town, my sense of foreboding growing with each mile. I regretted telling Will about the Haywoods' financial troubles. Had I known the truth, I would have kept it to myself to keep him out of harm's way. I said a silent prayer that we would catch Deborah White once and for all— and that she would never again bring harm to our family.

"That bloody woman! She's planned this down to the last detail. Bristol station will be packed," Alex growled. "The more people there are, the harder it will be to catch her."

"Scotland Yard won't get there fast enough, will they?" Dread gnawed at me.

"They'll be behind us for sure. They have a longer drive." Alex floored the gas pedal, pushing the Lagonda to its limits.

Like a never-ending motion picture, we zoomed past towns, farms, and everything in between. And at length, like all films, the drive was almost over. Alex eased up on the gas as we entered Bristol. With its harbor, aircraft factories, and significant railway station, the city was a prime target for air raids.

"Didn't the granary used to be there?" I gestured to a mound of rubble. The sight tugged at a memory of my first life when my father, my brother, and I came to Bristol to watch a horse race. We'd watched from the edge of the grandstand while the crowd buzzed with anticipation. The horses thundered past us, the embodiment of power and grace. Their jockeys, blurs of blue and orange, seemed to fly with their mounts.

We had cheered for a younger, untested horse endowed with bursts of speed and astonishing stamina. I could still see my father clapping and laughing; Lucca's grip on the rail, his eager eyes as he followed the race; the frenzied crowd—it all came back vividly.

"It did—that's what's left of it and the eight-thousand tons of grain it stored," Alex replied, bringing me back to the present.

"I see it, but I don't believe it." Again, the footprint of war came into focus.

"No one does."

Bristol changed a lot over the years and with the war. Nevertheless, our people's resilience kept the city moving and the stations running.

A sign loomed ahead: Bristol Temple Meads Railway Station.

"This will do." Alex parked the Lagonda between two large trucks, out of sight of the main entrance. "The less visible, the better."

My fingers wrapped around the door handle, ready to bolt.

Alex grabbed my arm. "Florence, you must be careful."

"I will."

I expected him to release me, but he didn't. "I mean it. Don't let your guard down, even for a second."

"You too." I met his intense gaze. "Remember, you are not invincible."

"Don't worry about me." His very words concerned me. They reminded me of the many times he had expressed a desire to settle Deborah White's debts—a debt far deeper than we fully understood, tied to what she had done to our son.

"We must think about Will," I warned. "Alex, you mustn't lose your head."

"I won't."

We crossed the parking lot and entered the station. The central hall bustled with activity—people filled the benches, moved between offices, visited ticket windows. The sea of strangers was chaotic and ever-shifting, a reminder of how easily someone could vanish in the crowd.

"Bloody hell," Alex hissed. "I knew it would be busy, but not this busy. If White is armed, she won't hesitate to hurt anyone in her way. We must avoid that at all costs."

"We need to catch her by surprise—don't give her time to react."

"Easier said than done." Alex stretched his neck, scanning the crowd. "Focus on people's faces and height. White is short and might be in disguise. Will is tall—he'll stand out. If you see her, find me or a porter. Don't approach her alone."

We split up and circled the great hall. I kept Alex in my peripheral vision, my focus shifting constantly. Moments later, I saw him dart through the throng. I bolted after him, but his speed and the way he cleared a path left me struggling to keep up. I climbed onto a bench to get a better view.

The man Alex pursued didn't resemble Will. Who was he? He turned his head slightly, and then I knew. My chest tightened with the same fear and unease I'd felt the first time I encountered him—his shrewd gaze, cold touch, and cryptic riddles. Mr. Vines.

I lost sight of the men as they disappeared into an adjacent corridor. Leaping off the bench, I sprinted after them, scanning every face in my path. Mrs. White couldn't be far. I did a double take at a woman by a telephone booth—no, not her. My gaze shifted beyond her to another. A scarf covered her hair, but her stance and silhouette were unmistakable. Deborah White. My heart pounded in sync with my racing footsteps as I closed the distance. Heavy with the weight of her deeds, I placed a hand on her shoulder. With a startled gasp, the woman spun around. "What in the world!"

"Ohh," I stammered. "I'm dreadfully sorry—forgive me. I mistook you for someone else."

She gave me a nasty look and walked away.

Was Mrs. White even here? Could she have sent Vines in her place? The thought circled my head as I neared the corridor where Alex and Vines had disappeared.

Then I saw her.

She noticed me at the same time, her wicked, catlike eyes locking onto mine. I sprinted after her, my legs churning with a speed I didn't know I had in me.

Mrs. White took off, scurrying into a deserted passage. I arrived just in time to see a door swing shut. Out of breath, I gazed over my shoulder toward the central area. No one paid us any attention; we were just another pair of figures in the rush of the station. In that split second, I made my decision. If there was another exit in the room she had entered, she could already be gone. I couldn't waste time finding help. I pushed after her.

The storage room was lit by two high windows overlooking a platform. Stacked crates formed tight rows, leaving little room to maneuver. From what I could see, there was no other way out. She was hiding somewhere amid the clutter.

"You must be careful." Alex's warning urged me to reconsider. No matter. This was a chance to put an end to her manipulations. It was a risk I had to take.

I contemplated the multiple directions I could take, my ears straining against the oppressive silence. She was waiting, watching, ready to strike when the moment was right. I took a tentative step into a narrow aisle. The door behind me creaked on its hinges. I turned.

Will entered and motioned for me to stay put. My heart surged—he must have seen me and followed. It took all my restraint not to run to him. He moved farther into the maze of crates, his eyes alert, his movements calculated. He was soon out of sight.

"I wanted to reel in one fish, not two." Mrs. White's cackling bounced off the ceiling, concealing her position. "This complicates matters." She'd lured me here. However, Will's arrival would make it a bit harder to kill me.

"This has gone far enough, Deborah," I called. "Come out and face me!"

"Far indeed. You just couldn't help yourself. You had to go inquiring about Mr. Sterling's son. Once again, you unearthed the past and forced my hand." She confirmed what I suspected. Somehow, she'd learned about my visit to Dr. Jones and, maybe even, the cemetery. She must have feared Mrs. Haywood would yield, revealing the truth and ending her blackmail scheme, her source of income. But I felt it was more than that. Mrs. White didn't want Alex to find his son, to claim the connection to his past, or find the closure that would finally allow him peace and love in his life.

Now, she knew her game was over. Capture was inevitable, and prison awaited her. Her only remaining victory would be to take my life. She had succeeded once before, but not this time. This time, I knew exactly who I was dealing with.

"Speaking of the Sterlings' son." I had to strike at her confidence. "Why don't you tell Will who his real parents are?"

There was no response. I had hit a nerve. Will surely heard but remained silent to guard his location.

"Tell Will the truth," I pressed on, my righteous anger boiling over as I tried to draw her out. "Tell him the Haywoods aren't his birth parents—that his father is Alexander Sterling. Tell him how you switched him with the Haywoods' deceased son at birth. Come on, Deborah! Tell him how you made Alex believe his son was dead. Tell him! Tell Will the truth!"

"Silence, you infernal creature!" she hissed, her voice venomous. "You know nothing about the past!"

"Oh, I know enough, believe me. Now, stop hiding." I inched farther down the aisle. "Don't be a coward. Face me!"

A sharp click broke the tension, followed by the pressure of something hard against my shoulder blade. A gun. I swung around and grabbed her arm. The gun went off, the bullet grazing my forearm. Pain ripped through me, and I screamed, hurling myself at her. We crashed into a pile of boxes, toppling them around us—one struck her arm, knocking the gun to the floor, while another pinned me beneath its weight.

Will appeared at the end of the aisle, gun in hand. I struggled to push the box off, but before I could rise, Mrs. White regained balance and retrieved her weapon. I kicked a crate at her and rolled out of sight. Two shots rang out. The door slammed against its frame, and moments later, Will knelt beside me.

"Mrs. Sterling, are you hurt?" He examined my arm.

"I'm fine. It's just a scratch."

"I took a shot at her but missed. I was afraid to hit you." His voice was drowned by the whistle of a train. "She's going to escape." He jumped to his feet and ran out.

I staggered after him, aching from the crates' impact, my arm burning. The platform stretched ahead as a freight train thundered past the station. Clusters of people milled about, but no guards were in sight. Then I saw Mrs. White—running like a soul unleashed from a hell of her own making. Will chased her, closing the gap with every stride.

At the far end, Alex was still pursuing Vines. Why didn't he have the man in hand already?

Will reached Mrs. White and yanked her to a halt. She whipped around and shot him—point-blank in the chest.

CHAPTER 19
~ PICKING UP THE PIECES ~

The blast reverberated through the platform, its echoes fading along the tracks. The acrid scent of gunpowder hung in the air as panic gripped the crowd. They scattered like startled birds.

Will collapsed onto the platform.

"Will! Oh, heavens! Will!" I dropped to my knees beside him. "Help! Someone help!" Blood seeped through his shirt.

Mrs. White advanced, her eyes blazing with hate. A scream lodged in my throat as she leveled her gun at me. I wasn't afraid to die, but terror consumed me at the thought of leaving my son helpless, writhing on the floor.

She pulled the trigger.

The gun failed to fire.

She squeezed again.

Again, it failed to discharge.

She spat a string of vile curses, then glanced past my shoulder, her face turning sickly pale.

I turned and saw Vines sprinting in our direction with Alex close on his heels. It was evident that Vines's presence was unexpected and unwelcome.

In that moment of distraction, I seized Will's gun from his holster and rose to my feet. "You'll burn in hell for the suffering you've caused." Now, I was the one aiming a weapon at her.

"I'll wait for you there," she hissed.

"Your wait will have no end."

"Put the gun down!" a porter yelled, bursting through a nearby door.

"Put it down!" another echoed.

Now they appeared.

Will let out a few agonizing sounds and then fell silent.

How could I simply let justice take its course? After preaching to Alex about keeping a sound mind and letting the law punish her, here I was, about to contradict everything I had said. My mind urged me to let her go, but my heart burned for vengeance. I wanted to see her blood spill, just like my son's. Rage—dark and destructive—coursed through my veins as I took in her mocking face. I loathed this woman. Life had given me the chance to settle the score, and the temptation was overwhelming.

"Florence, lower the gun!" Alex called out, drawing closer. Vines now secured in his grip. "Lower the gun."

"Shoot me!" Mrs. White taunted with a deranged laugh. "Shoot me!"

I glanced at my son, then at Alex, torn between fury and restraint.

"Of course you won't," Mrs. White sneered. "You're as weak as the woman you impersonate."

My finger hovered over the trigger, itching to pull it.

"She's not worth it. Put it down," Alex pleaded. "You aren't a killer. Florence, listen to me. I need you. I love you."

Alex's words reached me, grounding me, reminding me who I was. Love rose above the tide of hatred. Hate would fade, but love would endure. No, I wasn't a cold-blooded murderess, and a lifetime in prison, or hanging for that matter, would suit her better. I lowered the gun, my inner battle won. The most significant battle I had ever fought.

In a flash, one of the porters seized the weapon from my hand. The other stood by Mrs. White. I fell to my knees beside Will, who remained unconscious.

"Will, I'm here. Your father is here." I kissed his forehead. "Stay with us, my darling. Stay with us."

"I see you managed to find me," Mrs. White hissed at Mr. Vines, her venomous tone confirmed the strain in their relationship.

"I see I have found you too late," he replied, his gaze shifting to Will with a flicker of regret.

"Too late, indeed," she said, though her meaning was unclear—was she referring to Will or herself?

"Where's your puppet? You couldn't afford him any longer?" Mr. Vines sneered. "You should have kept him. He was worth every pound you paid him to watch your back. Without him, you'd have been long dead."

I knew then. The man I had seen with Mrs. White was her bodyguard, not to protect her from Scotland Yard, but from Vines. I would never have guessed.

"You should have kept your word when we returned to England. You should have stayed with me and away from the Sterlings. But no—you couldn't let go of your fixation on him, could you?" Vines gestured toward Alex. "Look at him! He has never loved you, and he never will. Can you get that through your thick skull now?"

The rumble of an incoming train filled the station, the ground vibrating beneath our feet. The fear was instant. If the train stopped, Mrs. White could blend into the crowd of disembarking passengers and slither away.

"You are a hopeless fool!" she snarled. "You are the one who couldn't let go of your fixation on me!"

To my relief, the train didn't slow down. It was another freight train, barreling through at a devilish speed.

"Are you sure about that?" Vines shouted over the clamor, wrenching himself free from Alex with a sudden jerk. "You have caused enough damage—and enough is enough." Before anyone could react, he shoved Mrs. White onto the tracks.

Her final scream—haunting and full of terror—pierced the air, the cry of a tormented spirit meeting its fate. I tore my gaze away, unable to bear the sight. Deborah White—the ever-present shadow in my life—was gone, swallowed by the screech of metal on rails.

Gone.

Alex grabbed Vines by the scruff of his neck and slammed him against the wall. He crumpled to the floor like a lifeless doll, his eyes staring blankly at the tracks, where the best and worst in him had finally met. Deep down, I felt a pang of sympathy for the man. Vines, Mrs. White's lover and accomplice had also been her greatest victim.

His undoing had been loving a woman with a heart of stone—a woman who had dragged him through a life of misery, never cared for him, and used him only to discard him. Yet, he had remained by her side, unfailingly loyal.

He'd stood by when she poisoned her husband, calling it an act of mercy. He'd been there when they first worked at Forti Radici and she caused my accident. He'd taken part in swapping the babies. He'd witnessed my arrival at Oak's Place and watched in silence as Mrs. White poisoned Alex and tried to rob him of his fortune. He'd fled New York, helping Deborah to escape the police.

And now, here he was again, at this critical junction in my life, ending his life alongside hers. Even if he escaped the gallows for killing her, he would never again know freedom.

"Keep your eyes on him," Alex ordered one of the porters. To the other, who stood in a trance as he surveyed the carnage on the tracks, he ordered, "Go get help! Now—go!"

Looking ill, the man scrambled inside the station.

"Alex, he is not responding," I sobbed.

Alex tore the sleeve off his shirt and pressed the fabric to Will's chest. "Florence . . . the wound . . . is near his heart."

"In the same spot where you took one for my father," I cried, then saw the blood on Alex's shirt. "You are hurt."

"Vines punched my incision. I'm fine," Alex replied through gritted teeth while he continued to work on our son. "Come on, Will, hang on. Hang on."

"Wake up, wake up," I implored, patting Will's face. A faint sound from his lips brought a fleeting hope.

"Keep talking to him," Alex instructed. I did.

Will mumbled something, his voice weak and garbled.

I looked at Alex, but he shook his head. Like me, he was unable to understand.

Will spoke again. This time I understood. "Mum."

"Mrs. Haywood is not here, but your father and I are by your side," I sobbed. "Stay with us, please."

A faint smile crossed his lips, and his eyes rested on me. "No, not Mrs. Haywood," he said softly. "You, Mrs. Sterling, my mother."

I couldn't breathe. He *knew*. Tears cascaded down my face and onto his chest, mingling with his precious blood. We were together at last. All three of us, a family.

How? I wondered in awe, but before I could ask, Will turned his gaze to Alex's.

"General—no—Pa. I'll carry the time we spent together with me. Those days in America were a gift. I loved Oak's Place, the monastery, and the people I met there. But most of all, I treasure the time I spent learning from you—your unwavering zeal to always do your best." Will paused, his breath labored. "Pa, Mum, I feel as if we were never apart, as if I had known you my whole life."

"I'm honored to be your father," Alex choked out. "You are much better than I could ever be. Now, stay with us. Stay awake."

"We love you," I whispered. "We have a lifetime to look forward to, to be together."

"No, Mum, we have an eternity to be together. I can soar through the sky now, faster than any airplane." His words came out broken and distant. "Adeline is waiting for me . . . she's so beautiful." His gaze seemed to wander beyond this mortal realm. "Mrs. Haywood is there too. I won't be alone."

"Mrs. Haywood?" Alex repeated. "He's delirious."

"No," I said. "She must have passed." A strong impression filled me— something had transpired during Will's brief unconsciousness. Had Mrs. Haywood finally had the chance to tell him the truth? Even though she hadn't known I was his mother in mortality—could she had learned it after passing?

"I love you." Will smiled, the sweetest expression I had ever seen.

"Until we meet again." His eyes closed, and his lungs released the last breath he would ever take.

A groan of agony tore from Alex's throat. I pressed Will's hand to my cheek. My son was gone, this time for good. Darkness enveloped me, dragging me into its depths.

"When the light seems to have gone from your soul, remember the dream." Dr. Jones's words echoed in my mind as clear as if he were standing beside me. With his counsel came the vivid remembrance of the dream—a dream had foreshadowed I would find my son, but also offered consolation for this very moment.

In it, Will had said, *"It's all right. I'm all right,"* and a profound peace had washed over me then. That same feeling enveloped me now. I breathed a little easier. Will was not just all right. Wherever he was, he was surrounded by love and complete contentment. We would be together again someday. I would hold on to that hope for the rest of my life.

I glanced at Alex, and my heart ached to see him on the brink of collapse. His eyes overflowing with tears, the veins in his neck pulsing erratically. In the days to come, I would share with him the dream and the solace it brought me. But for now, I reached for him, pulling him into an embrace.

We clung to each other with what little strength we had left, seeking comfort in the love that bound us, even as we wept for a beloved child taken too soon.

Alex and I strolled along the seashore at Keyhaven, the crash of waves blending with the steady pulse of our shared silence. As long as we were together, we could and would endure. There were days filled with hope and days overflowing with heartrending sadness. Nevertheless, we face them all together.

My gaze followed the gentle undulations of the sea, my thoughts adrift in the events of recent weeks.

Mr. Vines's inquest came and went like a terrifying nightmare, stirring our grief anew. For taking Deborah White's life, he was sentenced to hang. As for her, the wake of destruction and sorrow she left behind was, at times, unfathomable. I could only hope that with time, her name would fade into obscurity. It didn't deserve another second of our lives.

Will. My heart ached as sharply as it did the day I lost him. The wound was deep, and I doubted it would heal during this lifetime. Just as I had feared, Mrs. Haywood passed shortly after we left for Bristol. Will had cared deeply for her, and strangely, I found peace in the thought that, in the afterlife, she might mend the rift with her adopted son. I held no bitterness toward her. She loved Will fiercely, and for that, I was grateful. I could relate to her through my feelings for Eldad.

The image of the boy on the rocking horse Will had crafted formed in my mind. It was a bittersweet, constant reminder of what I had lost and gained. At last, I understood the all-encompassing love of a mother—that very affection Mrs. Allerton and Granny had for me. I had seen it in their eyes when I was scared during the long hours of the night. It was there when I hurt, when I cried, when I was frail and sick, and when the world felt like it would crush me. It always was and it always would be.

"You are thinking about Will," Alex stated.

"Always."

"Me too."

"He was so full of life."

"Wherever he is, he still is." Alex embraced me, comforting me with his gentle touch. "I'll be forever be grateful for the time we had with him. No one can ever take away the bonds of love we built together."

"Eternal bonds," I whispered, holding him tighter. "I just wish it didn't hurt this much."

"I know. But we must move on and help Eldad do the same. He has wounds of his own to heal."

"Do you think he is all right? I feel terrible leaving him home."

"He's likely enjoying every second of being spoiled by Zaira and Clarence." The pair were the newlyweds in town. After a brief honeymoon, they'd taken the reins at Forti Radici. As a wedding gift, Alex and I presented them with a parcel of land at the southern end of the manor. They had already begun planning their home, which included a large stable to support Clarence's dream of breeding horses.

"I'm afraid you are right," I said with a laugh.

"The little rascal has them wrapped around his finger," Alex added with a chuckle.

"I'm glad they decided to stay with us."

"It would have been hard to find someone we trust as much as them."

"Speaking of trust, it was generous of you to help Mr. Haywood retire and settle back on his farm," I remarked.

"Will would have wanted that. Old Haywood was a good father to him."

A low rumble drew our gazes to the trees. A military plane soon zoomed over us toward the sea.

"Will adored airplanes," I said, my eyes following its path as it skimmed the water and disappeared into the setting sun. "*I love you, Mum. I love you.*" Whether I heard the words in my head or carried on the breeze, I couldn't say.

The cabin stood still, wrapped in the quiet veil of night. Firelight flickered, casting dancing shadows on the walls. Alex spread a blanket before the grate, and we settled into its warmth. He looked serene, at peace with the war, with life, with himself. I wasn't there yet, so he remained my anchor in the storm.

The fire crackled, sending sparks out of the hearth, and the name popped into my head. "Dorothy."

"Dorothy who?" Alex asked, tugging off his boots.

"You seriously don't remember? There is no way you forgot her."

"That depends on who she is."

"How about the woman you sent to visit the devil?"

"Ahh." A smile crossed his eyes. "Poor Frankfort. You must have been very persuasive to get him to spill the details."

"Just like in the good old days. I batted my eyelashes, and he surrendered." I lied shamelessly, and he knew it. "No, seriously, Thomas divulged your dating habits of his own free will and choice."

"You know what, Florence?"

"What, Mr. Sterling?"

"I see you've fallen victim to the green-eyed monster. However, my lady, that was long ago."

"I still want to know what happened." I batted my eyelashes.

He laughed.

"Go on."

"Hmm . . . now that I think about it, she wasn't too hard on the eye."

"What's that supposed to mean?" I playfully punched his chest. He caught my fist before I could strike again.

"It means I'm just poking fun at you. But if you must know, she cornered me in Thomas's flat—in the kitchen, though she was determined to take me to the bedroom."

"Why would she want to do that?" I mocked.

"I can show you if you'd like."

I shook my head, suppressing a smile.

"All right, all right. I'll start from the beginning." His tone turned serious. "When I came home from the Great War, I was more lost than when I left. I don't even know how I accepted Frankfort's invitation to go out with them. I must've been drunk. Dorothy was agreeable at first, but by the end of the evening, she was out of place. Anytime something amused her, she'd touched my hand, my arm, any part of me she could get ahold of to emphasize her excitement. I felt like a caged, extremely irritated animal.

"Once we were alone, she forced herself on me. I rejected her. She asked if I was afraid of her. I told her I wasn't. She said she didn't believe me and suggested she would spend the night so I could prove her wrong. That's when I told her to go to the devil."

I couldn't help but feel a pang of sympathy for her—a beautiful woman, I imagined, helplessly falling for the handsome, wealthy widower. Who could resist that?

"I have to ask. Why? Any other man, especially a recent arrival from the war, would have been eager to set the record straight."

"Like I told you decades ago when Arianna corralled me, I don't like women who do the chasing. Besides, I was dealing with the war trauma and was quite bitter about your death. It was too much too soon."

"Did you ever see her again?" I ventured.

"No." He angled his body toward me and held my gaze with an intensity that warmed me more than the fire. "You know, you are the only woman I have ever truly loved."

"And you are the only man I have ever truly loved."

"And how do you love me, Miss Contini?" He leaned in, his lips brushing my cheek.

"Let's just say you own my soul," I whispered. "You always have and always will. Past, present, and future—always. How do you love me, Mr. Sterling?"

"Are you sure you want to know?" he murmured, his voice soft, sending a shiver through me.

"I do."

"Let's just say—your smile, your tears, your kisses, your scent, your touch—every part of you is embedded in my very bones. Without you, I am nothing." His lips found mine. "Is that enough?"

"It's more than enough, Mr. Sterling, more than enough."

CHAPTER 20
~ FOREVERMORE ~

I lay in bed, my heart beating quietly, steadily. I touched my face and looked at my hands, now marred by wrinkles—the imprints of a lifetime of joy and sadness. And now, at the end of it all, the hour had come to move on to my final home. I could hardly wait another minute to be with Alex and those I loved. I closed my eyes, and welcomed the memories that washed over me, carrying me back through some of the moments that had defined me.

The Second World War lasted six long, dreadful years. The United States, urged by the United Kingdom and forced into action by Japan's attack on Pearl Harbor, sealed the Allied victory. The mission Alex and Will took part in, became known as the Tizard Mission and proved critical in ending the Nazis' reign of terror.

Alex and I spent the rest of our lives at Forti Radici, often traveling to our haven at Keyhaven. We maintained the Victory Garden throughout the war, sharing its harvest with those in need. Four years into the conflict, we converted the manor into a convalescent home for wounded soldiers. Backed by his military experience, Alex's support was invaluable to the patients who arrived almost daily. I did my best to keep pace with him, but, as always, he remained one step ahead.

At times, it felt like the nightmare would never end, but it did. And the very first thing we did was travel to America to visit Granny and

Oak's Place. Granny lived a long, blessed life before following the course of humankind. Often, I wondered if she and her beloved priest would have a chance together in the hereafter. I had a strong feeling they would.

Mr. Snider and, later, his heirs, took excellent care of Oak's Place. He married a woman from Geneva, and together they built a hardworking family. After Granny's passing, Alex gifted the mansion to them.

A year after the war, Alex and I made our first trip to India together. India—oh, what fond memories I had of that place. It was there we conceived our second child. Since our firstborn had miraculously carried Alex's father's given name, William, we chose Marcus for our second, honoring my father. Not long later, we welcomed a baby girl, Margaret, named after Alex's mother. And, of course, we had our beloved Eldad. We taught him about his people's faith, courage, and resilience—things he must always honor. He grew up to become one of the most successful businessmen in England and a passionate advocate for human rights.

Over the years, day in and day out, the halls of Forti Radici echoed with the happy sounds of children's laughter and the pitter-patter of little feet. But the laugh I cherished most was Alex's. He gave me a life filled with joy. He gave me a family.

It had now been ten years since Mr. Sterling left me—ten long years that felt like a century. To his credit, he never failed to check on me. Each night, I felt his presence, his unwavering concern for my well-being. I heard his whisper in my ear, "Good night, my lady. I love you." I felt the brush of his lips against my forehead—until last night. For the first time in a decade, he hadn't come. I knew then he must be busy preparing for my arrival.

"Mother, we are here," Eldad announced, pulling me from my reverie.

I opened my eyes and beheld my children. "Eldad, Marcus, Margaret, there are no words to describe how proud I am of you. You have brought me such incredible joy."

"I will miss you, Mother," Margaret choked out, tears welling in her eyes.

"I won't be far."

"Say hello to Papa for us," Eldad said. *Papa.* Little Eldad had adored Alex. Alex had been a wonderful father to him. I smiled, recalling how, from the very beginning, Eldad would wander into our bedroom and refuse to leave. Alex would patiently coax him back to his bed, often staying to read until both fell asleep. Then, it was my turn to coax Alex back to our room.

"I will," I promised.

"Tell Father there will always be a Sterling in the army to make him proud," Marcus added. His features justified his name. He was the spitting image of his grandfather, General Marcus Contini. And like his father and grandfather, Marcus carried a deep-seated passion for serving his country.

"Consider it done."

"Don't worry about Forti Radici. There will always be a Sterling to care for it," Margaret said. "And as long as there is one of us here, your gladioli and roses will continue to bloom."

"Thank you, darling. Thank you."

"Father will be so happy to see you again," she added.

"I'm afraid to find out what he's been up to all this time without me or the army," I teased.

They laughed, the sound sweet and poignant. One by one, they kissed me and receded to the back of the bedroom, speaking in hushed voices. Margaret whispered something about her heart hurting too much, and Eldad comforted her in his arms.

I closed my eyes and drew a long breath. My life, one I had loved and despised, had come and gone. My journey in the mortal world—a place of joy and grief in equal measure—was now complete. Grief had been an unwelcome friend but a friend all the same—one that taught me to love deeper, hope more, and push beyond my comfort zone. I now realized that nothing mattered except for the things I would take with me into the next life, the knowledge that shaped my character and the bonds of love I forged and protected throughout my life. Those bonds would reunite me with my dear ones, keeping our family unit intact.

Life, I realized, was an intricately woven tapestry, each of us working together to produce a beautiful masterpiece of love, mercy, and justice.

Here, at the end of my path, one eternal truth was engraved in my soul— love was worth fighting for.

"You have done well, Florence," I told myself.

My spirit separated from its mortal host and stood beside the bed. Young again and full of vitality, I rejoiced in my newfound freedom from the burdens of age. With the wrinkles and frailties left behind, I was blessed with surreal energy. I could think, move, and feel as never before, not even during my out-of-body experiences. I was no longer subject to the elements; instead, I commanded them. It was an incredible, empowering gift.

I gazed at my children, their faces filled with emotion yet oblivious to the new dimension I had entered.

"Hello again!" Lucca greeted, suddenly appearing beside me, his eyes sparkling with life.

"I have missed you," I said, falling into his embrace.

"I wasn't far."

"I owe so much to you." Gratitude and love overwhelmed me for my dear brother.

"You have eternity to make it up to me." He smiled sweetly. "Are you ready?"

I was moving on. Nostalgia for the only world I had ever known swept over me. I would miss it—just a little. "May I?" I asked.

"I'll be right here keeping an eye on these three." Lucca winked. "Don't take too long."

I arrived at the monastery, now run by priests. Invisible, I wandered its halls, admiring the soaring arches and vibrant stained-glass windows —their depictions of the past alive with color. In the dormitories, memories of Higher Grounds flooded back. Gratitude swelled within me for those I loved—the girls, Sister Callahan, Father Thompson, and my dear Granny. I would see her soon.

I moved on to Oak's Place, and images of my miraculous arrival here hit me at once: Mrs. White's shock at my initial appearance, her hands shaking as she read my résumé; Mr. Vines's cold, calculating demeanor; me, walking down the hall to Mr. Sterling's office; his tall figure staring out the window as I stepped into his life once again; his eyes brimming with emotion as he turned and beheld me; our ride through the forest, the storm, and sleeping in his arms. Saying goodbye to this place proved more painful than I had imagined.

Next, I found myself in Keyhaven, strolling along the familiar shore. Hurst Castle Fortress stood resolutely against the blue sky, and the vast, endless ocean stretched before me. Both had brought me comfort and sorrow. I now bid them farewell. I merged with the trees, inhaling the fresh, salty air. Before long, I saw the cabin, our heaven on earth.

After escaping the German attack, Alex and I spent our first night as a married couple here. Seeing the contusions on his body from Krause's vicious attack, I'd said, *"I'm sorry about this."*

"My lady, for a single moment like this," he had responded, his cool lips tracing my cheek, *"I would take the beating all over again."* The memories were so tender, so raw, that I couldn't linger long. I hastened back to the manor.

I crossed green fields. In this lush, calm expanse, Alex and I met for the first time. Father's comrade turned out to be a handsome soldier who swept me off my feet. Finally, I entered the manor. Its grand halls filled with echoes of the life we had built together.

"It's not just a room, and you can't stay in it!" I'd told Alex outside Lucca's room.

"Would you rather I stay in yours?" he'd responded.

Our first breakfast together.

"Good morning, Miss Contini."

"There is nothing good about it."

"Well, it's good to see me, isn't it?"

"Are you off your trolley, or is it a side effect of the war?"

Outside my bedroom.

"Can you sew it on for me?" he'd asked, referring to a button.

"Why don't you sew it on yourself? Surely, you are capable of that much," I'd fired back.

"You don't know how to sew," he'd mocked.

"Of course I do, but it doesn't mean I'll mend your clothes."

"Nah. If you knew how to sew, you would be happy to help me out."

"Definitely off the trolley."

The night out in the garden.

"I'm in love with you, and I don't know how to express it any other way than—" Before I could process his words, his lips met mine.

Drawing my thoughts back to the present, I took a longing breath. I needed to see him, to be with him again. Ten years had been far too long.

I entered my bedroom.

"Ready now?" Lucca asked.

"Ready indeed." I cast one last glance at my children. "Goodbye, my darlings. I love you."

Lucca took my hand, and light engulfed us, carrying us into a sea of white. Gradually, it faded, revealing a path paved with jewels, leading to a city of crystalline beauty. Like a diamond cradling the sun, it gleamed against a sapphire sky. Within moments, we crossed its borders.

A gathering stood beneath the most vibrant trees I'd ever seen. Freed from the burdens of mortality, the people appeared younger than I remembered, yet remarkable as always. They knew and loved me for who I was. They had always cared for me more than they did for themselves. And oh, how I loved them! My parents were the first to step away from the group and rush to me.

"My dear daughter, welcome!" General Marcus Contini embraced me with the same tender strength I had always known.

"Oh, my darling Florence! How I've longed to hold you again!" My mother's voice broke as she moved toward me with effortless grace. Her dark hair cascaded down her shoulders, her fair skin luminous in the light. She was more beautiful than any of her portraits could ever capture.

I fell into her arms as though I had known her my entire life, as though we had never been apart. Perhaps, like Lucca, she'd always been near.

"Florence, I shouldn't say this, but you are a few minutes late," Mrs. Allerton teased, stepping forward with a broad smile. "But of course, I should have expected it—punctuality was never your strength."

"Mrs. Aller—" My voice broke with emotion.

"Bienvenue dans notre demeure céleste, mademoiselle," Mr. Leroy said as he followed behind her, kissing both my cheeks.

They made a stunning pair—youthful, radiant, freed from worldly cares. It felt as if I had just seen them yesterday, though decades had passed since the German attack that claimed their lives. Since then, I had learned there were many ways to be apart, but separation by time was the cruelest. *Time*. What was time now? Nothing but a memory.

"Have you forgotten about me?" Granny clasped me in her arms. Gone were her black habit and spectacles, replaced by a dazzling green dress. Her curly brown hair fell freely, unbound by a veil. She looked simply dazzling. "My dear, dear child."

"Granny! I have missed you terribly." I clung to her, my gaze drifting to a man nearby. His strikingly symmetrical features and poised stance radiated strength. He watched our reunion in silence, a smile touching his lips. "Is he . . .?" I whispered, more to myself than to her.

"Yes, dear," Granny replied, her voice tinged with pride. "That's him."

I had been right all along; she had been reunited with the priest she loved, bound together in immortality.

Once the greetings were over, laughter and joyful chatter filled the air. I was quickly brought up to date on their wonderful lives here, the knowledge passing from person to person with incredible velocity and understanding.

Suddenly, a pull stirred deep in my heart. Taking a breath, I turned—and there he was. Tall, handsome, and smiling just as I remembered him. My Will.

"Will!"

"Welcome home, Mum! We are together at last."

"My dear son!" I fell into his arms, and in that moment, my long-ago living dream became a reality. I now fully understood.

The church's bells had symbolized my inner connection to a higher power, the constant force guiding me to goodness and love. My journey through the forest mirrored the weariness, disappointments, and suffering I had endured in mortality. And now, the culmination of the dream—standing in the church and holding my son in my arms—was fulfilled. I had reached my eternal destination, where I was physically and spiritually whole. My two lives had finally, peacefully merged into one.

As if summoned by the warmth of the moment, a gorgeous young woman, the picture of refinement itself, joined us.

"Mum, this is Adeline. I've been eager for you to meet her," Will introduced.

I took her hands into mine. "Indeed, you are just as beautiful as Will said."

"Thank you, Mrs. Sterling," she replied shyly. "It's such a pleasure to meet you."

"The pleasure is all mine," I assured, and my attention shifted beyond them. My heart burned as if set aflame, for there he stood—a silhouette illuminated by the brightest light yet.

Alexander Sterling.

The man who had helped me endure everything, who had given me more than I ever dared dreamed possible, watched and waited with undying patience. He looked as young as the day I first met him in the fields of Forti Radici—broad shoulders, dark hair, blue eyes, and that mesmerizing smile.

I raced to him, stopping within arm's reach. Our gazes locked, and in his silence, I saw his struggle to control his emotions.

"You didn't come to see me last night, Mr. Sterling," I said playfully.

"I was too busy preparing for your arrival, my lady."

"Wasn't ten years long enough?"

"Not for the arrival of a queen."

"Well . . . I'm here."

"At last."

"What now, Mr. Sterling?"

"Now, Miss Contini, we spend eternity together."

"Sounds like a plan."

He pulled me into the security of his embrace and kissed me with a fervency I hadn't imagined possible, a passion that blended our souls into one. Eternity stretched before us. It would be good. Really, really good.

Thank you for reading! Did you enjoy? Please add your review because nothing helps an author more and encourages readers to take a chance on a book than a review.

And don't miss more from Marcia Armandi with THE GHOSTS OF LEWIS MANOR available now. Turn the page for the Author's Note, and then a sneak peek!

Also be sure to sign up for the City Owl Press newsletter to receive notice of all book releases!

AUTHOR'S NOTE

Although many of the events in *Alive* actually occurred, the times, dates, and details may have been changed to fit the story. A few points of interest:

- The sinking of the SS *Athenia*, the first UK ship to be sunk by Germany during World War II, occurred hours after England officially declared war on Germany on September 3, 1939, but it appears to have been an error in judgment by the captain of the German U-boat rather than an intentional act of war. While more than 100 were killed, over 1,200 survived.
- The bombing of Southampton occurred in December of 1940. Over 2,300 bombs and 30,000 incendiary devices were dropped, the resulting firestorm seen as far away as Cherbourg, France.
- England restricted the influx of Jewish refugees, allowing only about 10,000 to enter the country over the course of the war. Between 1938 and 1940, as part of the Kindertransport program, England also allowed 10,000 unaccompanied Jewish children to cross its borders for placement in foster homes and on farms. These were often the only family members who survived the Holocaust.

- The war interfered with the creation and distribution of many
  essential medicines (Germany had been a major player in the
  pharmaceutical industry prior to the war). In response, the
  Royal Botanic Gardens at Kew organized a plan to collect
  medicinal herbs from the countryside. Women's Institutes and
  Boy Scout troops were among the volunteers. One of the most
  important herbs gathered, foxglove, was necessary for treating
  heart conditions. Other herbs included nightshade, valerian,
  black horehound, wild thyme, and rosehip (valued for its high
  levels of vitamin C).

SNEAK PEEK OF THE GHOSTS OF LEWIS MANOR

Brockenhurst, the New Forest, England, 1942

As the train creaked into the station, my thoughts remained on the incident that had landed me here. I was not sure when I first became aware I could see the dead. In my nineteen years of life, they had hovered around the edges of my awareness like a faint melody heard from another room. When I was younger, they'd blended with the living well enough—the girl in an old-fashioned dress in the park who'd ignored my invitation to play, the old man with a blank look who'd stood on our porch one moment and was gone the next. The sightings were rare, and as an adult, I treated those old memories as dreams. That was, until the war started. The overwhelming number of disembodied spirits roaming the streets of the city could not be ignored.

Thankfully, most spirits—at least those *I'd* encountered—seemed oblivious to the world of the living, completely absorbed with whatever it was they did. They paid me no heed, and though seeing them had been slightly disconcerting, I considered them mostly benign. That was, until the boy called for my attention.

Being deceived to the point of endangering my family made me realize I might have to look more closely at this ability, for if I failed to comprehend what lay beyond the veil separating the living from the dead, I could find myself on the wrong side of it. The thought was grim. For if I were to ever understand the supernatural world, I would have to step farther in. But as I considered the possibility, goose bumps crawled up my arms, and fear of the unknown made me think better of it. I decided to brush away the uncomfortable thought as the train finally stopped, and I rose to gather my belongings. After all, I was here to escape the ghosts.

Alighting from the train, the first thing I noticed was the sky. Compared to the hellish brew of London, it was vast and endless—paradisal to behold. Yet dragging my suitcase across the platform, I felt the part of a vagabond, a refugee from the land of the dead. Piper sniffed the air, which had the refreshing scent of recent rain.

The other travelers brushed past me, impatiently trying to get on with their journeys. Feeling a little of that impatience myself, I readjusted Piper in my arms and took a fruitless lap around the station, avoiding the puddles as best I could. The groundskeepers of All Hallows, the Goswicks, were supposed to fetch me. But no one appeared to be looking for me.

Within minutes, I was the only person in sight except for the clerk behind the ticket window and a man wiping the water droplets off a black car in the parking lot. "Excuse me, sir," I said to the clerk. "Is there a way to call for a cab?"

His dark eyes rose to meet mine as he put down the pipe he had been smoking apparently nonstop, for he stood in a cloud of fumes. "How far are you going?"

"Burley. I understand it is a neighboring town?"

"That's correct, and Albert Craven"—he pointed at the man by the car—"offers local transportation." Looking at his wristwatch, he added, "You might want to speak to him right away. He usually leaves about now."

"I'm most obliged, sir."

Mr. Craven was a middle-aged man with a thick mustache and bushy eyebrows. Folding the cloth in his hand, he took a step back from his vehicle—an unmarked, older car I would have never guessed to be a cab—to make sure he hadn't missed any water spots. Piper growled as we approached, capturing his immediate attention.

"Good afternoon, sir. The clerk told me you are a cab driver. I'm in need of a lift to Burley."

"Indeed, I am." He extended his hand to me. "Craven, miss. Albert Craven."

"Seraphina Addington." I met his strong grip with my own.

"Burley, you said?"

"Yes."

"Not too far from here, about five miles. We can be there in a jiffy."

"Thank you." I was relieved, hoping that once I reached the Goswicks, I would regain a bit of that security which came from belonging somewhere.

After the incident in London, Father had contacted General John Lewis, an old comrade of his from the Great War, and accepted his previous offer to let me stay at his country house, away from the chaos of the conflict. Prior to becoming a general, John Lewis had been a familiar face, the image of an uncle in my mind. He was a wealthy and influential man but also acquainted with grief, having lost his wife at a young age and never remarried. Of course, we hadn't seen him since the war broke out.

"If you'll permit," the man said as he hefted my suitcase into the boot of the car. I settled into the back with Piper snuggled against the folds of my blue dress, which Mother insisted I wear, arguing that it matched my eyes and contrasted with my brown hair. I had acquiesced only to avoid an unnecessary confrontation on the day of my departure. Under any other circumstances, I would have worn slacks despite her disapproval. She was one of those who clung to the past, shunning twentieth-century styles.

The car left the station, making all sorts of racket and complaining of long-needed maintenance. The roads were lined with thatched-roof cottages that sat far back from the street, some with hydrangea hedges, others with evergreen shrubs. When we reached the end of the paved streets, Mr. Craven turned onto a rural road guarded by trees of every shape and sort. Through them, I caught glimpses of meadowland flowing through the ancient yews. It was breathtakingly green.

I was surprised to feel the unexpected beauty and calmness of my surroundings flood me, the contrast with what I had left behind startling. The war had taken so much from us, and we had quite rapidly adjusted to its ugliness—the sky dotted with black-and-red clouds of smoke as if heaven itself cried over the world; the explosions of the bombs followed by the shattering of windows; the mangled corpses; and for me, the spirits of the dead who walked aimlessly amid the rubble.

The New Forest, brimming with life, reminded me that our world was still beautiful, our people resilient. The war would end, and we would rise stronger and rebuild all that had been lost. Now that I was away from my family and needed a steadiness to allay my fears for them, I resolved to hold on to this belief more than ever.

Piper rearranged herself on the seat as we bumped along the muddy road. I ran my hand reassuringly through her fur, steadying my emotions at the same time. No doubt she would prefer the country to the air raids, which spared no one, tormenting humans and animals alike.

Apologetically, Mr. Craven explained, "The main road to Burley gets particularly nasty after a rainstorm. You must forgive me, but I'm taking a detour. A longer route through the forest. We don't want old Harvey getting stuck in the mud—no, surely not."

The car has a name. I smiled.

Up ahead, trotting gently along the roadside, a group of soldiers on horseback headed in our direction. Mr. Craven steered Harvey to the side of the road, if *road* was the proper name for this patch of mud in the woods.

"That's the Mounted Home Guard," he informed proudly. "They are volunteer soldiers operating out of Breamore. Great lads, they are. We also have both British and American troops stationed here, but thankfully, no bombs have fallen yet. Well, apart from Southampton, that is. The port is a target, but we've been spared farther inland."

"That's a mercy from heaven. Let us hope it remains like this." I had seen firsthand the erasure of history, brick and mortar, paper and binding. Hundreds of years destroyed in a matter of minutes.

"Where in Burley are you staying? Where should I let you out?"

"I'm not sure how to find it. I'm afraid I don't have an address."

"Don't fret, miss. In these parts, places have names. That's how we find them, not by numbers or anything like that."

"The name escapes me at the moment, but I'm a guest of General Lewis."

"Oh, I see. He is well known in the region—he owns the Burley mansion. The largest structure in the region." Just as he said that, a new thought seemed to startle him. "Wait, are you certain? The mansion currently serves as a military post—soldiers coming in and out all day. Not a good destination for a young lady, if you know what I mean."

The straightforward honesty of country folk was something I could get used to. "Agreed. No, I'm not going to the mansion. I understand the general owns a country house as well."

"You aren't speaking of All Hallows, are you?" His gaze found mine through the rearview mirror. For a split second, a shadow of disbelief crossed what I could see of his face.

"Yes, that sounds about right. I'll be staying there until things settle down in London."

He reached to loosen the collar of his shirt as if it suddenly strangled him. "That could be a long time...a long time indeed, to be in a house like that."

Was there something wrong with the house? Leaning forward, I asked, "Mr. Craven, what do you mean, 'in a house like that'?"

When he took longer than needed to respond, I knew he would not disclose the truth; however, I kept my gaze on him through the mirror until he did answer.

"It's one of the oldest houses in the region. Hundreds of years of history, you understand. I'm afraid All Hallows's fame will live forever. But it has been deserted since..."

"Since when?"

"An awfully long time...I didn't think it was habitable anymore."

"For my sake, I hope it is. But why is it famous? I imagine there are plenty of old houses around here competing for fame."

"Actually...since I've never been to the manor, I'm afraid my opinion wouldn't be an educated one." He cleared his throat, obviously unhappy with my questioning.

"I would still like to hear it."

"It's better that you wait to hear it from those familiar with the place." These last words he said with finality, putting an end to the subject.

His reason for not sharing was simply an excuse. Just as I considered pressing him further, the car slowed to almost an idling stage, but I couldn't see any reason for it. Piper lifted her head as high as she could, ears pointed, eyes wide open, in response to the unexpected change.

"Is anything the matter?"

"Miss, I thought you were going downtown. The manor is on the outskirts, and the roads are impossible during this weather. I'm afraid all I can do is let you out in town. Maybe you can spend the night there— rethink things?"

Rethink things? What did I have to rethink? Even if I wanted to stay in town, I had no money to spare. "Surely the roads can't be any worse than the ones we've traveled on."

In a faltering voice that betrayed his businesslike approach, he replied, "If the car gets stuck, it would be days before I could get any help. So, no, I can't drive you there." He glanced at the lowering sun. "No one would, at least not until tomorrow."

I said the first words that came to mind. "You must be having a laugh." I imagined Mother's response to such boldness, but after all, I had not come this far just to come this far. "There must be another way. Tell me there is."

He thought for a moment or two. By the way he fidgeted in his seat, I could tell he fought whatever idea he considered. At last, he let it out. "There is, but I don't recommend it. The forest is not safe for a woman to go about alone."

"It involves walking, then?"

He moved his head in assent.

I turned his words in my mind. There were areas in London where women felt unsafe to travel alone, daylight or not. I'd had to traverse them a time or two. This couldn't be any worse. *I should have brought Mother's frying pan.* I had seen her chase away several solicitors with it. It worked wonders.

"Walking Piper and I can handle. We just need directions."

He frowned as if saying, "*The foolishness of this woman will get her in trouble,*" but aloud, he said, "I can drop you off at the edge of Oker field. The manor is not far from there." He paused and then suggested yet again, "But I must insist that staying in town is a wise choice." The

n made me want to successfully brave the trail to All Hallows all
more.

"I'll take my chances."

With a severe expression of disapproval, Mr. Craven pressed his foot on the gas pedal. Harvey picked up speed, and at length, we came to a lane free of trees on one side. I leaned against the window to observe wild ponies roaming freely in the fields. If ponies were the type of threat my driver was worried about, my biggest challenge would be to keep Piper's excitement under control. She did not like anything, apart from her own kind, that had four legs, and she made sure they knew it.

The more I focused on the scenery, the more ponies I saw. "Oh my. There are so many of them."

"They belong to the commoners," Mr. Craven informed. "They have the right to graze their animals in the forest. A good thing too. The ponies and the cattle help maintain the landscape."

The vehicle made its way deeper into the woods, and soon the ponies were but a distant image. I was about to ask Mr. Craven how much longer we had when Harvey produced a jerking sound and came to a halt in the middle of nowhere. There were no houses in sight, just a welded wire fence guarding the meadow. Beyond that was a thickly wooded area. It was so still it didn't seem real.

I noticed Mr. Craven's hand tremble as he looked at his wristwatch. But the hour appeared to calm his nerves, for he said, "Oh, good." I imagined he meant that the remaining daylight was good enough for me to make the journey on foot. I certainly hoped that was the case, for time could be treacherous when moving against it.

With unexpected agility, he sprang from the car as though a fire burned unattended somewhere and opened the back door for me to follow suit. I stepped out and immediately felt my shoes—my nicest pair, meant to accompany the dress—sink into the wet ground. Piper jumped down after me.

"Remember, cross the field and go straight south through those trees. You'll see the manor soon enough." He flipped the boot open and quickly set my bag on the grass. Piper barked at the rushed handling of our property. "May I suggest you waste no time."

Civility, though I wasn't feeling it at the moment, called for me to say thank you. I handed him a few bills to cover the ride. He stashed them in his pocket without counting them.

"It's not too far. You'll be all right," he said, as if willing it to be true. Without further ado, he was back in his car. Harvey made a sharp turn, and with surprising speed, Mr. Craven drove away.

———————

Don't stop now. Keep reading with your copy of THE GHOSTS OF LEWIS MANOR available now.

Don't miss more from Marcia Armandi with THE GHOSTS OF LEWIS MANOR available now.

Seraphina must choose the lesser of two evils—the ghosts that haunt her or the murderer who hunts her.

Born with a rare ability—or curse, Seraphina can see and hear the dead. During the early days of the London Blitz, she is confronted with hundreds of lost souls wandering the streets.

As the war escalates, her parents send her away to the home of an old friend in the English countryside to preserve her sanity. But there are monsters lurking in the hallways and the surrounding woods of the mansion, not all of them are ghosts.

Seraphina must use her gift to help solve the gruesome mysteries of Lewis Manor's past in order to prevent her own murder in the present.

Please sign up for the City Owl Press newsletter for chances to win special subscriber-only contests and giveaways as well as receiving information on upcoming releases and special excerpts.

All reviews are **welcome** and **appreciated**. Please consider leaving one on your favorite social media and book buying sites.

Escape Your World. Get Lost in Ours! City Owl Press at www.cityowlpress.com.

ACKNOWLEDGMENTS

My deepest gratitude to Lisa Green. Thank you for your patience, hard work, and priceless advice in bringing *Alive* to its best version.

And a huge thanks to the entire team at City Owl Press for believing in me as an author. It is my pleasure to work with such fantastic people.

ABOUT THE AUTHOR

MARCIA ARMANDI was born and raised in Argentina. She is a soccer fanatic and loves listening to tango. Marcia studied International Family History Research and Writing.

After decades of compiling personal histories, she has developed a profound gratitude for the strength that can be found in families. So it is that through her fiction, Marcia explores the meaning of love and loyalty in times of fear, war, and finally, death.

 facebook.com/ArmandiMarcia

 x.com/MarciaArmandi

instagram.com/marciaarmandi

ABOUT THE PUBLISHER

City Owl Press is a cutting edge indie publishing company, bringing the world of romance and speculative fiction to discerning readers.

Escape Your World. Get Lost in Ours!

www.cityowlpress.com

facebook.com/CityOwlPress
x.com/cityowlpress
instagram.com/cityowlbooks
pinterest.com/cityowlpress
tiktok.com/@cityowlpress